LOST IN THE GILA

LOST IN THE GILA

LOIS GILBERT

FIVE STAR

A part of Gale, Cengage Learning

GALE
CENGAGE Learning

Detroit • New York • San Francisco • New Haven, Conn • Waterville, Maine • London

GALE
CENGAGE Learning™

LIBRARY OF CONGRESS CATALOGING-IN-PUBLICATION DATA

Gilbert, Lois.
   Lost in the Gila / by Lois Gilbert. — 1st ed.
     p. cm.
   ISBN-13: 978-1-59414-732-6 (alk. paper)
   ISBN-10: 1-59414-732-9 (alk. paper)
    1. Women anthropologists—Fiction. 2. Treasure troves—Fiction. 3. Gila River Valley (N.M. and Ariz.)—Fiction. I. Title.
   PS3557.I342235L67 2009
   813'.54—dc22   2008043355

First Edition. First Printing: February 2009.
Published in 2009 in conjunction with Tekno Books and Ed Gorman.

Printed in the United States of America
1 2 3 4 5 6 7 13 12 11 10 09

For all my loved ones.

My deepest thanks to Wayne Oakes, John Thorndike, Mary Gilbert, Lesley King, Jeanette Boyer, Bob Meyer, Liv Blumer, Susan Ginsburg, John Helfers, Alice Duncan, and Tiffany Schofield for their invaluable guidance and support.

CHAPTER ONE

The glass doors of the airport slide shut behind me, and I step into the dazzling light and warmth of May in Albuquerque. For most of the night I've been crammed into a window seat designed for pygmies, and I stretch out my shoulders and try to get the blood flowing again in my legs. The palms of my hands stick to the handle of my duffel, and my clothes smell like the dead air of the plane. But I'm finally here, and my pulse starts to gallop when I catch my first glimpse of the mesa west of the city.

After six months, the jinx has lifted. One more month without work would have taken me down to rice and beans and the prospect of waitressing, but now I have another chance. This time I'll be a model employee, I tell myself. I will not be a smart ass, I will not step on other people's toes, and I will not subvert the chain of command. For weeks now I've been counting the days to this moment, the moment I can begin a new assignment with a clean slate, working for the world's foremost archaeologist.

When the invitation came from Dr. Adam Richter, it felt like a miracle, a promise of work, professional redemption, and desperately needed cash. After I was fired from my last forensics job on a dig, I never thought I'd be hired by someone like him. Dr. Richter is a legend, his reputation secured by his brilliant writing on trading systems between Mesoamerica and Uto-Aztecan tribes of Arizona and New Mexico. And now I'm going

9

to be working with him on a mysterious site that no one, so far, has been willing to describe.

Whatever he's discovered has to be a major find since he's charmed grants out of *National Geographic,* the Archaeological Institute, and the National Science Foundation. But from the beginning, Dr. Richter's expedition has been shrouded in secrecy, and when we spoke over the phone he refused to give me any details about the site. All he'd say was that he urgently needed a forensic anthropologist in New Mexico within the next week. Maybe no one else was able to drop everything and fly out for an unspecified length of time to an unspecified job site, but it seems doubtful, given his stature in the field. I wondered about this after his call, and I still wonder. Why me?

A white van with the Archaeological Institute logo sits parked by the curb, and the driver stands next to it, leaning against the passenger side, scanning the crowd. Dressed in khaki slacks and a faded denim shirt, he's not handsome—his eyes are a little too close-set, his nose too thin, and his forehead too high—but there's a quiet self-possession in his bearing that makes me want to keep on looking. He's probably close to my age, in his early thirties. When he catches sight of me, he springs to attention and walks toward me without hesitating.

"Kate Donovan?"

"That's me," I say, extending a hand.

His handshake is brief, his palm callused and warm. "Glad you could make it. I'm the lithics man for the dig, Sam Gallagher." He stands there taking in my full measure, from the flyaway wisps at the crown of my head to the scuffed work boots on my feet. His eyes are calm, his gaze steady. Welcoming or not, it's hard to say.

"How was the flight?"

The sound of a plane taking off swallows my response and eliminates any chance of hearing a reply. Sam's eyes remain fixed on me, pale blue eyes, the color of a husky dog's, surrounded by spiky black lashes. His hair is dark, streaked from the sun, and it looks uneven, as if he cuts it himself. As we stand there awkwardly waiting for the jet to pass, I study the lines around his mouth and forehead, the archaeologist's testament to a life spent outdoors. There's no polite smile answering mine, so my mouth freezes into something that feels like a grimace as he continues to inspect me with his calm eyes. It takes an act of will not to run my hand over my unraveling braid, and I force myself to meet his stare.

The sound finally diminishes to a distant roar. "Dr. Richter said he'd pick me up," I say. "Is he here?"

After pausing for a fraction of a second, Sam shrugs. "I'm afraid he had some other business. You'll have to settle for me."

Something in his voice makes me hesitate, and I glance at the van, wondering what he's not telling me. But I try to adopt a cheerful tone, as if I'm grateful for his company. "Is it a long way to the site?"

He holds his hand out at waist level, tips it slightly this way and that, then lifts his chin toward the van. "Long enough, and we're burning daylight. What do you say we hit the road?"

My uneasiness builds as I drop my duffel bag at his feet and nudge the case of my tools closer to the van. Dr. Richter promised to fill me in on the details of the job on the way to the site, and I need the briefing. On the phone he'd been distracted, almost curt, as if he couldn't wait to get off the phone and move on to a hundred other more important things. There's an echo of this attitude in the businesslike way Sam bends down to hoist my duffel in both hands and stow it in the back of the van. He adjusts boxes of supplies that are already crammed into the cargo area to make room for my tools, then closes the van doors and tests the lock before he turns to face me.

"Ready?"

Without another word, we both climb in, and I brace myself against the seat as he pulls away from the terminal and steers around the curve of the airport exit.

I raise my voice over the river of traffic, still hoping for information. "Dr. Richter told me he's found evidence of the Teotihuacán culture here in New Mexico, but other than that I don't know a thing about the site."

Sam's eyebrow twitches like a lizard's tail. "You didn't talk to anybody in the press about this, did you?"

"No, of course not."

He pauses before he speaks, as if editing his thoughts. "You know the history of Teotihuacán."

"I know what little they've discovered."

Nobody really knows the history of Mexico's ruined city of Teotihuacán. It's one of the largest and most famous archaeological sites in the world, but no one really knows how it was built or why it was abandoned. Teotihuacán ruled ancient Mexico for five centuries before its inhabitants disappeared around 600 A.D., leaving an enormous ruined city of temples and pyramids. Not much writing survived, and what there is can't be translated. When the Aztecs discovered the abandoned city, they were convinced that the place had been built by a race of giants since only giants could have created such colossal buildings, and so they named it Teotihuacán: The Place of the Gods.

Sam takes his sunglasses from the dashboard, flicks open the earpieces and slides them on, hiding behind the mirrored surface. "This ruin will completely rewrite our theories about prehistoric cultures in North America."

There's no arrogance in his voice. He sounds like he's just stating a fact.

"Really," I say, letting the skepticism filter through. "Why wasn't it discovered before?"

He accelerates smoothly to merge with the southbound traffic on the interstate, then slouches back in his seat and drapes his hand over the wheel. "You'll see why when we get there. The site's in the middle of the Gila Wilderness—one of the most remote locations I've ever seen. No trails leading in or out."

I cast a dubious look at the gear shift. "Won't you need four wheel drive?"

"The van can only take us to the boundary. The wilderness has been closed to all motorized traffic since 1924, so we'll have to go in on horseback."

The prospect of a trail ride sends an agreeable tingle up my spine. My legs are still cramped from the plane, and I'm eager to be out in the open, away from cars and cities. But how far will we have to go before I can meet Dr. Richter and see what the expedition has actually uncovered? It's already been a long night, and it sounds like it's going to be an even longer day.

"Is it far?"

"Far enough. We have a four-hour drive to the outfitter's—that's about twenty miles north of Silver City. Another four or five hours on horseback to get to the site. But we'll ride through some beautiful terrain. It's pristine, untouched wilderness. You'll never hear the sound of an engine. They don't even let the hotshot crews use chainsaws to fight forest fires." His jaw relaxes slightly, and he leans back in his seat. "It's the southwest version of the Garden of Eden. And if we hustle, we'll get there by sunset."

I'm thirsty. At five in the afternoon, it's hot on the canyon floor, and a thin ribbon of sweat wanders down my back. My thighs ache as my roan plods along the trail, following two pack-mules loaded down with luggage, equipment and supplies. Sam leads the way across dry rolling hills dotted with juniper and scrub oak, or alpine meadows laced with aspen, or low hot canyons like this one. For three hours now we've been riding through forests that have never been cut, crossing small clear streams that tumble down mountainsides under moss-draped fir trees, and trotting through acres of wildflowers and fields of aromatic wild onion. The lack of sleep from the night before and the hypnotic sway of the horse lull me into a fitful, dreamy doze. I'm so tired I can barely keep my eyes open, and even though I'm eager to get to the site and see it for myself, I'm ready for a break from the saddle.

So far Sam has politely refused to answer any more of my questions about the site, and something in his voice reminds me of the clipped courtesy you hear in men obeying orders somebody else has given them, orders intended to hold you at bay, out of the loop and in the dark. Whenever I broach the topic, I can practically see the warning lights go off in his eyes: *Do Not Proceed. No Admittance Without Proper Authority, Which You Don't Have, Missy.* After a long day of fishing for information and getting nowhere, it's beginning to piss me off.

My chin touches my chest and I jerk awake, and then I see Sam stopped up ahead, watching me with that same look of patient, studied calm. I gouge my heels into the horse's sides, feeling self-conscious as I bounce forward in a rough trot.

"It won't be long now," he says when I draw alongside him. "We're almost there."

"Tell me what 'almost there' means in miles."

"Two or three. It's hard to judge with these switchbacks. But we're getting there."

He offers me a drink of water from his canteen, as if he knows mine is already empty. I take several long, delicious swallows, nearly emptying it, and the water floods my whole body with relief. I wipe my mouth with the back of my hand. "Thanks," I say, and pass the canteen back to him. His eyes remain on the ridgeline as he hooks the strap over his pommel then signals his horse to move forward.

Riding side by side, we climb steadily uphill toward the rim of the mesa. My horse snorts as the incline grows steeper, and I lean forward slightly and make what I hope are encouraging sounds as I pat its sweaty side.

Sam looks quickly at me, then away. "Richter said you were doing some work for the army. You still with them?"

"No." The silence lengthens between us as I try to think of an edited version of events I can give without incriminating myself. "Their funding for civilian consultants was cut, and I wasn't there long enough to have any seniority."

He nods. "Spencer Rowland didn't have anything to do with that, did he?"

I can feel the flush crawling up my neck. "What do you know about Spencer Rowland?"

"I was there, at Paquimé. You probably wouldn't remember me. You left the site about an hour after I arrived." His face is expressionless, but I can hear the judgment in his tone. "No one who saw you on your last day would ever forget it, though. You put on quite a show."

My ears begin to heat up. "It was a long time ago, Sam."

The landscape surrounding us reminds me a little of the basin and range country in northern Mexico, near the northeastern end of the Sierra Madre, where Paquimé flourished for three centuries. It was hot there, much hotter than this. That's what I remember most about the dig, the searing heat of Chihuahua in mid-July. Paquimé's terraced buildings and religious monuments were all made out of adobe brick, and by three in the afternoon the brick was hot enough to raise a blister on your palm.

He shrugs. "For what it's worth, the crew was sorry to see you go. They always said you were the best forensic anthropologist on the site."

This tribute floods me with gratitude, but I wonder if he's testing me for any sign of hubris. If he knows what happened at Paquimé, he must wonder if I'm still the reckless young woman I used to be, the rebel who dared to disobey The Boss.

"I guess Rowland had another opinion."

"Uncle Spence used to turn white if anybody mentioned your name. The crew hated him, so of course it was 'Kate Donovan' this and 'Kate Donovan' that for weeks after you left."

Warmth shoots up from the soles of my feet and washes over me. "Spencer Rowland is your uncle?"

Sam glances at me. "My mother's big brother."

The memory of Spencer Rowland's flushed face can still make the adrenaline hum through my veins. I don't want to think about him, don't want the thought of him staining my first day on this job. And it makes me squirm to realize Sam is related to the man who ruined my career. Sam knows all about it, then. He knows everything.

"By the time I arrived, I guess you were pretty fed up with him," he goes on, oblivious to my discomfort. The corner of his mouth tightens, but it's impossible to tell what he's thinking. In fact it's so hard to tell, I'm beginning to feel a little insulted. Is he *trying* to make me feel bad?

"If I'd known how many connections he had, I never would have opened my mouth." I say this with a little more force than tact might dictate, but to hell with it.

"Spence said he fired you because you dug up a body that was outside the permit area. Is that true?"

"There were extenuating circumstances."

"There usually are," Sam says mildly, and I cast a sharp look at him, checking for sarcasm. For half a second I let my mind skim the pile of might-have-beens and if-onlys that crop up whenever I think about that summer. It was one of the most humiliating moments of my life, to stand there while Spencer yelled at me in front of the crew. Yes, I was bad. I was stupid. But how many times do I have to go on apologizing for it? How many years of my professional life do I have to give up because of that fathead? I know where this conversation is headed, and I want no part of it.

"So what happened?" Sam asks.

"Sounds like your uncle already told you the story."

"I've heard Spencer's take on it. I wouldn't mind hearing yours."

I hesitate before answering, reluctant to break my own rule of never talking about it, but I'd hate to go on working with Sam if he believes even half of his uncle's version of events. No wonder he's been so guarded around me, so watchful, as if we're on opposing teams instead of a single expedition with a clear set of goals. Every time I approach the topic of what the Gila expedition has found—no matter how obliquely—I can almost see him retreat behind a wall of courtesy like a turtle tucking his head in his shell. Why all the secrecy? Won't it be clear enough when I get there? It doesn't make any sense, unless this is all some passive-aggressive bullshit because he thinks I'm a troublemaker with no respect for authority.

Maybe if I lure Sam into conversation, he'll tell me what I want to know about the Gila site. I'll talk; he'll talk. He'll ask a question; I'll ask a question, like normal people do all the time, especially if they've been stuck together for six or seven hours. It's amazing how tight-lipped he's been, all the way down to Silver City and up the two lane highway to the edge of the wilderness. Nothing but grunts and small talk when we stopped to pick up the mules and horses and load the supplies at the outfitter's. No conversation at all during the long hours of riding together toward some ruin, some burial, *something* related to Teotihuacán.

So I take a deep breath and begin, keeping my voice low, factual. "Rowland assigned me to a transect on the north boundary of the dig, the grave of a fourteenth century adult female, in pretty good condition. Not a fancy burial—she was probably a slave."

That was part of the problem, I always thought. Who cared about a female slave? With no grave goods of any value, Rowland certainly didn't. He'd filled out the government forms requesting permission to dig, and grossly underestimated the slave population buried on the outskirts of the permit area. I had to work four feet inside the boundary of the dig, and there was barely enough space to excavate the skeleton.

"I found a human toe bone next to her remains," I continue. "A phalange about this big." I hold up my thumb and forefinger about a quarter-inch apart.

"Juvenile?"

"That's what I thought. Rowland told me the toe bone was probably a charm or an amulet, and he didn't want me poking around, disturbing the ground outside the boundary, because it would mean a lot more paperwork. But I was convinced there was another skeleton nearby."

"And you dug it up."

"Well, yes."

"How?"

"At night. With a flashlight."

"No, I meant, how did you know where to look? The skeleton could have been anywhere within a dozen meters of that toe bone. A rodent could have dragged it off from the remains of the child."

I shrug, feeling uncomfortable under his scrutiny. Usually I avoid discussing anything that smacks of intuition with other scientists because of their typical reaction: eye-rolling looks of pity and disbelief.

The steady hoof beats of our horses syncopate the silence. My braid feels sticky at the back of my neck, and I swipe it free. *What the hell,* I think. *He'll probably find out sooner or later, and I might as well get it over with.* "I knew the skeleton was on the other side of the boundary. My hands knew."

"Your *hands* knew?"

"There's a kind of heaviness in my palms when there are bones nearby, lying in the earth." I glance at him, determined not to explain any further.

Sam looks as though he's trying not to laugh. "You mean you dowse for bones?"

How can I describe the lightheadedness that comes over me when I close my eyes and concentrate, the way my body feels pulled, like an iron filing to a magnet hidden in the earth? A strange chill passes over my skin when I'm close to a burial mound, even on a hot day like this. Just thinking about it makes me shiver. It doesn't always work, but it works often enough.

When I don't answer, Sam changes the subject. "Do you think finding the skeleton was worth losing your job?"

"Are you out of your mind? Of course not. That stunt cost me everything."

"But you were right. The skeleton of the little girl was exactly where you thought it would be."

The memory of her bones flashes through me, the striations from malnutrition, the brittle, chalky feel of her ribs. "Yes. She was there. She'd starved to death, like her mother." That was one of the ways the Mesoamericans disciplined slaves—if you got sick and couldn't work, they stopped feeding you.

Sam shakes his head. "That was one of the best preserved skeletons from the dig. And those sandals you found with her bones—they were perfect." Something about his praise seems artificial, as if he's testing me, prodding me for a response that will prove once and for all that I'm a loose cannon. Or as his uncle put it so sweetly, "a renegade opportunist."

I nod. "The pit house where the mother and child lived had burned down, so the bones and sandals were carbonized, making them impervious to rot. After the fire, the rain filled the ruin with a mud mixture of clay and ash, and that dried into a layer of dirt that was hard as cement—totally waterproof. That's why the skeleton was in such good shape. And there were two pairs of sandals. One made out of yucca fiber, the other made from human hair—the only articles of clothing recovered by the expedition."

"I noticed Uncle Spence didn't mind publishing your findings."

He was too much of a bastard to give me any credit, though. I can't say this. But I think it. I think it all the time.

Sam lifts the reins and lets them flap down against the horse's neck. "If you could go back to that summer, would you do it again?" He looks straight ahead, as if my answer doesn't matter much one way or the other, but something about his casual tone puts me on full alert. It crosses my mind that Richter might have put him up to asking me that question.

Probably, I think. "Never," I say out loud to Sam.

A smile flickers across his face. He doesn't believe me.

The truth is that I've always had trouble with boundaries, especially in this business. Archaeology is so intimate. Being on any expedition means exposing a civilization's past—digging up graves, sifting through garbage, cataloguing rooms, wardrobes, furnishings, utensils, and larders. It means poking into relationships between citizen and state, servant and master, husband and wife, mother and child. Discovery doesn't always come in neatly gridded slices of earth. Life is messy. It runs over boundaries, connects to the forbidden, and meanders in places we might not expect to find it. Maybe the neatly mapped lines of a dig are essential for gathering data, but archaeology is more than statistics. Understanding another culture is like understanding a work of art, and you have to observe it with humanity and compassion, as well as a calculator. It's not about grids and transects. It's about communities, and families, and how they lived.

I push these thoughts away and change the subject. "We're about a thousand miles north of where I'd expect to see Teotihuacáno remains. Do you know why Dr. Richter came out here looking for them?"

Sam whisks away a deer fly with the back of his hand. "For a long time he's been interested in the connections between Mesoamerica and the southwestern tribes in North America. You know there was extensive trade between the two regions."

This is old news. Dr. Richter was a pioneer in using an archaeological fingerprinting technique called neutron activation, and he had analyzed more than two thousand pieces of turquoise from thirty archaeological sites. The results confirmed what he'd suspected for years—the Cerrillos area in New Mexico was a major source of turquoise for Teotihuacán. Native American traders were mining the stone thousands of years ago and sending it down trade routes stretching all over ancient Mexico, from Casas Grandes to Chichen Itza in the Yucatan. In return the traders brought home macaw feathers, black coral and seashells, which weren't available to the Anasazi in New Mexico.

Sam glances up toward the rim of the canyon as he continues. "Two years ago he excavated the tomb of a priest in Tenochtitlan, just north of Teotihuacán."

My ears perk up at this—I've never heard of this excavation, and it has to be a major find.

"The walls of the tomb contained all kinds of glyphs and murals, and he spent months analyzing one mural in particular. The more he studied it alongside the glyphs, the more he was

21

convinced it was a stylized map. The glyphs told the story of the last ruler of Teotihuacán, and the map seemed to indicate that the king was about to make the trek north into what they called the *Gran Xiximeca*. You know that phrase?"

"The Land of the Barbarians," I say. Over a thousand years later, this would become the southwestern United States.

Sam nods. "According to Dr. Richter's interpretation of the glyphs, the last ruler of Teotihuacán must have died here in New Mexico."

A jolt of disbelief runs through me, and I study him to make sure this isn't a joke. A tomb on American soil for a king from the mysterious Teotihuacán culture would be the find of the century. "You found a tomb?"

His face changes, caution reasserting itself. A moment ticks by, then another, broken only by the sound of the horses' hooves pounding the dirt.

"Am I supposed to believe you didn't hear me?" I ask.

"I heard you."

"Well?"

"We found a lot more than a tomb, Kate. Hang on. Another mile or two and you'll be able to see the site for yourself."

We ride in silence for a few minutes. A small stream meanders for miles below us, a silver thread in a vast expanse that ends in the far-off silhouette of the Black Range. No power lines, no roads, no cities, no buildings of any kind obstruct the view. We're less than fifty miles from Silver City, only two hundred miles from Albuquerque, but it's another world up here. This is what the Teotihuacános saw more than a thousand years ago, this sun-soaked vista of mesas and canyons and mountains.

"What's it like, working for Dr. Richter?" I ask.

There's a tell-tale pause before Sam shrugs. "It's all right."

"That bad, huh?"

"Lately Richter and I haven't exactly seen eye to eye."

"About what?"

"It's complicated, Kate."

"Why is it complicated?"

Sam hesitates, then continues as if it goes against his better judgment to do so. "He's under a lot of pressure, and he doesn't always handle it well. The truth is, he left the site a few days ago. He's gone."

"Gone? Gone where?"

"Nobody knows. He walked off last Wednesday night, and we haven't seen him since."

Wednesday was four days ago. I tilt my head, expecting a punch line. "Walked off?"

"Things have been a little tense at the site. We're hoping he took a few days to cool off, get away from everybody. He could be back by now."

"Why would he need to get away from everybody?"

His lips tighten, and he shoots me a meaningful look. "It ain't a happy crew, Kate."

A blue-gray coil lies ahead of us on a sun-baked rock, and before I can absorb Sam's words I hear a sound like beads shaken in an empty gourd, an unmistakable shimmer of rattles. In a flash I'm lifted back and jerked forward as my horse rears and plunges up the trail, hooves clattering on gravel, raising a plume of dust. Panicked, I drop the reins and hang on to the saddle horn as the roan takes off in a stiff-legged run. I grip the horse with my knees as it gallops a hundred yards ahead to the rim of the canyon.

Up on top of the mesa the horse finally slows to a canter then ambles to a halt under a sky that opens into a navy blue vault, so vast and deeply colored it looks like an inverted ocean. Gasping, shaken by the ride, I press my hand to my chest and try to make my heart stop hammering against my rib cage. The horse tosses its mane then dips its head to crop at the sparse grass. The wind is strong enough to bring tears to my eyes. I feel dwarfed by the mesa, which extends at least a hundred miles to the north and fifty miles to the west, offering a view overlooking most of the Gila's three million acres.

The image of Dr. Richter lying in an arroyo with a broken leg flits through my mind, a picture that makes the emptiness of the landscape feel like a threat. The late afternoon sun burns my eyes as I scan the horizon. Every hour we've spent on the trail underscores the remoteness of the site, and the isolation gnaws at me. What if Dr. Richter's hurt? Or bitten by a rattlesnake, or pinned by a rock fall in a canyon? How long could he survive out here? Four days without water could kill him. So why does Sam seem so unconcerned about his absence?

A few minutes later Sam appears at the rim of the mesa, and I wait for him to catch up.

"Are you okay?" he calls.

"No harm done." But I still feel shaky, inside and out, stomach clenched, heart racing, my mind full of misgivings. I look out over the wide, rolling expanse of rock and grass. There's no sign of a trail, so I turn back to him, waiting for his lead.

Sam nods toward the far side of the mesa. "The site's over there, in that canyon to the south."

We continue at a trot across the mesa until we come to a halt at the edge of a cliff. Below us a stream winds through a narrow canyon, an oasis of sycamore and willow coming into leaf. At the mouth of the canyon I can see a flurry of activity near the base of the cliff facing us, a mile in the distance.

"Oh, my God," I whisper.

I stare, trying to comprehend what I'm seeing. *Impossible,* I think. It has to be an illusion, a trick of the light.

But there's no mistaking the form, a shape as familiar as the engraving on a dollar bill. The massive triangular wall juts out from the cliff that imprisons it, its broad expanse marked by vertical and horizontal seams. Half a dozen people work near the base, tiny as ants next to the monumental stonework.

It's a pyramid.

CHAPTER TWO

Once we reach the camp, the view of the pyramid on the other side of the canyon claims my attention with an almost physical force, a sight so unexpected it seems like a mirage. A fierce excitement wells up in me as I drink in the stark, uncompromising lines, its haughty presence in the wilderness.

For the first time I understand Dr. Richter's reluctance to talk about it over the phone and Sam's caution on the trip here. If the press caught wind of its existence, we'd be besieged by an army of reporters. And if the king of the fallen city of Teotihuacán died here, as this monument suggests, his people would have buried a king's ransom with him, to ease his passage into the afterlife. That fact alone could set off a stampede of treasure-hunters, and not even the National Guard could stop them.

Rising to a height of at least seventy feet, the pyramid has a broad, crumbling stairway of stone steps set at a dizzying, near-vertical rise, ascending three stacked platforms built in the unmistakable talud-tablero style of Teotihuacán. The tall stepped platforms are decorated on every corner with the plumed serpent Quetzalcoatl, its body in high relief and its three-dimensional head projecting beyond the revetment. Two more enormous heads of the serpent have been sculpted from the basalt and set on either side of the base of the stairway. The entire building looks as though it's been carved out of the rock face of the canyon wall facing me. Even though its south end is still buried in the cliff, the three platforms have been meticulously excavated from the earth on the north, east, and west sides.

I slide off the horse, wipe the dust from my face and try to get some feeling back in my legs. Sam begins unloading gear and equipment, and I tear my attention away from the pyramid to unbuckle the belly strap under my horse.

A man in a Dodgers baseball cap sees us and starts walking toward us.

"Is he back?" Sam calls out.

The man in the cap shakes his head. "Henry's been looking for him since you left. No sign yet."

"Son of a bitch," Sam mutters. They exchange a loaded glance before they walk a few feet away, out of earshot, their heads bent low in conversation.

A woman in her early fifties appears outside the nearest tent and approaches me. She has a strong face, thin and angular, and she carries herself with a natural authority. "I'm Sylvia, the ethno-botanist for the expedition. Dr. Richter's wife. You must be Miss Donovan."

I haven't been called "Miss" since high school, but I take her limp hand in mine. "Please, call me Kate. I was so sorry to hear Dr. Richter's not here. I was looking forward to meeting him."

My words create a distinct chill between us, and it's pretty clear to me she doesn't want to talk about her husband's disappearance. Her gaze skims the tangle of my hair, my wrinkled clothes and dusty boots, her mouth set in a thin line of disapproval. Her clothes are elegant for a dig: a fitted white shirt, with long, narrow black pants and silver-toed cowboy boots, and her dark hair is swept back in a bun, revealing turquoise discs on her earlobes.

She gestures toward the man talking to Sam. "I'm sure you've already recognized Michael Richter, my stepson."

I stare, belatedly registering the famous profile under the

baseball cap. Dr. Richter's son Michael and his wife, Isabelle, produced several highly respected films about archaeological sites around the world, from the tombs at Bahariya in Egypt to the Incan mummies found frozen in the Andes.

When Michael turns to glance our way, his haggard, lost look pricks me with sudden sympathy. I read somewhere that his wife died a few months ago. This must be his first film since her death. Although he's a handsome man with fair hair and warm brown eyes, there are shadows under his eyes, and his face seems gaunt, narrower than the face I remember from television.

Sylvia beckons him over, and he murmurs something to Sam before he turns and walks toward us. Her face softens as she reaches out to touch his back. "This is Miss Donovan. The bone woman."

"Michael," he says, and extends a hand.

"Kate," I say, and take it.

Sam approaches Sylvia with a question about where to store one of the boxes of supplies meant for her, and she leads him to the tent and directs him in stowing the equipment under the canvas awning. Michael and I hang back, out of their way.

Michael turns to me and smiles, the effort visible on his face as he searches for something to say. "How was the ride in?"

I smile, lift a shoulder, let it fall. "I have a few new blisters, and it's going to be a long time before I feel like doing any deep knee bends, but the landscape is incredible. Have you been here long?"

"A little over a week. I've been scouting the location to see what equipment the film crew will need to bring in later. Dad wasn't too happy about me coming in this early, but the suits at *National Geographic* want to make sure their money isn't going down another dry hole."

"Another dry hole? Has Dr. Richter ever come up empty?"

"Sure. My father's been trying to unravel this puzzle for years, and he's already gone through a fortune in funding."

"Sam told me your father's been gone from the site for a few days."

Michael winces, as if reluctant to talk about it, and nods. "He's had a few minor setbacks lately. I'm sure he's okay."

"Has he disappeared like this before?"

The doubt must be visible in my face because Michael touches my shoulder reassuringly. "Don't worry about it. He's probably soaking in a Jacuzzi in Silver City right now. He'll be back."

Sylvia walks toward us, her movements brisk, posture erect. "Let me show you the site before the sun sets, and then I'll introduce you to the rest of the crew." She tilts her head to indicate that I should follow her, and Michael gestures for me to go ahead of him.

I'd much rather explore the pyramid on my own, but Sylvia obviously wants to establish some kind of dominance, and it's easier to surrender. Still, it feels odd to walk away without Sam after spending the last ten hours with him, and I glance back to see what he's doing.

Sam takes no notice one way or the other. The saddle is off his horse, and he slides the blanket off and whacks it a few times to release the dirt. I wait a few seconds for him to look up, but he pays no more attention to me than to any of the other packages that have been safely delivered.

Sylvia leads Michael and me through the camp, past the scattered tents of the crew, beyond several dead piñon trees hung with laundry, up the narrow canyon toward a small stream that meanders through stands of sycamore and cottonwood.

As we walk toward the looming façade of the pyramid, I realize it's much farther away than it first appeared. The crew members I saw working around the base have disappeared, and the area surrounding the pyramid is deserted.

We enter thick clumps of willow that choke the creek and zigzag through tunnels in the dense brush. After we cross the stream, the ground rises in hummocks of big bluestem and rice grass. Most of the Gila wilderness is at least a mile high, and my lungs announce this to me with every step. Sylvia glides ahead easily as I fall behind, and Michael slows his stride to keep me company.

"How long are you planning to stay on the site, Kate?"

"As long as there are bones."

He laughs. "That's what we're all here for, I guess. You're from New York, right?"

"Upstate. Ithaca. But I spend most of my time traveling, working in the field."

"Then you must be an outdoor girl," he says. "Me, on the other hand, I woke up last night and saw the stars and thought, where the hell is the ceiling?"

I smile politely at the old joke. "Come on," I say. "You're an expert at this. I saw your documentary on the tombs at Bahariya, and that didn't look like any picnic."

"It was a tough assignment," he admits. "A hundred and twenty degrees on the set during the day. Most of the work had to be done in the middle of the night, to escape the heat. Isabelle used to set the alarm for midnight."

We lag farther and farther behind Sylvia, who forges on ahead of us. I wait for Michael to go on talking, but one look at his face tells me he can't talk about his dead wife without pain.

"You must miss her," I say softly.

He lets out a dry laugh. "By now Isabelle would have outlined the opening scene in the documentary and compiled a list of experts a mile long. My wife always gave me equal billing, but she was the one who ran the show."

Sylvia turns to wait for us, her arms crossed tightly against her chest, her back ramrod straight, and we pick up the pace.

"It seems like a small camp for such a big project," I say when we finally catch up to her.

"It's just a skeleton crew at the moment. My husband didn't want the news about the pyramid to leak to the press before he found the tomb. Of course we don't consider *National Geographic* 'the press,' do we?" she says to Michael with a touch of sarcasm.

"Certainly not," he says with a smile. "That would be a *terrible* insult."

Sylvia's face looks like a mask carved out of wood, even when she mentions the famous Dr. Adam Richter. *My husband.* But come on. Four days, and she's not going out of her mind?

When we finally emerge from the willow, the pyramid looms at least six stories above us. We approach slowly, ascending the slope toward the facing wall of stonework. I stare, unable to take my eyes off it.

"This is incredible," I say. "There just aren't any pyramids in this country."

"Well, there's the Luxor in Vegas," Michael says thoughtfully.

I laugh. "I have to admit, I feel like I'm looking at a movie set."

Sylvia gazes up at it with proprietary satisfaction. "You're one of the few people lucky enough to see it. The government has gone out of its way to help us keep it quiet because no one's prepared to handle a media invasion. This whole section of the wilderness will be closed to the public until we've finished the excavation."

Gingerly I touch the sculpted stone at the base of the pyramid, the corroded granite rough under my fingertips, still warm from the sun. "Why wasn't this discovered before?"

"It was completely buried in an earthquake several hundred years ago," Sylvia says. "A section of the mesa cracked off and covered it in a rockslide. It remained hidden for centuries, until one block at the bottom was exposed by a flash flood. My husband spent three years traversing this wilderness, searching for the king's tomb. When he saw the exposed block, he knew it was stone that had been worked, and immediately petitioned the government for permission to dig."

"Have you found any skeletons?" I ask.

Sylvia nods. "One. I discovered it, in fact. Come this way and I'll show it to you."

We trail after her as she steps over the strings used to mark the separate transects around the base of the pyramid, past a wheelbarrow full of excavated dirt with a screen lying on top, into a field thick with agave and rabbit brush.

She stops and removes a canvas tarp that covers a pit about four feet deep. I glance down at the pallor of bones against the darker soil in the hole. Clearly the skeleton was buried in a kneeling position, facing away from the pyramid, as if to guard whatever it contains. Most of a right arm lies loose on the ground beside it, its form tenuously articulated by withered cartilage.

"I excavated as much as I could, but I wanted you to see its position, so I left it like this," Sylvia says.

I kneel in the dirt to get a closer look, and a familiar heat builds in my hands as I fit the curve of the skull to the curve of my palm. My body feels weighted, tugged toward the earth, and the warmth spreads to my arms. The heat is always there when I'm close to old bones.

"It's a male."

"How can you tell?" Michael asks.

"You get a feel for it after a while," I murmur, tracing the surface of the skull. "See this mastoid process? It's smaller on a female. And this supra-orbital crest, along with these larger, more rugged muscle markings on the occipital bone. Definitely male."

"Is that twine around the hand?" Michael asks, looking down at the mummified tissue over the metacarpals.

"Braided human hair, probably," I say. "He must have had his hands tied behind his back when he was buried. You're looking at a human sacrifice. Nice work, Sylvia. Very delicately exposed." I glance up at her. "Have you photographed it?"

"My husband did, before he left." She tucks a strand of hair behind her ear and glances toward the cliff. There's a tiny pause before she begins speaking again. "He believes the man was sacrificed during the construction of the monument, as part of the dedication ceremony."

I study the exposed cranium. "Definitely early Mesoamerican. See how the front of the skull has been flattened? A wide, flat forehead was the height of glamour to them, a sign of gentility. They pressed boards against their babies' heads to shape them like this."

I point to a glimmer of white embedded in the soil near the clavicle. "Look at those teeth next to the neck vertebrae. I've seen the same thing in photographs of remains from Téotihuacan. Human sacrifices there wore collars made of human maxillae and mandibles, just like this. Did you find any slate disks in the grave? Any pyrite mirrors, or pieces of worked shell?"

"Several, in fact. I gave them to Sam to clean and catalog," Sylvia says.

"I'll want to take a look at those. They're part of the military costume worn by their warriors. It's amazing to think they came this far north."

"My husband believes the pyramid was constructed as a royal tomb, and the ruler is buried directly underneath it," she says.

Michael glances at me. "Do you think that's possible?"

Sylvia looks annoyed that he would question his father's

opinion, and I try to keep the doubt I feel from showing on my face. If they buried a king here, this pyramid would be like a neon sign, announcing the location of his tomb and all his burial goods. Would they risk that exposure in a strange territory filled with hostile native tribes?

"Sure," I tell Michael, trying to sound impartial. "I guess anything's possible. They discovered a burial chamber for an early ruler of Teotihuacán in the Pyramid of the Moon. Finding a pyramid here in New Mexico throws a wrench into everything we thought we knew about prehistoric cultures in this area."

Sylvia's voice is tight. "My husband has spent more time analyzing Mesoamerican writing than any other living person. If he believes a king is buried here, I believe it."

I smile and nod, anxious to let her know I have no intention of disputing Dr. Richter's expertise. Even though her husband has vanished without a trace and no one wants to talk about it, there's no way I'm going to challenge his opinion on my first day here.

Michael takes off his cap, scratches the back of his head, then settles the cap back over his hair and lowers the bill to shade his face from the harsh evening light. "You mind if I ask you a personal question? How'd you get into the business of digging up dead bodies?"

I rise from the edge of the grave, my gaze drawn to the bones embedded in the earth. *Because I love it,* I think, but most people can't understand that. No one seems to understand the joy this work gives me. A sensual, tactile thrill runs through me when I see bones gleaming in the dirt during an excavation. Bones are exquisite. Their form a miracle of utility and grace, and each bone tells a story about its owner. This one suffered from rickets; that one was a runner; this one starved to death; that one was well fed all the days of its life. Always, I'm seeing bones; even now, in the extension and retraction of Michael's hand as he waves a gnat away from his face. When Sylvia cocks her head, studying me, I can sense the fragile, seamed delicacy of her skull under her hair.

"Bones are beautiful. I've always loved them. After they've been polished by sand for a few hundred years, they look like ivory."

Michael purses his lips and lets out a long breath. "Sam said you've dug up your share of wet corpses, too."

Silently I wonder what else Sam has told him. "I take what I can get. Competition is fierce in this business. If you don't want to work for a coroner in Iowa or a medical investigator in some small town in Kansas, the Army Identification Lab is the only major employer for forensic anthropologists. They organize excursions to recover war casualties and identify human remains. I went to Iraq for them last summer." The searing heat of Baghdad in mid-summer was the worst I've ever encountered and made the stench from the bodies almost unbearable, but at the time I was desperate for work, thanks to Sam's uncle Spencer.

"Shall we move on?" Sylvia's face has the taut immobility of regular botox treatments, a face so rigid I'm sure it's incapable of frowning, but I can hear the strain in her voice. Tension glimmers there, sharp as a razor swathed in velvet.

We walk back in silence until we come to the corner of the pyramid where I pause to study the crumbling vertical walls.

She gestures toward steps hacked into the earth under the east side of the pyramid. "This is the tunnel."

As I walk closer I can see the steps lead down to an opening about four feet wide by six feet high, braced with wooden beams.

"The crew erected that framework of timbers," she continues. "We've excavated about thirty feet, so far."

"Digging him out looks like it's going to be dangerous," I say. This is an understatement. It looks like a nightmare, given the composition of the walls. The posts and beams in the framework appear to be too widely spaced to hold the loose rock in place. They've been skimping on materials, too—the timbers should be heavier, thicker, and they need rebar and wire mesh between the supports. But there's no rebar. No wire. No screen. Nothing but a rickety looking collection of boards to hold back the weight of a mountain.

She nods. "The interior is full of dirt and rubble, with no distinct passageways."

"The classic defense against looters," Michael says. "And that includes us."

Sylvia continues. "The tunnel has to be reinforced as we go deeper, because the rock isn't stable. We're making slow progress. We had a cave-in yesterday, and one of the volunteers was hurt."

"I don't envy the people who have to dig in there," I say.

Sylvia gives me a chilly smile. "I'm sure you think your skills would be best used elsewhere, Kate, but we have a small crew, and there's a lot of rock to move. You'll be digging with the others."

Her words jolt through me. "But Dr. Richter never said—"

She cuts me off. "Everyone digs. Those are my husband's orders." Her eyes meet mine in a challenging stare.

I say nothing, but glance at the perfect, shiny surface of her fingernails. If she can lift a shovel and keep that manicure intact, I'll be amazed.

Sylvia turns abruptly to lead us back toward the stream, and Michael and I fall into step behind her. He shakes his head and rolls his eyes, casting an apologetic look my way as the three of us walk away from the pyramid.

As we approach the edge of a clearing, the sound of raised voices echoes through the canyon. Both Michael and Sylvia slow down. Beyond the scrim of willow, I see an older man facing a muscular young Hispanic woman in her early twenties with a cap of short, wavy dark hair.

Clearly flushed with agitation, the woman crosses her arms over her chest in a way that manages to look belligerent as she speaks.

"That's Jessie Delgado," Sylvia says in a low voice. "One of the volunteers."

"Who's the man she's yelling at?" I whisper. He's in his sixties, at least, with long graying hair gathered into a scraggly ponytail, a narrow face and steel-rimmed spectacles. Built like a weathervane, his legs are alarmingly thin. He wears a snap-button cowboy shirt with the sleeves rolled up, and his forearms are covered with tattoos, the muscles like knotted rope.

"That's Henry," she says. "Henry Becker. My husband's right-hand man. His wife, Fidelia, cooks for the expedition."

"It's not here, damn it." Jessie Delgado's voice rises in the evening light and bounces off the stone wall of the pyramid. "You can't go on pretending it is."

Sylvia parts the willow and moves a little closer, her eyes sharp with alarm. Michael looks resigned to whatever is about to unfold between Jessie and Henry, and he and I step past the screen of brush.

Henry closes his eyes as if Jessie's giving him a headache. "We've been through all this."

"Look." She thrust her palms in front of his face. "You see these blisters? I work twice as hard as anybody else, whether Dr. Richter's here or not. And if it's so goddamn important to him, where the hell is he? Why doesn't he come back here and help us? It's been four fucking days!"

"He'll be here," Henry says. "And until he gives the order to stop tunneling, we're going to keep at it."

"Should we leave?" I whisper to Michael.

He shakes his head. "Sorry about this. Hang on—you have to

meet Henry sooner or later, and this is probably as good a time as any."

Jessie's voice is loud, insistent. "That tunnel is thirty feet long, and we haven't come up with a scrap of evidence that your precious king is buried anywhere near the pyramid."

"Not your decision, Jessie," Henry barks.

She glances at us hovering at the edge of the willow and lowers her voice when she turns back to Henry. "Come on. No shards, no tools, no burial treasure, no rooms, no hallways, nothing. We need to spread the search."

Henry shakes his head, but she ignores the warning and barrels ahead. "You're totally ignoring the pit house ruins and the midden up the canyon. Sam has found tons of pottery fragments up there."

"They're useless," Henry snaps. "I've seen them. Red on brown, all of it. Traded everywhere, mass produced—it's worthless. All it tells us is that the Teotihuacános were here, and we already know that from looking at the pyramid. It's not what we're after."

"But there are projectile points—"

He shakes his head and speaks in an explosion of impatience. "We aren't here to excavate some two-bit points."

Seen through the blur of my fatigue, the scene begins to take on a chaotic, fragmented, otherworldly quality. Watching Jessie Delgado is like watching a movie of the mistakes I made in Paquimé. *Stop,* I want to tell this girl. *He doesn't care what you think. He won't take your advice, and you'll only shoot yourself in the foot if you go on yelling at him.*

"You mean you have no interest in these people, how they lived, what they wore, what they ate?" she sputters. "You just want to find the royal treasury?"

"We're going to excavate that tunnel, and you're going to follow orders." His voice is like ice.

Jessie's back stiffens with frustration. "We had a serious cave-in today, while you were out looking for Dr. Richter. Will has a gash in his head that didn't stop bleeding for an hour. He could have been killed. It's not safe."

Sylvia takes another step toward them, beyond the edge of the willow thicket, and Henry straightens. Michael follows her and I join them in the clearing. More than anything I want to set up my tent, crawl inside and bask in solitude. My eyes are gritty with fatigue, and I'm hungry and wobbly on my legs from the long ride into camp. But I can't see any way out of this uncomfortable exchange without calling attention to myself.

Henry glances at Sylvia, who gives him a barely perceptible shrug, and then he turns back to Jessie. "You know how long Sugiyama tunneled into the Pyramid of the Moon before he located a tomb?"

"Three and a half months," Jessie says, eyeing us sullenly.

"And how long have we been tunneling?"

"Five weeks."

"We're not running a democracy, Jessie. Dr. Richter says dig here, I'm gonna dig. And as long as I'm in charge, you will too."

A bruised, embarrassed red appears in Jessie's cheeks, and she mumbles under her breath, so low and fast I almost miss it. *"No es el patron, usted."*

You are not the boss.

"What was that?" Henry's voice is sharp.

"You don't want to know, *sir*," she spits out. And then she turns on her heel and walks briskly back toward camp.

Chapter Three

As the sun touches the western horizon, I finish staking out my tent on top of a small rise overlooking the creek. My gear lies scattered in loosely organized piles, but I'm ready to leave it where it is and go down to the creek to wash off the dirt from the trail ride. I shove my bra and dirty socks and underpants into my pockets, hoping to do some laundry before it gets too dark.

As I zip up the door to keep the mosquitoes out, I see Sam emerging from a large six-man army-surplus tent across the clearing. A canvas awning attached to his tent shelters a long work table covered with the tools of his trade and heaps of stone debris. The tent has been pitched by a low, flat basalt formation that affords him a natural work space.

He glances up and catches me staring, and I wave, a little self-conscious about the underwear bulging from my pockets.

He holds up an empty water bottle. "I was just going to the stream. Is that where you're headed?"

I nod and shrug.

"Mind some company?" he asks, walking toward me.

Well, this is a change of attitude, I think, looking at his friendly, open smile. He has a great smile, with perfectly even white teeth that seem to glow against the suntanned darkness of his skin. "Not at all."

We walk together past a scattering of basalt boulders in a field of Indian rice grass, toward the thicket of willow lining the stream. The pyramid looms over the canyon, its stones the color of blood in the low light of the setting sun.

When we're out of earshot of the other tents, Sam says "I guess you heard the fight between Jessie and Henry."

"I was right there. Is Henry really in charge now?"

"He seems to think so. And he's not the kind of guy you want to argue with."

I wonder why Henry thinks he's in charge. Does Henry know where Richter is? It's hard to believe Richter would disappear without telling anybody where he was going, especially when the crew was in the middle of a dangerous excavation into a mountain of rubble. I hate the thought of working in that tunnel.

"Have you seen any sign of a burial under the pyramid?" I ask.

Sam shakes his head. "No. Jessie's right about that."

"Why do you think they built it?"

"It might be a kind of tombstone, a mark of respect, but if a king was buried here, in hostile Mogollon territory, I don't think they'd advertise the tomb with a monument like that. The Teotihuacános wouldn't expose his body and his burial treasure to enemy raiders."

Exactly what I thought when Michael asked me for my opinion. "Have you said anything to Dr. Richter about it?"

"Sure. But he's not ready to give up digging yet. And he has a point. Over the past few years Sugiyama has found scores of burials under the Pyramid of the Moon and the Feathered Serpent Pyramid in Teotihuacán."

I look up at the cliffs rimming the canyon and think of the wide open mesa above us. "Can't we survey the surrounding area?"

"We don't have the permits." An edge of exasperation comes into his voice. "And getting them will be a nightmare if anything's happened to Dr. Richter. He knows how to shmooze the local tribes and the bureaucrats at the Forest Service. The state, the feds and the tribes all have to agree before we can get permission to extend the boundaries of the dig."

Permits. The key to any expedition. Sam's right: without our missing expedition leader, getting them will be next to impossible. "Has the crew been searching for Dr. Richter?"

Sam shakes his head glumly. "Henry's been looking, but he insists everybody else keep working on the tunnel. I have to admit, I'm getting a little worried, Kate. I thought he'd be back by now. If he's not sitting in a hotel in Silver City, this expedition is screwed."

My stomach tightens, and a panicky rush of adrenaline zips through me as I consider the possibilities that lie ahead. "We'll go on excavating without him, won't we?"

Sam glances at the darkening sky and the blocky silhouette of the mesa looming above us. "I don't know," he murmurs. "But I'll tell you one thing. Ever since I got here, I've had a weird feeling about this place."

His words ripple through me, as though he'd drawn a feather down the back of my neck. For a moment there's no sound at all except for the wind whispering through the canyon. "Dr. Richter must have a cell phone. He could call for help if he needs it."

"Cell phones don't work out here. There's a satellite phone in Sylvia's tent, but if Richter's called her, she hasn't mentioned it. Sylvia and Henry keep saying he'll turn up."

We emerge from the willow thicket to stand by the stream. It's a quiet, shallow creek with a sandy bottom, and the overhanging branches of willow give it the private, intimate feeling of an enclosed room. We both pause in the tall grass for a moment, hands in pockets, watching air bubbles rise from the sand and float to the surface, then slip downstream. In spite of

the peaceful setting, worry gnaws at me, and my stomach twists
with anxiety at all the questions I've asked that Sam can't
answer.

"Sylvia told me you want to see the artifacts we took from
the burial she found," Sam says abruptly. "Come over for dinner when you're finished here, and I'll show them to you."

Before I can thank him, he melts off into the brush.

By the time I finish hanging my things out to dry and start
walking over to Sam's campsite, the smell of cooking hangs over
the canyon. Steam from boiling potatoes fills the air, along with
the odor of Coleman fuel and the silence of people intent on
eating after a day of hard labor. It's chilly now, and the leaves
on the sycamores rustle in the wind.

Sam sits on the broad expanse of basalt next to his tent, stir-
ring a pot that steams and bubbles over a two-burner stove. He
looks up when he sees me enter the clearing. "I hope you're
hungry, because I made enough noodles for an army."

"Starved," I admit. "But why aren't we eating with the others?"

"I told Fiddle we'd fend for ourselves tonight. I didn't think
we'd make it back in time for dinner, but you can go over there
if you want. Would you rather eat with the crew?"

"No. This is great. I'm exhausted, to tell you the truth." The
artifacts from the burial are neatly laid out in rows on the rock
beside him, and I finger the disks, tracing the glyphs carved on
both sides. It amazes me to see these ancient, handmade relics,
excavated so far away from where I'd expect to find them.

"Have a seat," he says, gesturing to the other side of the rock.
"I'm making macaroni with tuna." He brushes his hands over
his khakis and rummages in a net bag beside the stove, extract-
ing an onion and a green pepper. His hands are calm, unhur-

43

ried as he shaves off a few slices from the green pepper with his pocketknife.

Coyotes yip in the distance as Sam divides the noodles, and we begin to eat. The food is terrible in the way that most camping food is terrible, canned and mushy, but my appetite is sharp from the long day outside. We eat under a sky that fades from rose to indigo to a pale darkness pricked by stars. The pyramid looks even more ghostly in this half-light, a monolithic presence looming from the canyon wall, and it seems to waken and breathe at night. Through the lattice of branches I can see the exposed face of the pyramid, and the gargoyle silhouette of Quetzalcoatl guarding the dark expanse of stone and mortar.

"Were you with Dr. Richter when he found the pyramid?" I ask, my mouth full.

Sam looks up. "Yup. Henry was with us, too. The three of us had been scouting the wilderness on and off for a year. As soon as we uncovered the stonework and saw the dimensions of the thing, we went crazy."

I put down my plate and curl my arms around my knees. "What's Henry's background?"

Sam pauses as he lifts a loaded fork to his mouth. "Henry's a survivalist. He and his wife have a ranch at the edge of the Pecos wilderness, east of Santa Fe. No well, no neighbors. They have a rain cachement system and solar power. Totally off the grid. Plus a hell of a gun collection, according to Dr. Richter."

"Does he have a gun here?" The thought makes me uneasy.

"He's got a small arsenal in his tent."

I roll my eyes. "Does he shoot his own meat, or what?"

Sam laughs. It's the first time I've ever heard him laugh. The chuckle starts low in his chest and bubbles out in an oddly musical note of delight, followed by an audible postscript of appreciation, like a sigh. It's a pleasant, reassuring sound. I'd like to make him laugh again.

"Henry's been with Dr. Richter forever, so he can pretty

much do whatever he wants on a dig," he says. "He told me once that Dr. Richter paid for his college education."

That seems odd. Henry looks like he's at least sixty, close to Dr. Richter's age, too old to be a protégé. With the tattoos and ponytail, he reminds me more of a retired biker than an archaeologist.

Sam chews thoughtfully. "Henry's a brilliant guy. Has a couple of master's degrees, one in cultural anthropology and one in Russian literature. No people skills, though. No people skills at all. Did you meet his wife Fiddle yet? She's our cook."

"No. Not yet."

"What about Jason? He's Richter's younger son."

"I met Michael. I didn't know Dr. Richter had another son."

A twig snaps in the darkness beyond the scattered juniper trees. Sam glances over his shoulder and searches the shadows. After a few seconds he turns back to me, his voice lowered. "Didn't you see the story about Jason last summer? It made national news."

"I must have been in Iraq."

"For a couple of years Jason worked as a bond analyst for Lehman Brothers. He was a Wall Street hot-shot, a millionaire by the time he turned twenty-three. Then the feds indicted him for securities fraud. He ratted out a few of his friends and got off with probation, but that finished his career. Now his parole agreement puts him in his parents' custody. That's the only reason he's here. Wherever they go, he goes."

I ponder this. The black sheep, shackled to his parents. He must be miserable, unless he always had a secret hankering to be an archaeologist. "Does he have any experience in the field?"

"Jason hates archaeology. His mother claims he's doing all kinds of work, but I've never seen him lift a finger to help us out."

I measure Sam for a beat or two, feeling my way toward a

question that's been lurking in me since our talk on the trail, but I'm not sure he'll answer. "Sam, did you have anything to do with getting Richter to hire me?"

He keeps his head down, focusing on the food. A scrub jay cackles from the top of the sycamore, and the wind dies to a rare stillness as he chews and swallows. "Once Sylvia found that human sacrifice, we had to get somebody in here fast, but our funds are low. So I told Richter about you. Told him you'd had some trouble in Paquimé and might be willing to work for less than the usual fee. You were the only forensic anthropologist we could get for the money he was offering."

He takes one last bite, chews and swallows. "Of course once he locates the king's tomb, the grant money will start pouring in. Then he'll be able to afford the best in the business."

After an awkward pause he glances up and catches the look on my face. "Not that you aren't qualified," he adds kindly. "Everybody says you have a knack for reading bones."

The insult sizzles through me, and I put down my fork. "Why didn't you tell me this before, Sam?"

He pauses, fork in mid-air. "Tell you what?"

"That Richter's going to get rid of me as soon as he gets enough money to hire somebody else!"

He stares at me with those ice-blue eyes, pale as glaciers, a cool, appraising look. All warmth gone. He inspects me and waits. The moment lasts long enough to make me uncomfortable, and I glance away first. The truth of the situation is obvious. I'll do whatever I'm asked to do for the chance to work on this dig, and we both know it.

For a moment self-pity engulfs me. I'll never have a clean slate. All those years of mucking around in labs, weighing out livers and spleens, struggling through chemistry and human evolutionary anatomy and pathology—I wasted them all in one hot rush of anger at that bastard Spencer Rowland, and my face burns as I realize Sam sees me as a charity case.

He lifts his chin toward the pan. "You want some more?"

I shake my head. "No thanks." I start to gather the dishes, but Sam stops me with a hand on my wrist.

"Don't worry about those. I'll do them while you look at the artifacts."

He scratches a match, lights a Coleman lantern and hangs it from a line suspended between his tent and a dead piñon, illuminating the rock where I sit. Quietly he stacks the dishes and throws a towel over his shoulder before he walks off toward the creek.

After he leaves I groan out loud and scrub my face with my hands, as if I could wipe away the past. But what did I expect? Spencer Rowland will haunt me for the rest of my life, and his nephew isn't about to let bygones be bygones. I'm cheap labor. Easy to hire, easy to fire.

Unless.

Who knows? If I show Richter I'm not just cheap, not just a dispensable hack, but a model of organization and immaculate field work, the kind of work that makes me vital to the success of the expedition—then maybe I can change Richter's mind.

I stare at my hands, flex them open, and turn to the rows of artifacts shining in the pool of lamplight. A flicker of warmth tickles the center of my palms as I hold them over the slate disks that gleam beside jagged bits of pyrite and shells that have been drilled and sanded. There are several pieces of broken pottery, and I select one of the curved pot shards. The fragment is roughly triangular, with an eroded reddish glaze on one side. For a few moments I rub the glaze absently, trying to imagine the people who touched this fragment before me.

I've done this before. I know how to close my eyes and sink into myself. I know I can release the garbage, the worry, the mistakes in my past, and become still.

I breathe. I let go. I become blank.

My jaw relaxes, and my shoulders slump. Neck, arms, legs, hands, feet turn limp, heavy, rooted to the rock where I sit. I hold the shard loosely in my palm, and let my breath in and out.

Slowly, without fanfare or warning, an image comes to me. An open pit. A turquoise sky. Ground the color of blood. I can see workers in the barren landscape, wearing nothing but breechcloths, their skin the color of copper. They dig up the red earth and sift it through cloth into baskets. I can see the sheen of sweat on their backs, and hear them chant in a language I've never heard, a steady, hypnotic thrumming that comes from their bodies as they dig. I can feel the sound in the pit of my stomach, and a wave of goose bumps washes over me, followed by a familiar warmth. My head feels light, open, unbound, sensing another world that lies out of reach, on the other side of time.

Abruptly I open my eyes. Sam sits beside me, drying our bowls with a bandana. How long has he been sitting there? I put the shard back, a little shaken by the vivid, sun-drenched image of those people bending to their baskets. It seemed so real, almost more real than the flickering light of the lantern swinging above me. The pale darkness beyond the light seems filled with ghosts. The willow and sycamore by the stream move in the wind, filling the night with shadows that seem alive.

"They must have been desperate," I say quietly.

Sam retrieves a canvas bag from the other side of the rock and slides the bowls and silver inside. "Who?"

"The people who made these things." I hold up the pot shard, turning it in the moonlight.

"Teotihuacán had already burned to the ground by the time they arrived here," he says, leaning back on one elbow to take the shard in his hand. "Yeah, I'd say they were desperate. They were refugees."

"I still can't believe they came this far. To cross the mountains, the desert—it would take them a year to come this far north, into the *Gran Xiximeca.*"

He holds his hand over mine and gently tips the shard back into my palm. "That's what I don't get. Why did they come here? The Mogollon tribes must have been hostile to them. It seems like a suicide mission."

I turn the shard in my hand, studying it. "They knew there were turquoise mines up here."

"They called it the god-stone," Sam murmurs. "Turquoise held enormous power for them."

"Maybe they thought the mines would restore their strength as a nation. They must have brought an army with them, to seize the mines from the native tribes."

He stares at me, taking his time. "That's what I think. They used their army to quarry the rock and build the pyramid."

"It makes sense. If the king traveled here, he would have had an elite force, the inner circle of the court. That would have included architects and masons and sculptors."

Sam leans forward, elbows propped on his knees, hands loosely clasped in front of him. "Dr. Richter thinks the priests may have sacrificed the king, in a last bid to restore the power of the empire. What do you think? Wouldn't that be heresy? Like killing a god?"

The fact that he thinks I have an answer soothes my wounded ego a little, and I try to bend what I know to fit Richter's theory. "Usually a human sacrifice was culled from the slaves or the lower classes. In their mythology, one of their gods was sacrificed to ensure the daily return of the sun. If they were looking for a new dawn for their empire, they might go ahead and kill the king. They thought he was divine. He may have even agreed to it, to save his people."

Sam remains silent, staring into space, lost in thought.

"But you don't think the king is buried in the pyramid," I say.

He turns and looks directly at me, and I feel a sudden rapid murmur of blood in my ears, a faint, warning tingle.

"No," he says. He stands, rustles in his net bag and pulls out two apples. "Dessert," he says as he polishes one on his shirt, then hands it to me.

"Where do you think the king is buried, Sam?"

He smiles that non-committal half-smile, as if he's known all along that I'd ask. "You could make an educated guess."

"Me? Why?"

"Think about it. Think about what we saw in Paquimé."

"You mean the caves?"

"Exactly." He nods to the mesa above us, a black silhouette in the moonlight. "A hundred thousand years ago there was a chain of volcanoes up there. When you look at the canyon wall you can see the layers of basalt from each successive eruption— millions of tons of lava. Think about what that means."

"Lava tubes."

"Bingo."

I think about it. If lava oozes out across terrain that isn't too steep or too flat, the surface of the river of lava solidifies like a pipe when it touches cool air, allowing the liquid lava inside it to run downhill.

I can picture it: the river of lava forging a path downhill, extending for miles. Once the eruptions ceased, the lava would drain away, leaving pipelines and caves. In Mesoamerica, these caves were often used to bury the dead.

"Just like Téotihuacan," I murmur.

"Just like that," he says, and bites into his apple.

I can't sleep. I lie awake in my tent and think about the bones that wait for me, the human sacrifice in the hole outside the pyramid. Was he buried alive? Or was his neck broken, his throat slit? By the time that young man was sacrificed for the glory of Teotihuacán, their religion had changed from an emphasis on the creation myth to a cult of war, and blood-letting rituals were as common as their barbaric treatment of slaves. There are rooms at Casas Grandes no more than three feet high, where slaves lived out their whole lives, never allowed to stand without crouching, leaving them too weak to revolt.

I think about the necklace of human teeth around the skeleton of the young warrior in the hole. How many warriors had to die to insure a safe passage into the afterlife for their ruler? What happened to the rest of their people? Where did they go? And why hasn't the dig uncovered any other human remains?

Before Dr. Richter focused on building the tunnel, the crew obviously spent a few weeks excavating the area surrounding the pyramid. But only one human sacrifice has been found, when there should be dozens. An army lived here. Where are their bones?

For centuries Teotihuacán was the wealthiest nation in the western world. They must have brought as much of their wealth with them as an army could carry, and since this treasury hasn't been found anywhere in the new world, their riches must still be here, hidden in the landscape that surrounds us.

Pressing the stem of my watch to illuminate the dial, I moan when I see it's already one a.m. My eyelids feel like lead, but my mind hums with anxiety, too fretful to drift toward sleep, needling me with questions I can't answer. Where the hell is Dr. Richter? If he's really all right, four days is a cruel amount of time to leave the dig with no explanation given how many people here are depending on him. And if he's hurt, why hasn't the crew found any trace of him?

I sigh, punch the bag of laundry I'm using for a pillow and turn over.

CHAPTER FOUR

In the morning the sky changes from rose to pearl to blue as I walk down to the stream to splash water in my face. When I return to the tent I take my time organizing tools, locating work gloves and arranging the bedding. After a long night of fitful sleep my body aches in a number of original ways, and the chill of the morning seeps through my shirt, emphasizing every unhappy muscle. The first night is always a killer out in the field, with nothing but an inch of foam and a down sleeping bag between my back and the cold dirt.

The thought of joining the others to dig in the tunnel makes me slow to wrap up my tools and put them away. I zip up the tent, rise to my feet and gaze at the pale sky above the cliffs. In the distance a chevron of sandhill cranes quivers overhead. My eyes strain to see their silhouettes against the brightness; I've always loved watching them. But they're moving away from me, their soft cries receding as they disappear completely in the haze.

It makes me feel blue, watching them vanish, and it brings back a memory of going with my dad to the Brooktondale Cemetery to visit my mom. I must have been about nine or ten. It was May, probably, because the lilacs were out, and I remember the sound of the bees working the hedges. My dad sat under the oak tree that shaded her plot, while I traced the rough, cool letters chiseled into the glassy surface of the marble: "Margaret Gallagher Donovan, beloved wife and mother."

My heart felt dead, ripped out and buried with her, and an overwhelming sadness clung to me while Dad talked about how stubborn and funny and pretty she was, and how much she loved me before the cancer took her away. I sat down on her grave, closed my eyes and splayed out my fingers against the mound of fresh dirt that covered her. My dad's voice mixed with the drone of the bees, and I let myself go limp, soft, falling straight down to a place below sleep. It was safe there. Empty, and dark, but not lonely. I felt the nearness of her body, her bones, while I was sitting there. It was like unplugging my ears, or opening my eyes. Nothing extraordinary, nothing I tried to do, exactly—I just allowed myself to do it. I listened with my hands to the bones underneath us and felt the heaviness in my arms drawing my palms to the earth. Her face flashed through my mind, a young woman's face, not the face I remembered from her long brutal bout with cancer, but a mother who looked young and alive and happy to see me. She had brown eyes and thick dark hair, just like me. I could feel her hug me, and there was an echo of laughter around her as she gazed at me and smoothed the hair from my forehead.

When I opened my eyes again I saw my dad staring at me, head cocked, eyebrows quirked up in puzzled interest. "Katie? You feel all right?"

I nodded. I felt good. But I knew, looking at his sad face, that I was doing something he couldn't do. He couldn't feel her, and he'd never feel her again.

Maggie Gallagher Donovan had been in her third year of medical school at Cornell when she met Frank Donovan, and he always felt guilty about the dream she gave up to marry him when she became pregnant with my brother Peter. There was never any doubt that he wanted me to live the life my mom didn't have a chance to live. While other daddies read fairy tales to their little girls at bedtime, he read aloud to me from her tattered copy of Gray's Anatomy. Instead of the Barbie doll I longed for on my seventh birthday, he gave me a plastic model of the Visible Man. Eventually I forgot about Barbie and fell in love with the mysteries made clear in the scale models I received every year: the human heart, the mini-skeleton with its own stand, and for my twelfth birthday, the human reproductive organs—both male and female. All the way through my years in elementary school, junior high and high school, he nagged me to take accelerated courses, especially in math and science. He taught himself chemistry, algebra and calculus to help me get through my exams, and if I brought home anything less than a B, it was cause for a week of black looks and long-suffering sighs.

But when I started med school I realized I didn't want to be the kind of doctor my mother wanted to be. There was no way I could put on a lab coat every morning and work in a cubicle, facing insoluble problems that I could only refer to specialists or the benign pathologies that bored the life out of me. HMOs were asking their doctors for an impossible efficiency, allowing no more than four and a half minutes to diagnose and write out a prescription, and I knew that kind of life would kill me.

I wanted to go into forensics, and study the ancient bones left to us from cultures that have vanished from the planet. It was the dead who spoke to me. And I had a knack for listening.

So I gravitated toward archaeology, and the peculiar isolation of this work. Working on archaeological expeditions means hopping from one contract to the next, packing up and flying off at a moment's notice for two months or two years at a time. I've never met a man who could tolerate my dipping into and out of his life according to my work schedule, and the few times I let myself have a romantic fling with a fellow crew member, I had my heart broken when the contract was up and we had to go off and lead different lives. The long distance love affair doesn't work. It never works. You tell each other you'll write, but you don't write. He says he'll call, but he doesn't call. An email or two might show up in your Inbox, but in the end you have to swear off love, or you start feeling like an addict who's run out of drugs.

Of course the tiniest gesture—a smile, a touch, even the sight of a man walking away from me—can throw me off and make me want things that are dangerous to want. Last night, for instance, talking to Sam. It was nothing, really—he tipped the pot shard into my hand, and grazed my fingers with the side of his palm. Just that. A touch that lasted no more than a second. Less than that, probably. He didn't mean anything by it, I'm sure. And yet the memory of it ripples through me now, and something repressed and starved leaps up in recognition, electrified by an old hunger that begins to stir inside me. Most of the time I can ignore this need for touch, for contact, for love, and then it will flash across my body in a sudden heat.

So I watch this glimmer of attraction, the little nudge in his direction from the stray thoughts that come to me. What I might say the next time I see Sam. How I might make him laugh again and look at me. How I'll stand, or walk, or talk in front of him. I smother these thoughts, stomp them out like sparks near a pile of tinder-dry kindling. I had to bury that Kate a long time ago, and I have no intention of letting her screw up my life now.

The clatter of dishes guides me to the mess tent, where a stocky woman with bushy gray hair stands at a picnic bench near the kitchen, her arms sunk into a tub of soapy water. "Breakfast starts at seven," she says, lifting her arm out of the tub and looking pointedly at her black diver's watch. "You missed it."

"I'm Kate," I say. "I just arrived yesterday. Nobody told me the schedule for meals."

"Figures," the woman grunts.

"I'll run back to the tent and grab a granola bar," I say, turning to go.

"Sit," she says, wiping her hands on her overalls. She walks over to a six-burner Coleman stove on a nearby work bench, scoops a ladle into one of the pots and dumps the contents into a plastic bowl. "Here," she says, holding it out to me. "Spoons are in the green bag on the table. You'll have to wash your dishes when you're finished."

"Is there any coffee?" I ask meekly.

"Not any more."

The oatmeal is stone-cold and tastes like glue, but I eat it without complaint, reluctant to offend her any further. Sam's comment about Henry having no people skills comes back to me, and I guess the same thing could be said about his wife.

"I'm Fidelia," she says, drying her hands on a filthy dishtowel. "But everybody calls me Fiddle."

Silently I wonder if that's a good thing or a bad thing. "Nice to meet you."

"You're the bone lady," she says, staring at me.

I nod politely. "You could say that." When the oatmeal hits my stomach it feels like wet cement.

She crosses her arms in front of her ample chest and leans back against the work bench, her beady blue eyes boring into me. "So you dig up dead people, or what?"

"Usually they've already been excavated." I cup a hand over my mouth to spit out a raisin that's harder than my molars. "Have you catered for digs before?"

"No. I ran my own restaurant in Albuquerque."

Somehow the past tense doesn't surprise me.

Fiddle pulls a pack of cigarettes from her shirt pocket, taps one out and lights it. "Just so you know, lunch is at noon and dinner's at six." She exhales a plume of smoke in my direction. "Not that anybody gives a crap what I say. People come; people go. They do what they want. Not a word to me about their plans." She waves the cigarette toward the stove, the work bench, the cartons of supplies. "They think all this takes care of itself."

No wonder people go, I think, dragging my spoon through the oatmeal.

"Richter sails out of here, no warning," Fiddle mutters to herself. "Never offers to pick up fresh eggs or meat in Silver City, oh no." She sucks in a lungful of smoke, squinting at me as if I'm to blame. "Not him. He's a big shot. He can't be bothered."

"You think he went to Silver City?"

She shrugs. "Who knows? But if he doesn't turn up soon . . ." An odd smile plays across her face. "Then everything changes, doesn't it?"

Fiddle drops the cigarette and grinds it into the dirt with the heel of her boot then opens a large steel cooler under the work table behind her. Reaching in, she lifts out the skinned carcass of a jackrabbit. It dangles loosely from her fist as she holds it up by the feet for my inspection. The flesh gleams pinkly, the color suggesting a fresh kill. It holds the sweet odor of wild game, nothing like the stale muted smell of meat available in a supermarket.

"Lunch," she says, and slaps it down on the picnic bench, directly across from where I'm sitting. She stretches it out with the brisk efficiency of a woman who could probably skin and roast a mule for dinner. The carcass glistens in the morning light as she takes a canvas bundle from the work table and unrolls it to reveal a set of kitchen and hunting knives nested in slots sewn into the canvas. Sliding one of the knives out of its pocket, she holds it to the light, testing the edge for sharpness. This is no kitchen knife—it looks like a military weapon, a dagger with a blood groove running down the center of a stainless steel blade that's been polished to a mirror sheen.

Grunting in satisfaction, Fiddle spreads the carcass and presses the tip of the dagger against the hip joint, separating the ball of the femur cleanly from the socket of the pelvis. The blade sinks into the flesh like a hot needle piercing wax, and the tissue falls away from the bone.

"Nice cut," I tell her.

A murmur of voices rises from the bank of willow next to the mess tent, and we both look up at the interruption.

Sylvia emerges from the thicket and walks toward us, accompanied by a man in his early twenties. Her makeup has been flawlessly applied, her hair piled on top of her head in a loose chignon, with dark curling tendrils and wisps that float around her face. She wears a snug embroidered vest over a tailored white shirt with black jeans and pointed black cowboy boots.

I put my bowl down on the picnic bench, stand and offer them both a tentative smile.

Ignoring Fiddle, Sylvia pushes the young man forward slightly. "Jason, this is Kate Donovan. Kate, this is my son, Jason."

Dressed carefully in belted shorts and an immaculate white cotton shirt that fits tightly against his shoulders, Jason Richter is a walking ad for Abercrombie & Fitch, while his face looks like a masculine version of Sylvia's: broad, high cheekbones, hooked nose, and eyes so dark the pupils melt into the irises. A gold watch on his wrist flashes in the light of the morning sun.

"Jason's one of our volunteers," Sylvia says, sliding a possessive arm around his waist. Her face softens as she brushes a stray lock of hair back from his forehead. "He's been a great help to us on this expedition."

Jason twitches away from her as his mother strokes his hair. I push my hands deep into my pockets and glance uneasily toward

Fiddle, who watches them intently. *No,* I think. Fiddle's not watching both of them. She's watching Sylvia. Fiddle barely glances at her hands as the knife whisks through flesh, as if she's butchered a thousand rabbits.

Sylvia's attention flows to her son and only her son, adoration written across her face. "It's been wonderful for us to have this much time together. He's been so busy these last few years."

Busy? I think. There's a great euphemism for dodging criminal prosecution.

"So you're the rainmaker," he says, looking me over. "Here to solve all our problems."

I hesitate, unsure what to say, and finally shrug in what I hope is a friendly, noncommittal way.

A corner of his mouth curls up as his eyes remain locked on mine, his gaze sharp, probing, waiting for me to flinch. "Sam says you have a talent for hocus-pocus. Telepathy, psychic vibes, fortune telling, that kind of thing—so is it true? Are you a good witch or a bad witch?"

The back of my neck stiffens at Jason's tone.

"Jason." Sylvia's voice holds a warning.

He gives his mother a cool glance before his gaze shifts past her shoulder and fixes on a figure in the distance, striding toward us. "Here comes your real problem."

Henry approaches us, brow furrowed, his expression dark. "What are you doing here, Jason?" he calls out. "Why aren't you in the tunnel?"

"Yes, I did sleep well, thanks so much for asking. And how about you, Henry? How did you sleep?" Jason's tone remains unruffled, but there's a slight emphasis on the last question.

Henry stares at Jason, who meets his gaze in a visual tug-of-war, and a hush descends over the clearing, as if the canyon walls themselves are appraising this exchange.

"Leave him alone, Henry," Sylvia says quietly.

Henry reaches out abruptly and grabs Jason's arm. "You're coming with me, son. No more excuses. We had a deal."

Jason yanks his arm away, and Sylvia slides between them. "Stop it," she says. "He's been through enough. He doesn't have to account to you for his every move."

"Oh, I think he does," Henry says.

Jason leans toward his mother. "I'll be in my tent. Come over when you have a chance to talk." As he turns away from them his mouth tightens in a self-satisfied smile, a smile they don't see. He catches me looking at him, and the smile vanishes. He holds my gaze for a second, then saunters off toward the creek.

"You have to stop treating him like a child, Henry," Sylvia says. "There's no point in making him hate you." She looks off at the cliffs beyond the pyramid. "Why aren't you looking for Adam?"

Henry casts a sidelong glance at Fiddle, then stares at the ground. Something about the way he doesn't quite look at Sylvia draws my attention like a magnet. He and Sylvia aren't standing particularly close to one another. Her face is smooth, expressionless as always. Henry keeps his features still. He doesn't touch her, and she doesn't touch him. But there's something in the way they don't look at each other. The way they don't move away from each other. The tension in their bodies, the alertness. Sylvia fingers her collar, and Henry glances at her fingers, then away.

Henry and Sylvia are having an affair. There's absolutely no doubt in my mind. I don't want to know this. I don't need to know it.

I steal a look at Fiddle standing at the table in front of the butchered rabbit, the knife still in her hand, her gaze leveled at Sylvia like a marksman taking aim. Her mouth is a hard, pinched line.

"It's been four days," Henry says quietly. "He could be in

Vegas, for Christ's sake. He'll come back when he's ready to come back."

"I left a message with his service in Washington," Sylvia says in an undertone. "And his secretary at UNM."

"If he checks his messages, he'll be back."

She shakes her head, her voice no more than a whisper, and I strain to catch what she says. "That's a big 'if,' Henry."

Henry reaches out and touches her arm. Sylvia leans toward him slightly, her head bowed, and then she turns away and walks back to her tent.

Fiddle watches her leave, and her cheeks slowly turn a dull, mottled red. Suddenly I feel a pang of pity for her. She must be close to sixty. Pot-bellied, sagging, her skin rough and cracked— she's no match for Sylvia's slim elegance. She turns away, squats next to the work table and begins unloading cans from a box, slapping each one down on the table with unnecessary force.

Henry's face closes like a cupboard as he turns toward me, his customary hostility back in place. "You're late. Follow me."

Without another word he walks off toward the sound of a pickax ringing out as steel strikes stone. The others must have already assembled at the pyramid.

I trot after Henry and try to absorb the scene I just witnessed. Does anyone else know about the affair between Henry and Sylvia? It leaves me with a small, cold sliver of worry, like a thorn stuck in my chest. I wonder if Richter knew, and whether or not that had something to do with his departure.

The pyramid casts a long shadow over the crew, and the tunnel yawns like a dark mouth at the base of the east wall. My stomach rumbles nervously at the thought of working in there, under thousands of tons of dirt and rock, with only a few shaky-looking posts and beams to support the subterranean passageway. A line of workers has already formed in front of the hole in the pyramid, to ferry buckets of rock from hand to hand.

Henry points to a vacant spot in the ragged line of crew members in front of the tunnel, and I step into it. "Welcome to the bucket brigade," he says. There's no smile with the words, no friendliness at all. With arms and legs like wire, his whole body looks like a Giacometti sculpture, right down to the forward tilt as he hustles back to the mouth of the tunnel, all business, rush and duty.

Without any wasted motion he nods to Michael, who hands him a large pail filled with rocks, which Henry passes to me. It must weigh at least sixty pounds, and I immediately let it drop.

Sam emerges from behind a pile of rubble thirty yards away, walks over, and takes the pail from me. "Morning, Kate. You ready to pick up the pace? Our tailings go over there." He nods toward the mound of dirt he just left and walks away, showing no visible sign of strain at the weight.

A few seconds later Henry brings another bucketful of rock back to me, and I walk it over to Sam. This bucket is even heavier, and I have to drag it.

"Why aren't we using a wheelbarrow?" I ask Sam, pitching my voice so Henry won't hear me. "This is ridiculous."

"One of them is broken, and the other one's inside the tunnel." He catches the look on my face. "Be grateful you're out in the fresh air, Kate. It's worse in there."

Before long I find out what he means. We rotate at thirty-minute intervals, and after half an hour of carrying buckets of rock and dirt, it's my turn to dig. As soon as I approach the dark opening, a young man emerges from the tunnel. A dirty bandage covers his head under the hard hat.

"I'm Will," he says. "Glad to have you on board, Kate." He hands me his pick, shovel, and hard-hat with the miner's lamp attached, and then he gives me an exhausted smile that gleams in the black dust on his face. "Good luck." The sincerity in his voice alarms me, and I watch him limp off to the back of the line. He must be the volunteer who was hurt in the cave-in yesterday. If I were in his shoes I don't think I'd risk going back to work in there.

Cold air pours over me as I enter the dark throat of the tunnel. The walls rattle from the force of the pickax blows echoing in the vault, while dirt sifts down continuously in the gloom. *Bam. Bam. Bam.* Every thud makes the boards creak in the braces, and in the dull beam of my headlamp I can see the timbers vibrate from the assault. When I reach Jessie she throws me a hostile look.

"This is such a fucking waste." Her chest heaves with effort as she stoops to pick up a rock, tosses it in a wheelbarrow full of tailings, and bends down to grab another.

Following her lead, I lift a rock the size of a bowling ball and chuck it on the pile. "Do you want to take a rest?"

Jessie ignores my suggestion. She grabs the pick and swings it until a hail of dirt comes down on both of us. "That's all we've found here," she says, breathing hard, wiping the dust from her eyes. "Dirt and basalt. Lots and lots of basalt."

"There should be something to indicate a burial, if there was one." I wipe the dirt from my eyes and scan the tunnel walls in the faint light of our lamps. "Statuary. Mosaics. Murals. Something."

Jessie grunts as she swings the pick. "Try telling that to Henry."

We work in silence for a few minutes before I ask her the question that's been nagging me ever since I arrived at the camp. "You think Dr. Richter will come back?"

Her movements slow, then stop. "I don't know."

"Michael said he's done this kind of thing before."

"Never like this," Jessie says.

"You've worked with him before?"

In the unsteady light of my headlamp I see her glance at me. "I know he'd never put this expedition in jeopardy. There's no way he'd go off for four days without telling me."

Jessie looks like she's barely twenty, pretty and smooth-skinned but tough, like a kid who's been raised in the barrio. Not exactly the type I'd expect Richter to confide in, and nothing at all like Sylvia.

She throws down the pick and takes up the shovel, plants one foot on the lip and pushes it into the pile of debris, then tips the shovel into the wheelbarrow. "If you want to see some artifacts, come over to the pit house ruins Sam and I have been excavating."

"I'd like that. Sylvia didn't show me those."

"I'm not surprised." Jessie finishes shoveling the loose pile of gravel into the wheelbarrow, then hoists the pick and hits the wall with a resounding whack.

"What have you found in the ruins?"

"Not much, really, but there are a few interesting bits and pieces. Some tools. A few spear points, broken bowls, and lots of shards. The pit houses were primitive, but it's where these people lived while they were building the pyramid."

"Any bones?"

"No. It's strange. It's like they all just disappeared. Maybe there was the same kind of Diaspora there was in Mexico after Teotihuacán fell, and they joined the Mogollon or the Anasazi."

"I doubt it," I say. "Their skulls are distinctive. If an anthropologist ever found any in this area, I would have heard about it."

I lean over to lift a rock, twist to drop it in the wheelbarrow, and feel a sickeningly familiar stitch in my back, right down there in the *longissimus dorsii*, the same muscle that always gives me trouble when I'm digging. Damn. I've been working less than an hour. It's been nearly a year since I did any archaeol-

ogy, and I'm out of shape.

Slowly I straighten my spine and massage the small of my back with my fists. It's not just the work that makes my muscles knot up. There's a free-floating tension in the camp, an anxiety that lurks in everyone I've met, a communal dread that infects all of them. The air is thick with secrets, and hostility runs through the crew like the heaviness that builds before a hurricane. As far as I can see, Henry's not fooling anybody. He's barely treading water here.

Jessie batters the stone with her pick, hurling herself into every arc like a logger trying to fell a redwood in one swing. I look down at the wheelbarrow and try to imagine pushing the heavy load up the corridor of the tunnel without groaning out loud.

The dust makes me cough. "I think this is full."

Without hesitating she throws the pick to the ground, lifts the handles of the barrow and pushes the load of rock into the tunnel, where the bobbing light of her headlamp quickly disappears in the inky blackness.

As soon as she leaves, I prop the shovel against a post and open my palms to the walls surrounding me. Slowly I turn my hands in every direction, casting for bones. Nothing. Not a glimmer, not a twitch, no tingle of heat. My hands remain cold, indifferent.

The clatter of the wheelbarrow rolling down the passageway fills the tunnel. Jessie pushes it to a stop in front of me and lets it drop, then bends over and lifts the pickax from the ground as if it weighs no more than a garden hoe. No sign of fatigue in her movements. The girl is pure muscle, tall and lean and built like a gazelle. Wiping her brow with the back of her arm, the pick rests easily on her shoulder as she stares at the wall ahead.

"Can you believe this shit?" she mutters. "There's nothing here. I mean, think about it. They found more than twelve

hundred burials at the site for the Pyramid of the Moon in Teotihuacán, with tons of artifacts. All we have is one lousy human sacrifice."

Silently I agree but pick up my shovel and press the blade into the pile of debris, then dump the load in the wheelbarrow.

She takes in a deep breath and lets it out in a long, exasperated sigh. "Goddamn Henry. We're digging into a mountain of rubble just because he wants to throw his weight around. He must have the tiniest dick in the universe."

The beam from a miner's headlamp switches on behind us, cutting through the blackness, startling me like the touch of a cattle prod. "I'll take your place, Jessie."

She whirls around to face the light. "Jesus, Henry. Do you have to creep around like that?" She ignores the hand he extends to take the pick, tosses the pickax on the ground and stomps off toward fresh air and daylight.

Henry shoulders his way past me, lifts the pick and hammers the wall with repeated blows, while I shovel the tailings. Dust rains down from the ceiling of the tunnel in an ominous and constant whisper of instability while the timbers groan in the shadows.

Henry grunts and sweats and curses, and my ears grow numb from the ringing of steel against rock. His agitation fills the space, making it even more claustrophobic, and I fight the urge to throw down my shovel and walk out.

"You try," he says, coughing, and hands the pick to me.

The pickax is heavy, and when I swing it into the black wall of rock the impact jars every bone in my body. The strained muscle in my back screams in protest and sends a cascade of pain down my legs. I lift the pick again as he barks out a correction.

"Higher!"

I continue, half-tempted to drive the pick into his foot.

The minutes tick by. Nothing turns up. No hidden chambers, no murals, not a shred of evidence that there are any tombs hidden inside the stone façade of the pyramid. Dirt infiltrates my eyes, my nose, my ears. Every pore feels choked with dust, and when I swallow I can feel the grit between my teeth.

The pyramid seems implacable, its secrets buried forever. And I'd bet the last fifty dollars in my checking account that Sam is right—the tombs we're looking for aren't in the pyramid. The pyramid is no more than a decoy.

Chapter Five

In the evening I snatch the remaining hours of daylight to finish excavating the skeleton, hoping to complete my measurements before sunset, and as I work the familiar routine absorbs me completely. My tools are always soothing to handle: calipers in a range of sizes, jointed boards, six-feet-long telescoping rulers, made of polished wood and steel—each one fits my hand with reassuring familiarity. I love their low-tech simplicity, their classic exactness. But it's the bones I love the most, with their smooth ivory texture, their solid, fossilized weight in my hand.

After a few hours of careful digging, I know the long bones are all here, in addition to the skull and the pelvis, and I'm grateful for that, since these are the critical bones for making any estimates about height, weight, and age. In addition to the long bones, there are twelve pairs of ribs, the sternum, both scapulas, both clavicles and all twenty-four vertebrae. Altogether I find one hundred and sixty-six bones. Rodents must have picked off some of the phalanges and metacarpals and a few of the smaller bones of the wrist and ankle.

When I look up I see Sam standing at the edge of the canvas I've spread out near the pit to hold the skeleton. In the low evening light his features seem softer, fresher. His hair is wet, and a fleck of shaving foam dots his earlobe.

He squats to my level, hands resting comfortably on his knees, looking relaxed, calm. It's attractive, that calm. I can feel myself being drawn to it, wanting to smile, wanting to say something that will make him smile.

"You look happy," he says.

I look at the bone I hold in my hand. A femur. The thigh bone. Beautifully preserved by the desert sand, the shape itself seems exquisite. I flirt the dust from the smooth surface with my brush, trace the grooves and notches, study the rough eminence where the ligaments were once attached.

"Look at this," I say, and present the femur to him.

"What does it tell you?" he asks, holding the bone.

"The height of the skeleton, for one thing." By the time I measure each long bone and feed the numbers into my calculator, I'm sure the results will confirm what I already suspect. "This was a young male. No more than eighteen to twenty years old, five feet six at the most. He probably weighed about a hundred and twenty pounds."

Sam peers at the fossilized marrow before he hands it back to me. "There are crystals in here."

I nod. Mineralization of the bones is well advanced, and the marrow in several of the long bones has been replaced by quartz crystals.

"Take a look at this one," I urge Sam, holding out the magnifying glass and the fourth cervical vertebra.

He exchanges the femur for the vertebra and the magnifying glass. "What am I looking for?" he asks, scanning the bone.

"See that V-shaped notch?"

"Barely. Isn't that from a rodent gnawing on the bone?"

"Rodents make scooped indentations that are more rounded. See? Like that one." I point out a few parallel gouges for comparison. "This notch was made by a knife or a dagger—you can see how it must have thickened toward the middle of the blade."

He squints at the mark, turning the bone under the magnifying glass. "You sure about that? It's nearly invisible."

It's a tiny mark, but it tells the story of his death. "Someone stabbed him in the neck, just under the jaw. They had to cut through two inches of flesh and gristle to make this little nick on the bone. A thrust hard enough to slice through all the muscles, nerves and cartilage of his throat, hard enough to scratch the bone. With his jugular vein severed he would have bled to death within seconds."

Sam raises an eyebrow and hands the vertebra and magnifying glass back to me. "I'll have to take your word for it. Are you going to take any samples of tissue for DNA analysis?"

I nod. "They'll go with my report. Then I'll photograph the bones, wrap them up and put them aside for reburial by the Apache, or whatever tribe finally claims them."

I sink back on my knees and wipe the sand from my forehead, suddenly exhausted. My back is on fire from leaning over the skeleton, and fatigue drops over me like a shroud. It's only been one day, but it feels like a week.

"Sam, I'm going to need some money before too long. Dr. Richter told me he'd reimburse me for my flight as soon as I arrived, and I was hoping I could ride out to Silver City next week and wire some money to my account. Do you think Henry or Sylvia could cut me a check?"

He picks up one of the heel bones, the calcaneum, turns it in his fingers and studies it in silence, then puts it back on the tarp. "Dr. Richter was going to see the money guys at *National Geographic* and the Archaeological Institute next week. Without their okay, he's pretty strapped for cash right now."

"I don't need much. Just a few hundred dollars."

Sam shrugs. "For the moment, he's broke."

I cock my head, waiting for him to clarify that last sentence. He remains silent, and returns my gaze without even a hint of apology.

"But he'll get the money, won't he?" I ask.

"If nothing's happened to him."

"What about Sylvia? Do you think she could give me an advance?"

"There's no money, Kate."

His words sink into my brain and detonate. How much longer can I stay here without a paycheck? My credit cards have been pushed to the limit, and I'm already two months behind with the rent. More to the point, why am I working so hard if I'm not getting paid?

Because I have one shot at this, I remind myself. Because if I don't perform well enough to make them believe I'm the best candidate for the job, I'm finished, and they'll fire me even if Richter comes back with a bundle of grant money. Sam's already told me they plan to dump me and hire the best, just as soon as they can afford to.

I stare at the pyramid looming above us, then let my gaze fall to the bones at my feet. There's nothing I can say. Nothing I can do, except quit and go home. But then what? What would I do? Beg the bank for another loan? Take the waitress job? No way. I have one chance, and this time I'm not going to blow it. The gathering dusk casts a web of shadows over us, and the air feels suddenly cold.

Even after a quick bath in the icy water of the creek, I feel gritty. The birds have quieted for the night, and the first stars appear above the cliffs hemming in the canyon. A light breeze rustles the leaves of the sycamores. I unzip the screen door of my tent and bend to enter, ready to stretch out in my sleeping bag for the rest of the night.

"Sam!" someone calls out.

I rise and brush my hands against my jeans, suddenly aware of the sound of raised voices filtering through the trees.

Michael rushes into the clearing, hurrying toward Sam's tent, stumbling over rocks, clearly upset.

Sam's head pops out of the door to his tent. "What's the matter?"

Michael glances over his shoulder toward the ruckus coming from north side of the campsite, and I head over to the two of them.

"It's Henry and Jason." Michael gestures toward the sound, his breathing ragged. "They're fighting again. Can you help me break it up?"

Sam is already tugging on his boots and leaves them untied as they take off toward the stream without another word. I hesitate a moment, then hustle after them.

Past the creek, on the other side of the willow thicket, the twilight reveals Jason and Henry squared off, fists clenched, looking like they want to kill each other. Jason weighs at least twenty pounds more than Henry, and he's forty years younger, but Jason looks soft, with a little paunch that hangs over his belt. I've seen Henry swing a pick and lift a hundred buckets of rock. There's no doubt about it: Henry will win.

Michael edges forward cautiously, touches Henry's shoulder and mutters something inaudible in his ear. Henry's eyes never leave Jason's, and he shakes Michael off and steps toward Jason, snatching him by the collar. "Don't you lie to *me*, son." He hauls him close, nearly lifting him off his feet.

Abruptly Jason's fist lashes out and connects with the side of Henry's face, and before we can stop him Henry slings him down in the dirt. Jason grabs Henry's long ponytail on his way down, and Henry lets out a grunt and falls on top of him. The two of them roll on the ground, red-faced and locked in combat. Within seconds their shirts are torn, Jason's nose erupts with blood, and a long scratch appears on the side of Henry's face. Michael and Sam rush forward to pull the men apart as Henry scrambles to his feet, his eyes wild.

Jason's face is white with fury. A brilliant streak of blood issues from his nose, spattering his shirt with red. "You stay the hell away from me!"

I shrink back, shaken by the rage in his voice, wishing I could disappear before they notice me standing here, but I don't dare move.

"If I ever hear you've been up to your dirty tricks again I'll break every bone in your body," Henry snarls, struggling to free himself from Michael.

Sylvia enters the clearing and dashes toward the center of the group, then halts in her tracks at the sight of Jason's face. "What have you done to him?" she shouts at Henry, then rips the silk scarf from her throat and presses it to the stream of blood coming from her son's nose. Jason clutches the cloth to his face and wrenches away from Sam's grasp.

Henry jerks himself away from Michael's arms and approaches Sylvia. "Did you know your boy was using the satellite phone in your tent? Did you know he was talking to his friends in New York every night?"

"Why shouldn't he talk to his friends?" she snaps. "For God's sake, he's a grown man."

"Half of them are in jail, Sylvia," Henry growls. "They're crooks."

In the dying light his words take on a strange menace, and I wonder if the stress of Richter's absence has finally tipped Henry over the edge. For a long, bizarre moment Jason and Henry stare at each other, their eyes glittering with rage.

"What are you, my parole officer?" Jason finally sputters.

"We had a deal, Jason." Henry bites off the end of each word. "You're working on a classified government project. There will be no calls to your friends from this site. Is that clear?"

"You're a joke," Jason says. "You have no authority over me. You haven't even found anything worth stealing."

"Is that why you're here? Now that you've been kicked off Wall Street, you think you can loot this site for your friends back home?"

"Stop it, both of you," Sylvia shouts. "This is ridiculous, Henry. You're only going to antagonize him."

"Too late," Jason mutters.

Sylvia touches Henry's arm and softens her voice. "He's been through hell, Henry. Please, give him a chance. For me."

Shafts of light from the setting sun poke through the trees into the clearing, and suddenly Henry turns and looks right at me. Every hair on the back of my neck stiffens at the expression on his face.

"This is between us," he says in a low, frightening voice. "Stay out of it." His malevolent gaze swings toward Sam and Michael. "All of you. Just stay the hell out of it."

I wake abruptly from a vivid, threatening dream, something about somebody trying to hide a dead body and stuffing it into a closet in my apartment. The dream clings to me as I struggle up from the depths of sleep and break through the surface of the present. I'm stiff all over from sleeping on the ground, and I stretch and check my watch. It's only five a.m. Dark outside, and the camp is silent.

The thought of working in the tunnel all day fills me with a deep, hopeless chill in the pit of my stomach. I don't want to work in the tunnel. I don't want to pound rock with a pick or shovel basalt rubble into a bucket when every ounce of intuition I have tells me it's pointless. I don't want to pretend everything is fine when the expedition leader is gone, and no one knows whether he's dead or alive. At this point, it will be hard to forgive Dr. Richter if he is alive. The same restlessness that infected me in Paquimé is here again, and my brain grinds away, thinking long irritable thoughts. I didn't sweat out eight years of medical school to dig into a pile of rubble, no matter how glamorous the pyramid looks from the outside. I'm a forensic anthropologist, goddamn it, not a ditch digger, not some expendable piece of muscle who will put up with an egomaniac like Henry. I'm not even getting paid, and after another fitful night of sleep on the hard ground, that thought rankles more than any other.

Unfortunately Henry was right about one thing: the artifacts Sam and Jessie have excavated from the pit houses have no real significance, except for the fact that they're here, a thousand miles from where anyone might expect them to be. No more human sacrifices have turned up. No burials of any kind. It doesn't make sense. Twelve centuries ago this valley was occupied by a royal court and enough soldiers and sculptors and masons to construct the pyramid. So where are they? Where are the bones?

As I pull the sleeping bag up to my chin, Sam's words about the lava tubes drift through my head, and I think longingly of the mesa and the caves that might be up there. How many mornings do I have left in this place if Dr. Richter doesn't show up? How long can the dig function without funds, without a leader? I shiver at the memory of Jason and Henry, brawling on the ground. It's pretty clear Sylvia won't be able to control either one of them much longer. No one is happy here.

I yawn and scratch my scalp and stretch my aching joints, then squirm around searching for a more comfortable position on the hard ground. Digging in the tunnel won't begin for another three hours, and there's no way I'll be able to go back to sleep. It's hardly enough time to search for lava tubes, but there's plenty of time to climb the mesa and take a look. With this thought I'm wide awake, filled with the urge to get up and go.

The pre-dawn light in the east promises a clear and sunny day ahead. Quickly I pull on a pair of jeans, hiking boots, T-shirt and a hat, then stuff a bottle of water, a granola bar and a few tools in my day pack, along with my field notebook and a topographical map. On impulse I take the Polaroid camera that my dad gave me before I went to Iraq last summer, along with a few packs of film. I zip the tent behind me as quietly as possible and set off at a brisk pace, eager to leave the camp before anyone sees me wandering off.

It's a steep half-mile climb out of the canyon, and by the time I reach the top of the mesa I'm breathing hard. Up here the trees are low, pressed back to the earth by the wind, and the broad-shouldered humps of bedrock are scattered with shrubs: yucca, beargrass, prickly poppy, and agave. The dawn flares along the eastern horizon and the wind pushes me forward. The views are fantastic, and as I walk I feel the release in my shoulders, which ache from digging and the tension in the camp.

It's good to be up above it all, out of the confines of the canyon, and I wander without much plan or thought about doing a careful survey. The rising sun sends daggers of light toward me, and the shadows shrink so quickly it looks as if the earth itself is rushing toward day. The plants seem unusually glossy and strong up here, and even the stands of prickly pear look lush with health this far from cars and smog and pedestrians.

Five hundred million years earlier, during the Paleozoic and Mesozoic eras, the seas advanced and swallowed the land where I walk now, leaving sediments rich in marine fossils. During the Cretaceous Period, hundreds of millions of years later, there was a tremendous squeezing that uplifted the region in a great series of folds, like wrinkles in a carpet. Erosion carved the mountains, exposing their hard rock cores, and great quantities of sand and clay were spread to bordering plains and plateaus.

About forty million years ago, near the end of the Eocene Epoch, volcanoes erupted, then erupted again a few million years later. Streams and rivers cut canyons and deep gorges across the mountains and mesas of New Mexico. So much geology is exposed here in the high desert, and it's exhilarating to see it all laid out before me for a hundred miles in any direction. To the north, silhouettes of volcanic cones rim the mesa, and a lone butte towers to the west where the canyon land ends. All around me the landscape blazes with morning sunlight. I drift over the dips and rises of the mesa, walking toward the volcanic cones on the horizon.

After hiking a few miles without finding so much as a pot shard, I climb a low rise and stretch out on the ground to bask in the early morning sun. The air is cool, the sun warm, and I sprawl on the grass and let my muscles go slack. The grass bends to the wind as a few ragged clouds gather along the western horizon. Claret cup cacti open to the light, offering a chalice of rose-red petals to the bees that hug the ground. New grass pushes up among the clumps of knee-high blue grama.

The breeze plays across my face, bringing the smell of sun-warmed dirt. The heat from the ground cradles me, inviting sleep, while the sound of the bees working the prickly pear blooms lulls me into a lazy, vacant daydream, where images drift through my mind like pollen.

Half-dozing, I cast my thoughts back to the Teotihuacános who made the journey here. There's a timelessness to this place, and it's easy to imagine them living here. Hunting, foraging, building the pyramid. Coping with the shock of becoming refugees after they'd spent their lives ruling others.

A moment later I sink into the abyss of fatigue that's dogged me ever since I arrived in Albuquerque. My eyes close. Images flicker through me, a parade of landscapes and faces, and then a welcoming cloak of lethargy covers me like a shroud. I lie there, unable to move.

When I open my eyes again an unnatural brightness seeps into the edge of my vision, and I can almost feel the People, in another time, a different reality, a reality that feels as close as the wilderness around me. Every thorn on the cholla, every rock and blade of grass seems clear and particular in the morning light.

As I lie there my point of view effortlessly ascends, like a hawk gaining altitude, soaring higher and higher. In this half-dream I look down and see a procession of mourners move along the ground below me, a column of hundreds of people walking toward the largest volcanic cone on the mesa.

Clothed in richly dyed cotton mantles and elaborately carved headgear adorned with quetzal feathers, the parade glitters below me. Two men at the head of the procession carry a large shield of gold that reflects the rays of the sun, and the sound of their voices spirals up to me like smoke. Behind the men with the golden shield, four priests carry a pallet on their shoulders, like an offering, with a small figure lying on it. A boy. A boy with a mask over his face. The boy is dead.

Abruptly my eyes fly open, and a chill ripples over my skin at the image of the dead child that lingers in my mind. My brain feels muddy with sleep, caught between worlds, and I rub my face, trying to erase the ghosts that hover close to me. The sun is high overhead, and I realize I must have dozed off for more than a few minutes. With an effort I sit up, adjust my hat, rise to my feet and brush myself off, lightheaded from the heat

I check my watch. It's late. Almost noon.

Damn, I think. I'm in big trouble. By now everyone back at camp must be wondering where I am. They've already been working all morning, digging in the tunnel, ferrying buckets of basalt and dirt out of the belly of the pyramid. I'm already late—what difference will it make if I explore a little further? I look around, trying to get my bearings.

The largest volcanic cone rises directly in front of me to the north, its contour softly rounded like a breast. From this angle

it looks exactly like Cerro Gordo, the holy mountain of Teotihuacán, the embodiment of the goddess they worshipped.

The temples of Teotihuacán were laid out precisely on a
north-south axis, and from the center of their main street, the
Avenue of the Dead, the summit of Cerro Gordo could be seen
towering above the apex of the Pyramid of the Moon.

The hair on my arms begins to rise as I realize I've been lying on the ground halfway between the pyramid and the largest
volcanic cone on the mesa, along a north-south axis. Why hasn't
anyone noticed the orientation of this volcano to the pyramid?
Even though it's at least twenty miles away, it seems obvious
that the pyramid was built to face the volcano. Maybe Dr.
Richter saw the relationship and dismissed it, but I'm convinced
the tomb of the king must lie somewhere along this axis.

I walk on toward the volcano, scanning the ground for the
tell-tale spill of broken basalt that could indicate an opening to
a lava tube. The mesa seems to expand as I walk, becoming
larger, a sea of grass under the limitless curve of the sky. It feels
wonderful to skim the ground in long scissoring strides, to walk
off the guilt of missing a day of work, and the anxiety of what
might happen to me if I don't return to the camp with
something to show for it.

Another hour of walking reveals nothing, and I fall into the
rhythm of walking for its own sake, a mindless push toward the
volcanic cone. By now I know I'll never reach it. It's too far, at
least another ten or fifteen miles. By now I don't care.

At first the mound ahead appears to be no more than another
rise in a mesa full of dips and rises, but as I walk closer I see
how it's gently, almost imperceptibly rounded in all directions,
a dome of earth and rock about fifty feet across. Underneath
the tufts of blue grama grass there are large slabs of basalt.

Slowly I circle it, heart racing. The palms of my hands begin
to throb. Struggling to remain objective, I note the cholla and

prickly pear on the south side of the mound, the fine-grained hills of harvester ants, and the clumps of bluestem and grama grass, which are thicker on the rise. These slight variations in the terrain are all familiar, all signs of a ruin. My eyes zero in on the rubble of large basalt slabs on the north side of the mound and a small hole between the boulders.

The hole is hardly bigger than the palm of my hand, but it draws me closer. Several smaller rocks cover one side of it, and when I drag the stones away I can see the hole is larger than it first appeared.

I kick at the layer of dirt around the top edge and a clump of earth gives way, revealing a shaft that slants down into the basalt. Cautiously, I bend over to peer inside, and see the tunnel disappear into blackness. My heartbeat accelerates into a jumpy staccato rhythm, a quick skitter of expectation. A chill emanates from the mouth of the tunnel like a cold breath, and the back of my neck begins to tingle.

With my bare hands I break away the clumps of blue grama that cling to the base of the entrance to the hole. It's easy to scoop the shallow dirt aside to enlarge the shaft in the rock. The tunnel is bigger than I thought, large enough to accommodate me if I wriggle in on my belly.

With steadily mounting excitement I take off my hat, snap off the elastic at the bottom of my braid and pull my hair back in a tight ponytail to keep the flyaway wisps out of my face. Before I can talk myself out of it, I pull out my penlight, click it on, hold it between my teeth and enter the hole head first.

The walls of the shaft are cold, the passage thick with cobwebs that catch on my face and trail over my hair. I swab my face and spit out the strands, then look down the passage. There's hardly room to take a deep breath, and I can feel my pack scrape the rock above me as I inch forward. In the beam of the penlight a centipede flutters across the stone and shimmies into a crevice I'll have to pass over if I keep going.

What the hell do you think you're doing? I ask myself. What if you get stuck? Do you really want to die out here, caught like an animal in a trap?

Panic seizes me, and I scuttle backwards, my shirt riding up to my armpits in my eagerness to get out. At last I pop free of the tunnel and crouch in the open air for a minute, breathing hard. The hole remains mute, open-mouthed, still.

Feeling foolish, I peer back down into the tunnel. I can't turn my back on it and go back to camp. How can I abandon whatever prize might lie at the bottom? Buffeted by the rising wind, I shout into the hole to flush any resident wildlife. "Hey! Anybody home?" My words vanish into the earth, answered only by a whiff of cooler air.

My skin crawls at the thought of entering that tight dark space, but I have to try. I kick the slab of basalt over the opening, testing its solidity. It doesn't budge.

I take a deep breath and force myself back in.

Except for the narrow beam from the pen light, the blackness inside the tunnel is absolute. I wrestle my way forward on my elbows and pray there are no snakes. I try to forget everything I've ever heard about the balls of rattlers that spend the winter clumped together, sheltered in places just like this. The air temperature falls at least thirty degrees as I slide down the frigid corridor, and the shaft continues to slope steeply as I edge down, ten feet, then twenty, the passage just wide enough to permit my shoulders and hips, but not high enough for me to crawl. If there's no room to turn around at the bottom I'll have to do this again, uphill and backwards, just to get out. I shove that thought away and wriggle forward.

After what feels like a hundred yards of scraping along on my belly, the shaft swells and opens into a cavern in the rock, a place big enough for me to stand. In the thin beam of light I can see the cave is roughly rectangular, about eighteen by twelve by fifteen feet high. A faint musk of guano hangs in the air.

The walls have been whitewashed and intricately painted with murals. Each picture is bordered with row upon row of glyphs, the surface in pristine condition, untouched by time, as bright as if the paint were wet. As I play the light over the walls my breath comes in short gasps, and I'm caught in a wave of elation so great it almost feels like fear.

My eyes burn as I realize where I am, and what I've found.

The mummy of a child lies on a low altar in the center of the room, swathed in the trappings of a prince, necklace laid upon necklace, with enormous earrings of carved and polished jade. The face is covered with a tiny funerary mask made of alabaster, inlaid with turquoise, serpentine and shell mosaic, and animal skins cover most of the body in tightly wrapped strips of rabbit fur interwoven with turkey feathers.

Suddenly I'm overwhelmed, stricken by the sight of the child I saw in my dream. He's so small, so young. My eyes sting with tears for this tiny, desiccated body before me, and the culture that placed him here with so much reverence, so much hope.

Delicately, tenderly, I lift the mask away from the skull with trembling hands and see that necrophagic insects have eaten some of the soft parts of the face. My light bounces off white bone under a lock of black hair still attached to a scrap of leathery scalp above the skull.

It's impossible to determine the sex of the child accurately in the gloom of the cave, with the cranium only partly revealed, but I know it's male. The skull stares at me, the skin around its mouth held in the fixed and silent scream of the boy who died centuries ago. Most of the mummies I've excavated present this fearful grimace, as if they've died in extreme pain. No matter how peaceful the death, the jaw sags and the skin shrinks, exposing teeth in what looks like terror. Was he assassinated? Did he fall sick and die in exile? I study the sutures that are visible in the cranium, then turn my attention to the teeth and skin-covered neck and clavicle below the slack lower jaw. There's a turquoise bead lying on the tissue that was once his tongue. His people must have placed it there, as food for the journey.

How small he is, I marvel: only three feet tall. Judging by the size of the body and the dental formation and eruption, I'm fairly sure he was only five or six years old when he died. The cranial suture closures aren't as reliable an indicator as the teeth, but they're what I'd expect in a five year old boy.

Carefully I replace the funerary mask, knowing Dr. Richter would have my head on a platter if he knew I'd touched the mummy without documenting it first. Moving quickly and quietly, I set the pack on the floor, draw out my Polaroid camera and take a picture of the figure, using the flash.

Instantly the cave explodes in a rush and clatter of wings as a dozen bats fly by my head and out through the tunnel. When my heart starts beating again I take twenty more photographs, then place them in a row on the floor to let them dry while the images emerge. The tape measure lies at the bottom of my pack, and I extract it to take measurements of the cave, the mummy, and the mummy's position within it. While I hold the penlight in my teeth, I draw an outline of the cave in my field notebook, sketching the location of the mummy and the artifacts.

The glyphs on the ceiling look nothing like the random, graffiti-like scatter of tribal signs I've seen before in New Mexico. These are dense, orderly rows of pictographs. I copy the designs in my notebook, my hands shaking at the enormity of what I'm transcribing. Teotihuacán writings are extremely rare even in Mexico, and the walls in this cave are covered with them.

The methodical work calms my breathing, and the growing catalog of artifacts fills me with excitement. I can't wait to see them all in daylight. This is clearly a royal burial, far richer than the one Sugiyama found at Téotihuacan in 2002. A gold shield almost thirty inches across lies propped against the altar holding the child. Obsidian sculptures, gold figurines and a large array of knives, blades, beads and pendants lie scattered around the body. On either side of the mummy I see the tiny bones of birds—hawks or falcons—and one corner of the cave holds the skeleton of a larger animal in the remains of a wooden cage. Possibly a jaguar, which may have been buried alive.

At the foot of the wrapped corpse lies an object that at first glance looks like no more than a block of wood, but when I examine it more closely I see the faded glyphs that have been painted on it. Its bulk comes from sheaves of deerskin pressed between two thin pieces of wood. My heart nearly stops as the meaning of its form dawns on me. It's a book, one of the first books ever produced on the planet. I'm looking at a codex.

Codices are extremely rare. Typically they contain rows of writing on a long piece of deerskin or pressed bark, folded accordion-style between two wooden sheets that are used as end pieces. There are only a handful in existence, and no one has ever found a codex from the mysterious Teotihuacán culture. The implications of such a find ripple through me like a shock wave, and I take another dozen pictures of its placement in the tomb.

Against the wall are three large pots, covered in delicate geometrical designs, the most impressive ceramics I've ever seen from Mesoamerica or the southwest. Storage jars for a dead king. I shine the penlight inside one and see it's filled with tiny ears of corn, each cob no bigger than my finger. The next jar holds seeds of some kind, and the last is filled with polished olivella shells, an ancient form of money.

A ceremonial dagger with an obsidian blade is centered on the wrapped package of the corpse, and even in the gloom I know it's a stunning piece. Its handle is a solid, carved piece of jade.

My fingers fly as I fill page after page with notes and drawings. A fierce joy churns in me, a longing to bring others to share this, but another part of me feels reluctant to leave, to expose this intimate, holy place. Eventually I'll crawl out and alert the crew to the body and artifacts, and then the cave will be excavated by the whole team. But it will never again be this hushed, this pristine.

When I finish taking notes I shut off the flashlight for a moment and let the darkness cover me. It's so opaque I can't see the silhouette of my hand in front of my face. The silence is as pure as the darkness, untouched by any rustle or whisper from above. No birdsong, no wind penetrates the stone.

The blackness feels thick, thick as the earth itself, and as the seconds tick by it seems to exert a light pressure. How frightening it would be, to be buried alive here, bound in this suffocating darkness. I hope the boy didn't suffer that fate.

When I flick the flashlight back on, my heart jerks with relief as the beam pierces the blackness. I cast one final, longing look at the body and the treasures surrounding it. Is there anything I've forgotten to do? The photographs and notes and drawings should provide more than enough evidence to anyone that the dig will have to be relocated.

Unfortunately the cave is at least six miles away from the pyramid. How hard will it be to get the permits we need to begin excavating this site? Could they deny us the permits until Dr. Richter returns? What if he doesn't come back?

In the presence of so many riches, that thought is painful, impossible to contemplate, and I smother it immediately. Instead I think about the crew and what they'll say when they see what I've found.

This thought is purely irresistible. A grin blooms on my face as I admit it to myself: I'm ready to show off. I want to hear the gasps, the murmurs of appreciation and envy, and feel the heat of admiring glances. I want to rub Henry's nose in the fact that I found the tomb in a single day, and I only found it because I had the gumption to take off and look for it, instead of following orders and lining up with all the other drones at the tunnel. Most of all, I want to see the look on Sam's face. This is what you can find, if you let yourself wander past the boundaries.

Gripping the penlight again in my teeth, I lie down at the mouth of the tunnel and scrabble my way back up the steep shaft. At the top I wriggle out and stand panting in the bright dry air, exhilarated by the intoxication of discovery.

I drop the pack and do my happy dance, arms churning, legs pumping, head bobbing in a wild celebration of the find of the century. This is going to rewrite every text on prehistoric Southwest cultures. My name will be in every newspaper, every magazine, every publication that cites the discovery of this tomb. I'll be famous! That thought fills me like champagne, and I giggle out loud.

But before I can start signing autographs, I have to make sure I can find the site again, and that won't be easy. The mesa stretches for miles in every direction, and there are no landmarks to distinguish the barely perceptible mound of the ruin. I unroll the USGS map Sam gave me and mark the location of the entrance to the cave as accurately as I can, then photograph the hole and the surrounding landscape. Pulling out my notebook again, I fill four more pages with notes and drawings of the shaft and the landmarks around it.

For a moment I tense, thinking of the others waiting for me, wondering where I am, and then I relax as I study the notebook and flick through pages filled with drawings and descriptions of the artifacts. Let them wait. They'll understand when they see what I'm holding in my hand.

After sliding the map, camera, photos and notebook into my pack, I spend several minutes covering the entrance with brush and dirt, disguising the point of entry from any backpacker who might wander by. It hardly seems necessary on this empty tableland. The hole was already naturally camouflaged, and obviously it hasn't been disturbed for the last fourteen centuries. It's going to be hard to find it again, even with my map.

It's a long hike back, and the sun sinks low on the horizon as I trudge toward the camp. A small tingle of anxiety grows into a sharper fear as I cover the ground. Have I done everything by the book? Photographs, drawings, map, list of artifacts, measurements—everything has been meticulously recorded in my field notes. But the closer I get to the camp, the more my stomach tightens with worry.

Henry and Sylvia will be grateful. They have to be.

Chapter Six

Henry sits with Sylvia in front of his tent at an outdoor work table, the two of them engaged in a hushed conversation. They stop speaking when they see me approach, and Henry frowns in an unspoken warning that he's displeased.

"Where have you been?" Sylvia says, giving me an exasperated look.

I withdraw the topographic map from my pack and place it carefully on the table between them.

"Well?" Henry says impatiently, waiting for my answer.

I gesture to the rolled map on the table. "I found the tomb."

"Really," Sylvia says, glancing at the paper tube.

Henry's face tightens like a knot. "Where is it?"

I unroll the USGS map and point to the "X" I made to mark the spot. "Here. There's a shaft in the basalt that leads to a burial chamber."

"A burial chamber," Sylvia repeats, her voice stiff with disbelief. Both of them look as if they've bitten a lemon, their faces pinched, expressions sour with distrust.

My hands begin to sweat. "There's a beautifully preserved mummy of a child, along with a huge cache of offerings and artifacts. It has to be a royal burial."

"You spent the whole day exploring on your own?" she says, her voice cold with accusation.

How can they be so hostile? The map marks one of the great lost treasures of history, and I'm telling them I can lead them right to it. "I took photographs, made notes and drawings of every major artifact and its placement. I can show you exactly where the cave is located." I extract the photographs from my pack and slide the stack across the table toward Sylvia.

Will materializes at the edge of the tamarisk and walks toward us. "You found a mummy?"

Jessie appears close behind him. "What's going on?"

They crowd forward and cast hungry looks at the photographs in Sylvia's hands. She fans them out and glances briefly at them before she tips them toward her chest, obscuring them from view.

"You had no right to run off prospecting for treasure." Henry's quiet tone fails to conceal his fury. "You could go to jail for this, Kate. We have no permit to conduct a survey up there. When you entered the tomb you committed a crime."

"I wasn't trying to steal anything," I protest, but he holds up one hand to cut me off.

"This isn't a scavenger hunt, Kate." Sylvia places the photographs face down on top of the map and hides them under her hand.

My neck tingles with anger. To call an archaeologist a scavenger is the worst possible insult. A hectic flush crawls up my neck and suffuses my face, and I tighten my jaw to avoid yelling at her. "I took notes on the horizontal and vertical context of every artifact. I took measurements. I took photographs. I listed everything I found in that cave."

Jason walks up to the edge of the circle, and Will and Jessie reluctantly make room for him as he shoulders Jessie aside to look at the map. "How many artifacts are we talking about?"

"Hundreds," I say. "The mummy is surrounded by huge pots filled with corn and beads and shells. The whole cavern is full of artifacts and sculptures. There's even a codex."

"A codex!" Jessie cries in a hushed whisper, and she and Will nudge each other, eyes wide, faces split into grins.

"The walls of the cave are covered in murals and writing. It's all untouched, in perfect condition."

Jason leans forward to get a better look at the map, then bends over the table and touches Sylvia's fingers, which are still clutching the photographs. She hesitates. He strokes her knuckles, back and forth, twice, taking his time, and finally she loosens her grasp. Delicately he slides his fingers under the stack of photos and lifts them one by one to the dying light.

"Mmm," he purrs, flipping through the pictures. "I like this." He transfers the photos to his left hand and takes the map from the table to study it.

Sylvia clears her throat. He flicks a glance at her before he slowly hands the map and photos to me. Numbly I place them in my backpack, while the murmurs of appreciation from Jessie and Will subside.

"Why did you walk away from your duties, Kate?" she asks.

The gathering dusk gathers me into it, and I feel a steady erosion of spirit as I watch her face. There won't be any celebration tonight. No heartfelt thanks, no pats on the back, no victory parade around the camp. "Won't the government need some kind of proof of what we've found? I thought the photographs and the map would help us get the permits. We'll need to excavate as soon as possible."

"Don't you realize what an awkward position you've put us in?" she says. "My husband is still missing. Without him, we can't expand the perimeter of the dig."

Henry looks at Sylvia. "I could go to Silver City, talk to the Forest Service, try to transfer the existing permits to my name and see about getting one to cover the mesa."

"You're not qualified, Henry," she says.

Jason catches my eye and lifts an eyebrow, then licks his lips to control the smile that lurks there.

Henry stares at her, his mouth a thin line. "Then what do you suggest? If what Kate says is true, we have to act."

"Not until Adam returns."

"And if he doesn't?"

Sylvia rises from the table, barring further questions. "He will." Her chin lifts, and she stares at me in cold defiance. "Now if you'll excuse us, Henry and I have other matters to discuss."

I shoulder my way past the others and walk to my tent in a daze, unable to believe the fate of the expedition hangs on Sylvia's reluctance to do anything while Dr. Richter is gone. Surely she doesn't have the power to delay the next logical step in expanding the scope of the dig. How can she insist we do nothing, while a royal treasury sits unprotected just a few miles from here?

I crawl into my tent and dump the pack with the map and the photos on the sleeping bag. Bitterness washes through me as I think of all my daydreams about being given a hero's welcome, and soon I'm bogged down in the muck of doubt and regret. Was it really so terrible to enter the cave? Sylvia and Henry are right, in a way. I had no permission to conduct a survey up there on the mesa. But given the dimension of this find, won't the government rush a permit through? I don't know. I've always hated paperwork, and the permit process for expanding an archaeological excavation is a nightmare, from what I've heard. I wince at the memory of her sharp words. Spencer Rowland screamed at me in Paquimé when I suggested he should expand the perimeter of the dig. He claimed it could mean months, even years of delay. Maybe he was right. Maybe Sylvia is right. Maybe I was too caught up in the passion of discovery, but even now I can't see how she can remain unmoved by it.

Too restless and miserable to remain in the tent, I re-emerge to see the sky flooded with the dark reds and purples of the dying sun, bathing the campsite in the color of blood. Paper rustles in the neighboring campsite, where Sam sits on his flat rock, digging into a bag of saltines. I walk over there, hoping for comfort.

"Hey," I say, still feeling morose.

"Kate," he says, and lifts a fork in greeting. "Where the hell have you been?"

I shake my head, suddenly close to tears.

His face changes when he sees my mood. "Come on, join me. I have sardines and cheese and a few crackers that aren't too stale. You missed dinner."

I sit with him on his rock, elbows propped on my knees. "Sam, I may have done something terrible."

He smiles as he spears a sardine. "You played hooky, girl. You do the crime, you do the time."

"I found the tomb."

He halts the fork halfway to his mouth. Then he lowers it slowly back to the tin. "Where?"

"Up on the mesa."

Slowly he places the tin of sardines back down on the rock. "You're sure."

"It's incredible! The treasures in it could fill a museum. It's at the bottom of a shaft, a whole burial room. Perfect, untouched. Walls full of writing. A codex. The mummy is nearly intact."

He lets out a low whistle. "How far is it from here?"

"Maybe six miles."

"Kate, Kate, what have you done?" His voice is an urgent whisper. "We don't have permission to scout up there. Dr. Richter's claim is only for this canyon. The permit doesn't cover the mesa."

"But when the Forest Service hears about this, they'll have to grant us a new permit. It's a staggering collection of artifacts."

He gives me a worried look. "It's not so easy, Kate. It's not up to the Forest Service alone. The bureaucracy could take months, especially without Richter. Those Indian tribes can tie us up in red tape forever, if they think their ancestors' graves are being excavated."

"But it's the find of a lifetime! There must be some way we can push the paperwork through."

"Maybe. But right now it's just a big pile of loot, open to all takers. Whatever you do, don't tell the volunteers about it."

"It's too late," I say, miserable now. "They already know."

"For Christ's sake," he mutters, covering his face with his hands and then raking his fingers through his hair. "How could you be so stupid? Didn't you even stop to think about the trouble that could cause?"

His questions ignite the resentment that's been building ever since Sylvia and Henry scolded me for entering the tomb, and I snap. "If it weren't for you, none of this would have happened. You were the one who went on and on about the lava tubes up on the mesa."

Sam rolls his eyes. "I never thought you'd take off on your own private expedition."

My eyes narrow as I consider how he dangled the bait in front of me, hinting at something he was probably too timid to explore on his own. "Didn't you? I think you wanted me to find it, Sam. You'd heard the stories from the crew in Paquimé. You had an idea of where the tomb might be, and all you had to do was give me a little push in the right direction so I'd be the one to take the heat for straying outside the boundaries of the dig. But you'd be here to catalog the treasure once I'd uncovered it for you, wouldn't you?"

His expression freezes and hardens, and his voice takes on a nasty edge. "Interesting how you see yourself as a victim, when you walk off and do whatever the hell you want."

I stare at him, amazed. "And you're going to hold it against me? Sam, don't you get it? You won't have to dig in the tunnel anymore."

"Why the hell didn't you ask me to go with you? Why did you have to go off on your own?"

Irritation boils over into a recklessness that feels too satisfying to squash. "Because you wouldn't have come with me, that's why. You do as you're told. You've been bought and paid for—and that's more than some of us can say."

He shakes his head as if I've lost my mind. "Christ, Kate. Grow the fuck up. You haven't learned a thing since Paquimé. You think anyone's going to hire you after this? You don't want to work with a team—you want to go out hot-dogging on your own. You don't care whose toes you step on, or whether or not you expose the tomb to any backpacker who sees your tracks and follows them right to the treasure. Who knows? Maybe all you really want is an interview on Oprah. Maybe you want to be a star."

Dumfounded by this shower of accusations, I say the first thing that pops into my head. "You're jealous."

"I'm not jealous." His voice is loud, his face dark.

"Screw you," I say. "At least I had the guts to go look for the tomb, when you didn't have the balls to do it yourself."

"I think you'd better leave," he says quietly.

Furious, I rise to my feet and turn my back on him, lifting my middle finger in farewell.

A few minutes later I'm armed with my towel and fresh clothes and stomped down to the creek to bathe, imagining a dozen more tart comebacks I could have leveled at Sam. How dare he accuse me of not being a team player? My hands are red, cracked and blistered, my back aches, and I'm not even getting paid. And now that I've found the thing they've all been searching for, everybody's mad at me.

95

I push past the willow to a secluded pool in the stream, and crouch to touch the water rippling by my feet. Even though it's bone-chillingly cold, I need to wash myself, if only to scour away the memory of Sam's cold expression and the fear that's beginning to sprout in me like a fungus. What will I do if I'm fired from this job? Was Sam right? Would anyone ever hire me again? Not if Richter files a written reprimand with the American Board of Forensic Examiners or the American Anthropological Association. Jesus. They could fine me. They could even suspend my license.

Peeling off my clothes, I wade in, then hurl myself under and scrub at my face with sand from the bottom. When I come up gasping I see Sylvia standing on a flat rock in a shallow part of the stream, watching me. My clothes are behind her. I'm suddenly aware of my naked body and feel awkward, overexposed.

"Sorry if I startled you." Sylvia walks over to the heap of my discarded clothes, picks up the towel and hands it to me.

"Thanks," I say, wading out and wrapping it around my torso.

She removes her shoes, rolls up the cuffs of her slacks and wades in, then throws her head back to stare at the stars that are just beginning to appear in the sky. With her hands on her hips, she shifts her weight from foot to foot, seemingly relaxed, as if we're old friends.

Stooping to pick up a clean pair of jeans, I hop a little as I pull them on, then wrestle a sweat shirt over my head, squeeze the water out of my hair and shake it back. Sylvia remains silent, and I wait to see what she wants.

Finally she speaks. "You must have had a thrilling day." Her face is unreadable in the twilight, her tone neutral.

This tiny concession thaws some of the ice between us. "It was amazing."

She takes a deep breath, then smiles stiffly. "I don't want you to think we're completely ungrateful."

Well, it's not a parade, but it's the first glimmer of recognition I've had, and an acute longing rises in me, a need as physical as hunger, to tell her everything: the vision I had of the funeral procession, the fear I felt descending the shaft, how the bats startled me, how the discovery of that small body in the tomb sent a shiver of sadness through me. But I suspect Sylvia hasn't come here to offer congratulations.

She stirs the water with her foot, not meeting my eyes. "I know you must be excited about the discovery, and I'm sure you're eager to discuss it with the rest of the crew. But if you show the site to the others before my husband can arrange the permit to excavate, it could be dangerous."

I hug the wet towel to my body. "You don't trust the crew?"

She shrugs. "It's been difficult without Adam. Jessie and Sam are obviously critical of Henry. Unfortunately my son has been persuaded by some of their complaints." She picks up a twig that floats by and breaks it in her fingers, then throws the pieces of wood into the water. "Frankly I'm a little worried about Jason. He's been telling Will and Jessie that he has a fortune from his Wall Street career hidden in an offshore account in the Caymans. But it's not true. He's broke. The lawyers and the government took everything we had. My husband and I had to give up our own life savings just to keep him out of jail."

I stare at her, trying to read between the lines. Could this be why there's no more grant money, and why there's only a skeleton crew of ten people to excavate the pyramid? Would Richter have spent government funds to rescue his son from jail?

The water gives her voice an underpinning of smooth, rushing sound, and I wonder where this is leading, and why Sylvia has chosen to confide in me. She turns to me, her eyes large, luminous in the twilight. "Jason is young. He's impressionable. All I'm asking is that you don't put temptation in his path."

"So you don't want me to reveal the whereabouts of the cave to anyone."

"Exactly. At least until we get the new permit."

"Fine."

She studies me for a long moment. "Sam said you were a wild card. A little too impulsive, a little too casual about following orders. But this is important, Kate. Do you understand me?"

Heat blooms in my solar plexus, as if Sylvia has struck me there. It's an insult, and she meant it to be an insult. If I screw this up, there's no doubt in my mind that she has the power to get rid of me, and the thought of leaving the dig now is unbearable. Not before I've seen and touched and stroked and catalogued every artifact from the tomb, not before I've measured the bones of the child king and studied every millimeter of the cave.

"I understand."

My tone must say more than I intend because when Sylvia speaks again her voice is smooth as caramel, as if to apologize. "We'll give you full credit for discovering the tomb, of course."

I don't say a word. I fold the damp towel, lay it across my arm and gather the rest of my things.

When I look up Sylvia locks eyes with me, and her voice hardens. "The tomb has been there for centuries, Kate. You can afford to wait a little while longer."

"It's been a long day," I say.

"Of course."

I walk away, my arms and legs numb, my breathing shallow as I head for the sanctuary of my tent. Lightning flickers along the horizon, illuminating the camp. A cold wind springs up, and I wrap my arms around my towel and dirty clothes and hug myself as I walk. The conversation with Sylvia lingers like a shroud, and it chills me to realize how little I know about the people around me, and how large a prize is at stake, waiting in the ground, unguarded.

Someone in camp has started a fire, and the smell of piñon smoke hangs in the evening air. There's a murmur of conversation, a rustle of wind, the crackle of logs in the fire, and beyond that, no sound. No trucks in the distance, no car doors slamming, no jets overhead. The moon is a beacon in the dusk.

When I come within sight of my tent I see a flashlight beam moving inside the blue nylon walls, and at first I pause, confused, thinking I must have mistaken my tent for one of the others. But even by moonlight I recognize the stand of brush oak and the big boulder to the rear, and as I draw closer I see my dirty socks hanging from the line outside the door.

Someone is in my tent.

Behind the thin fabric I see the silhouette of a figure flipping through a book, holding a flashlight on the pages.

"Kate!" The sound comes from right behind me, and I whirl around, startled. Henry appears at the edge of the brush and seizes my arm, his voice unnaturally loud. "I've been looking everywhere for you. We need a poker player—you up for it?"

His breath smells like whiskey, and his eyes glitter with an agitated intensity that I don't trust. "Not now," I say, struggling to pull my arm free, whipping around just in time to see the flashlight in my tent go off.

Crossing in front of me, he blocks my view of the tent and pushes me toward the willow thicket. His mouth spreads wide in a jack-o-lantern grin. "Come on, we need to celebrate. Fiddle volunteered a bottle of Yukon Jack. Let's get happy."

He staggers into the thicket, dragging me along with him. The dense brush obliterates my view of the tent, and whoever was in it.

"Let me go, Henry!" Desperate to get away from him, I dig my nails into his hand.

"Damn!" he cries, and flings me off. "What's the matter with you?" he mutters, glaring at me.

I turn without a word and run back to my tent. It's dark and empty. Whoever was looking through my things has disappeared, but the contents of my daypack lie strewn across the bedroll. The camera is open, the film removed. A deepening sense of unreality envelops me as I take in the scattered tools.

My field notes, photographs and the map to the cave are gone.

Chapter Seven

Laughter breaks out from the clearing beyond the shadow of the piñons, and I flail through the trees toward the sound. Jessie, Will, and Jason stand in a ring around a campfire, passing a bottle that holds an amber glow in the firelight.

"No more tunnel," Jessie says in a loud, happy voice, lifting her tin cup in a toast. Shoulders relaxed, feet planted wide apart, she's the picture of exuberance.

Jason matches her gesture with the bottle, then tilts his head back and takes a long pull. His white shirt gleams in the darkness, a glowing contrast to the filthy bandage on Will's head. Will's clothes are the color of basalt dust, and the side of his face is smeared with dirt. He leans close and whispers something in Jason's ear, and they both snicker.

For one crazy moment I wonder if their good humor comes from ransacking my tent and walking off with a map worth millions. The thought clings to me, and when I speak my voice sounds unnaturally harsh.

"Did any of you see someone in my tent?" I shout over their laughter.

Jessie turns to me, the smile lingering on her face. "Why? What's the matter?"

"Somebody took the map to the cave. The photos, all my notes—they're gone." My voice sounds ragged, close to breaking.

Her eyes widen in alarm. "Shit."

"How long have you been here?" I ask her.

"I built the fire about twenty minutes ago. I heard someone moving around in your tent, but I figured it was you."

"You didn't see anyone go in or out of it?"

Jessie glances at the dark silhouettes of piñon between the tent and the firelight and shakes her head.

"Maybe we should tell Henry," Will says, his voice slurred.

I whirl around, peering beyond the trees. Where did Henry go? The branches shift in the wind, but there's no sign of him.

"Please, don't get up. Let me tell him." Jason giggles, swaying slightly on his feet, but he makes no move to leave. "It would be my pleasure." Adjusting his face to a more somber expression, he passes the bottle to Will.

Michael emerges from the shadows, and his face lights up with relief when he sees me. "There you are. Where the heck have you been, Kate? I was worried about you."

"Didn't you hear the news?" Jessie asks him. "Kate found the tomb."

He stops in mid-stride, the smile frozen on his face, lips parted, eyes lit up with questions. "Where?"

"Up on the mesa," I say. "About six miles from here."

His expression slides into surprise, then pleasure, and he walks over and claps me on the back. "Kate, that's wonderful. You must be thrilled."

His praise brings a prickle of tears to my eyes, and I press my hands to my face and shake my head. "Someone was in my tent a few minutes ago. They took all my notes, my photos, and the map to the tomb."

"But you could still find it, right?" he asks.

My throat tightens with tears held at bay. "It's like an ocean of land up there, Michael. Every dip and rise looks like a thousand others. I covered the opening, and there aren't any landmarks. Even with the map, I was worried about finding it again. It was pure luck that I stumbled across it at all."

"We'll find it," Will says as he takes the bottle from Henry and tilts it to his lips. He swallows, then wipes his mouth with the back of his hand. "First thing tomorrow, we'll go up there, grid off the mesa, do a full-scale search."

"No, Will. You can't." Michael's voice is soft.

"What are you talking about?" Will says. "We have to find it."

Michael shakes his head. "We can't go near that spot. Not yet. Not until we get the permit to excavate."

"Screw that," Jason says, and takes another swig from the bottle.

"It's a felony, Jason," Michael says. "If they catch you violating the ARPA, they'll slap a fine on you before you even take a pot shard out of that tomb. If you take anything at all, you could be sued for millions. Not to mention the years you could spend in jail." He gives his half brother a long, level look.

"ARPA? What the hell is that?" Jason asks.

"Archaeological Resources Protection Act," I say. Everything Michael said is true. The implications of what I've done yawn before me, and the abyss of all the bad things that could happen widens with every passing moment.

Jessie speaks up. "So you're telling us we should just forget about the tomb until the Feds hand over some paperwork? That's insane."

There are shadows under Michael's eyes, so dark in the firelight they look like bruises. "It's not just the paperwork. We'll need round-the-clock security. People camp out in this wilderness for months, years at a time. Poachers. Ex-cons. Bandits. They live on what they can trap or hunt. If one of them happens to see you go into the tomb, we're laying it wide open to them."

"One quick trip, and they'd have a codex," Jason mutters.

"A codex?" Michael asks, staring at me. "You found a codex?"

I rake my hands through my hair. "What if somebody steals it? This is a nightmare."

Jessie gives me a sympathetic look. "Is there anything we can do?"

I shake my head impatiently. "There's someone I have to see." I turn away and hustle through the dark humps of piñons as a dull roar of thunder ripples through the canyon, and a moment later rain spatters down like cold fingertips. Lightning cracks overhead, bright as magnesium, followed almost immediately by a boom that vibrates the ground.

Sylvia's tent stands next to a makeshift drying shed created from tent poles and a canvas tarp, with bundled plant specimens hanging from a clothesline underneath it. Lantern light glows from within the tent, and I hurry toward the awning, out of the rain.

Without waiting for an invitation, I lift the flap of the opening and stand shivering for a moment on the threshold. It's surprisingly spacious inside the tent, and my gaze shifts from the shadowed silhouettes of leaves bundled with string hanging from the center pole, to the net bags of dry food suspended above the sleek, lightweight furniture. The scent of sage fills the air.

Sylvia looks up from a canvas butterfly chair placed by a low table, and I can see the shadow of someone slumped in the chair opposite, his back toward me, his head hidden by the chair.

"What are you doing here, Kate?" The half-light makes it difficult to judge her expression, but her voice sounds calm enough.

Anger swells in my throat, beating in time with my pulse. "Someone stole the map to the tomb." I take a step toward her.

"You were the decoy, weren't you? Whoever was in my tent needed enough time to find my notes. You came to the river to distract me, to make sure I didn't break in on him, didn't you?"

Sylvia smoothes back her hair and straightens in her chair, facing me like a queen from her throne. "You've never met my husband, have you, Kate?"

The man in the chair stands slowly and turns. In spite of his rumpled clothes and the week's worth of stubble on his face, Dr. Richter is an imposing man, with silver hair cut close to his skull and a lean face, austere and reserved.

Seeing him sends a jolt of adrenaline through my body, and my heart hammers in my chest as his eyes fix on me. In the lamplight his deep-set eyes look black, like hot coal. His energy seems to focus in them—brilliant, interrogative eyes that take me in at a glance.

"A pleasure," he says, and grasps my hand.

"It's a privilege to meet you, sir." Cheeks flaming, I force myself to return his gaze. "I'm relieved to see you're all right. We were all worried."

"Jessie Delgado in particular," Sylvia murmurs.

Dr. Richter continues to hold my hand as he studies my face. "I understand you found the tomb."

Sylvia's eyes narrow, a knife aimed at his back. "Adam was just telling me he's been in Silver City, trying to secure more funding for the dig."

There's a slight, almost indiscernible edge of sarcasm in her voice, and for a moment I wonder what's going on between them. If the only reason Dr. Richter left the camp was to take care of business in Silver City, why couldn't he have told the crew?

The corners of his mouth tighten, and his smile remains fixed as he continues to examine me. "Apparently you've had an exciting day, Kate."

He lifts my notebook from the seat of his chair and holds it loosely in his right hand. "It was clever of you to find the tomb," he says, stroking the familiar cloth binding. "Unfortunately, it's going to be awkward for us."

For a moment I rock back on my heels, too overwhelmed to speak. My gaze darts around the room, searching. My map lies spread out on the table, weighted down by the Polaroid photos of the artifacts.

Gusts of rain pelt the canvas walls of the tent, growing into a steady drumming downpour, while Dr. Richter watches me with a gentle air of condescension. Turning to his wife, he says "Sylvia? Could you explain?"

"The tomb doesn't belong to you, Kate," Sylvia says evenly. "Adam has been searching for this site for years. He found the pyramid when everyone else dismissed it as a fantasy, and he would have found the tomb if you hadn't gone off on a reckless treasure hunt of your own. It was his work that allowed you to find it. I'm sure you can understand that."

"You think that gives you the right to rummage through my things and steal my notes? All you had to do was ask. I would gladly have given them to you."

Dr. Richter gives me a rueful smile. "I'm sure you would have. We were concerned that you might also hand out copies of your notes to anyone else who asked for them. We had to confiscate them before you could do that."

Stunned by the detached way he admits it, I take a step back. My body begins to tremble, and I glance from one to the other. "You could have told me why you were concerned. You could have—"

Sylvia's voice rises. "Don't you see what this means? You've announced the archaeological equivalent of Fort Knox several miles from here, outside of our jurisdiction, outside the area we're permitted to excavate. The tomb is completely unsecured, on public land."

My legs feel like rubber. "So you'll have to get another permit."

Dr. Richter rubs his brow with thumb and forefinger. "It's more time consuming than you can imagine, Kate. Federal, state, local, and tribal governments all have to agree on the merit of our claim. Tomorrow I'll verify the location of the tomb and assess the scope of the permits we'll need, and then I'll head back to Silver City to rework the entire proposal. Until the permit comes through, we have to make sure the location of the cave is kept secure. And that means no one will go anywhere near that tomb."

He and Sylvia exchange a look before he continues. "We've also decided that no one will be allowed to leave until I return. With luck, I should be back in two or three weeks."

Frozen with incomprehension, I stare at him. "This is your notion of security? To steal my notes, hold us hostage here and keep us away from the tomb until you come back? Dr. Richter, this is insane. You can't be serious."

Sylvia crosses her legs and leans back in her chair, hands clasped loosely in her lap. "You've read the fine print in your contract. Our security clause is very tight. No one can leave the site without our approval. If you're foolish enough to leave without that approval, you could be sued for breach of contract, and your license would be revoked."

My stomach shrinks at the thought of the power they hold over me. There's no doubt in my mind that they could undo all my years of education, experience and hard work with the stroke of a pen.

Dr. Richter gives me a tight, humorless smile. "When this story breaks, the press will descend on us. We have to be prepared for that. A codex is lying up there, a few feet underground. It's a prize worth dying for, Kate."

Sylvia continues, without a trace of remorse in her voice. "We're delighted you found the tomb. But sometimes an archaeologist can become too attached, too proprietary about her individual discoveries. From now on it will be vital for every crew member to follow orders, and so far you haven't shown any willingness to do that. As soon as Adam returns from Silver City we'll release you from your contract."

"You're firing me?" I ask in disbelief, turning to Dr. Richter.

He lifts his palms and lets them fall.

"How much longer were you prepared to tunnel under the pyramid? Six months? A year?" My voice comes out higher and louder than I want it to, but I don't care.

"We would have found the tomb eventually, without your interference."

"But I've discovered the burial that will be the highlight of your career. How can you fire me?" The ghost of all my failures looms large and dark and cold in my belly, and my throat closes over the knot of fear welling up inside.

His voice is soft, like velvet over steel. "Kate. Without trust, we have nothing. The ability to follow protocol is paramount on an expedition as sensitive as this one. As soon as I return from Silver City with the necessary permits, you'll be free to go."

For a moment I stare at him, dumfounded, and then in the blink of an eye, disbelief turns to fury. Too angry to speak, I rush out of the tent and into the rain, immediately blinded by the slashing downpour. The rain feels icy as it blows against my face, but I walk in a numb trance, chilled to the bone before I've gone a hundred yards. The wet, heavy brush slaps against my face as I struggle through the mud-slicked paths between the tents. The pyramid looks malevolent in the glare of the bright and constant cracks of lightning, and thunder rolls across the heavens while sleet hammers my face.

Sam's tent glows in the darkness, and I run toward it, fumble with the zipper and slide through the opening in the rain-soaked fabric. I stand dripping at the threshold, taking in the smell of clothes and sweat, muddy boots and damp socks. Rain slaps the sides of the tent, making a racket. The walls are softly illuminated with lantern light, and the rain beating on the waterproof canvas would be soothing if I hadn't just been fired. Jessie lies sprawled on Sam's cot, while Michael and Sam sit in camp chairs next to the bed, and they all look up in surprise at the intrusion.

Sam's face stiffens at the sight of me, and suddenly a wave of shame floods through me. He was right, and I was wrong. And now, looking at his face, I know I'll never have the chance to redeem myself. I failed, and he knows it, and the fact that this is how he'll remember me stings almost as much as losing my job.

The moment seems to hang between us forever, until his face softens and he rises from his chair. "You're soaked. Come on in, Kate, have a seat."

Sam takes a towel from a pile of clothes on the floor and tosses it to me, then ushers me to his chair while Jessie sits up and makes room for him on the cot.

"We've been worried about you," Michael says.

Jessie examines my face. "Did you find out who stole your map?"

"Dr. Richter," I say grimly. "He just fired me."

"No," she whispers. "He came back? He's all right?"

"He's back, but he won't be here long." I lean forward and let my head sink into my hands. "He told me he's riding out to Silver City as soon as he inspects the cave and figures out what permits he'll need. None of us are allowed to go near the tomb or leave the camp until he gets back, and that could take weeks."

"How can he fire you?" Michael says. "You found the tomb he spent ten years looking for."

"He says I had no permission to survey the mesa, and Sylvia

said I didn't follow orders." I raise my eyes to meet his. "It's a mess. If I'm not allowed to work, I can't imagine staying here until he gets back."

"We could confront him," Jessie says. "All of us, together."

"No," Sam says. "Let him go to Silver City. By the time he returns, he might reconsider."

I feel a dull ache in my chest, heavy as a stone. Silence fills the space between us, broken only by the rain and the tent walls billowing restlessly in the gusts of wind.

"I bet anything this was Sylvia's idea," Jessie says. "Maybe I could find a way to get him alone and talk to him."

Michael rolls his eyes at Sam, who shakes his head.

"It won't work, Jessie," Michael says. "You go in there wagging your tail, asking for favors, and Sylvia's going to figure out a way to fire you, too."

She glances away, not meeting our eyes, a stubborn set to her mouth. "Sooner or later he has to leave that tent."

Michael reaches out and touches Jessie's arm. "I know he makes you feel special, honey, but he always goes back to Sylvia. That's how it ends. That's how it always ends."

Jessie looks stricken, and two bright spots of color appear in her cheeks. Sam pokes Michael with his foot.

"I'm sorry, but it's the truth," Michael says softly. "I just don't want her to get hurt."

"Lighten up, Mike," Sam says.

"Is there any way we can go around Richter?" I ask.

Sam snorts. "Not unless you want to kill him."

Jessie lets out a strained laugh, and takes a deep swig from the flask.

"Could you talk to him, Michael?" I ask. "He might listen to you."

He takes a deep breath and lets it out between pursed lips, his eyes mournful. "I'm not exactly his favorite person right now. He was pretty ticked off when the suits at *National Geo* insisted I come out here to scout the site for the film. I'm not sure it would do you much good if I stuck up for you."

"Does Jason have any influence over your dad?" Jessie asks him. "Maybe he could talk to him about letting Kate stay."

Michael makes a face and scratches the back of his head. "They can't stand each other. Jason will always be a loser in Dad's eyes, and Jason knows it. He'll never escape the expectations that go along with being Adam Richter's son."

"You did," I point out.

"I just found a way to work in the same game. Lots of people call me Adam. I get congratulated all the time for Dad's achievements, and I don't even bother to correct them. But Jason's latest escapade made him a little too notorious for him to get away with that."

Sam silently offers me the bottle, and I tip it to my lips and feel the liquid burn my throat. It tastes like Scotch, but I wouldn't care if it was gasoline. I want to drain it.

Sam nods as if he can read my mind, and I take another deep pull. When I look around at the others, they have the blurred look of people who have been drinking hard all evening. Jessie's face is unnaturally flushed, and her eyes seem too bright. Sam's torso tilts sideways at a precarious angle, as if an invisible burden weighs him down and will eventually make him topple.

Michael continues, his legs sprawled out in front of him, arms behind his head, eyes half closed. "Sylvia's been pretending Jason is part of the team here, but he'll never be anything more than slave labor to my dad. There's no way Dad's going to let him get anywhere near that tomb."

"Even after the permit comes through?" Jessie asks, leaning back on her elbow.

"Even then. I don't know why, but Dad doesn't trust Jason, doesn't even like him, really. Never has."

"Jason's not going to like being excluded from the excavation," Jessie says. "He was really excited about the codex."

A steamroller headache begins to pound between my ears. I have to get out of here. The whole subject of Richter makes me crazy, and if I sit around here much longer I'll probably say something I regret. The others exchange terse comments while my thoughts boomerang off in one direction after another. Finally I stand, too agitated to remain. "I'm going back to my tent."

Sam's blue gaze pins me for a few seconds. Something I can't identify flits across his face, but he says nothing, just passes me a flashlight from the table by his cot.

"Thanks," I say. "I'll bring it back in the morning."

Jessie lifts a hand in a half-hearted farewell, and I duck out the door.

As I raise my head from the flap I see a dark figure scuttle away from the side wall of Sam's tent, then dart across the stretch of basalt toward the thicket of willow that lines the creek. Startled, I flick the beam of the flashlight toward the shadows and catch the gleam of a profile, wet with rain, disappearing into the brush.

It's Jason.

CHAPTER EIGHT

In the harsh morning light I can see fine lines radiating from Dr. Richter's eyes and seaming his face, lines that reveal his age. As we gather at the base of the pyramid, he draws himself up to his full patrician height and squares his shoulders, like Caesar sensing mutiny in the senate. He called this meeting, but his sour expression lets us know it's only a formality, a burden he'd rather avoid.

None of us looks good. Jason, Will, Michael, Sam, Jessie—we all look disheveled, bleary from hangovers and not enough sleep. Sylvia's hair hangs loose around her shoulders, and she wears rumpled khakis and work boots. Henry wears an old leather hunting vest, pockets bristling with shotgun shells. His black Stetson dips low over his brow, and he seems nervous, shifting from foot to foot, avoiding eye contact.

Sylvia leans close to Richter, murmuring something I can't hear.

He shakes his head and mutters a single word, "No."

She touches the sleeve of his denim work shirt, whispering, imploring him. His gaze sweeps over the rest of us, frowning as he pulls away from her, still shaking his head, no, no, no.

Jason, Jessie, Will, Michael, Sam and I—the whole crew, except for Fiddle—wait for them to finish arguing. All of us carry packs, and Dr. Richter knows why. Every other member of the crew wants to see the tomb, and I want to save my career.

Sylvia raises her voice to a hiss just loud enough for me to hear. "I've been with you every step of the way, haven't I?"

He lets out a brief, humorless laugh. "When you weren't otherwise occupied."

The skin on her face seems to draw tighter against the bone, sharpening her features. Red splotches appear on her cheeks, and her eyes flash with warning. "I deserve this, Adam. I've waited for this."

He plucks her hand away from his arm. "You'll have your chance after the permits come through. You can wait that long."

Richter sends a meaningful glance toward Henry before he lifts his voice to address us all. "As soon as I've recorded the location of the tomb in the GPS, I'll return here before sunset. Tomorrow morning I'll leave at dawn for Silver City. With any luck we'll begin excavating in two or three weeks, after I've secured the necessary permits and more funding."

Sam edges his way toward Richter, his hands pushed deep in his pockets. "I packed the magnetometer. We can take readings of the adjacent rock to see if any other tombs are up there."

"You're not invited, Sam." Richter's voice is weary, but there's no mistaking the determination in it. "I'm going alone. The fewer tracks, the better."

Sam's cheeks turn a dull red under his tan. "You can't leave me hanging here, Adam. We're in this together."

Henry glares at Sam. "If anyone goes with him, it's me."

Dr. Richter flicks one hand through the air, cutting them off. "Stop it. All of you. I'm not saying this again. I'm going up there by myself, and that's final."

I step forward, my heart fluttering like a bird beating its wings against the bars of my rib cage. This is my last chance. Not just today, not just for this expedition, but for the rest of my life. Everything hinges on this moment, and what I say next will mean the difference between excavating the find of the century or a life spent serving burgers to frat boys.

"You won't find it." My voice cracks with tension.

Richter inspects me coldly. "I have the map, Kate."

I shrug, trying to appear neutral. "I can't vouch for the accuracy of the map. I'm a doctor, not a geographer."

He hesitates. "I have the Polaroids and your notes. You made drawings of the surrounding terrain."

I try to appear apologetic. "You're heading into miles and miles of flat, rolling mesa. Piñon, cactus, layers of basalt . . . it all looks the same. Sure, I took the photos, made some notes and drawings, but the hole leading to the tomb—it's tiny, and I covered it up before I left. You'll never find it without me."

Richter gives me a speculative look, as if I might be bluffing. "I'll take my chances." He turns away, ignoring me.

I can't help myself. I open my mouth and plunge in. "How much time can you afford to lose looking for it? You'll never find it in one day if I don't go."

He stiffens and turns back to me, his coal-black eyes blazing. "That sounds like a threat, Kate."

I remain silent, feeling the tightrope of his disapproval swaying under me. One breath and I could fall. So I stop breathing.

Richter holds my eyes for a few seconds, and the more I squirm, the better he likes it. Confidence flows into him as he sees my discomfort. This is not the warm, kindly patriarch who entertains viewers in his PBS documentaries. Without a camera trained on him, Dr. Richter is a ruthless egomaniac, and I can tell by the hostility in the crew that they share my opinion. To know Dr. Richter is to hate him.

Amusement curls his lip, but there's no warmth there. His eyes scan the crew, dismissing me, restlessly searching until his gaze lights on Michael's face.

"Michael, I'll need to speak to you in private before I go."

Michael hesitates. "You sure about going up there by yourself, Dad? You might need Kate, if the map . . ." His voice trails off as he sees the chill in his father's eyes. "Or I could go with you. If I show the suits at *National Geo* some raw footage of the tomb, they'll send you a blank check. The Feds will take weeks if you leave it up to them. Let me head up there with you."

Dr. Richter's attention seems to drift as he studies his son. He's looking right at him, but he doesn't respond to Michael's question.

"Dad?" Michael asks. "You okay?"

Richter blinks, smiles. "I'm fine, kiddo. But I'm going by myself." He looks at the rest of the crew and waves a hand, his way of letting us know the meeting is over.

Then he stares at me, pointing his index finger at my face as if he's holding a gun. "You. Follow me."

I hurry in Richter's wake as he strides toward his tent, parting the group clustered at the base of the pyramid like a hawk scattering a flock of sparrows. Resentment lingers in the air, along with something darker, something more sinister. Doesn't he feel it? It's hard to believe anyone could create so much antagonism and not be affected by it.

He walks past Sylvia's drying shed and ducks under the bundled plant specimens hanging from the clothesline, then flings open the canvas door of their tent. Early morning light streams across the work table inside, and the scent of herbs fills my nostrils as I enter. Richter crosses to the work table, where he begins to sort through a sheaf of papers.

"Sit," he commands me, not bothering to look up.

I ease myself into the butterfly chair he occupied last night, tensed and waiting for whatever comes next.

He perches on the edge of the table, takes a yellow legal pad from the stack of books and papers and uses a pencil to take notes. "Once you left camp, how long did it take you to reach the tomb?" He taps the pad with the pencil impatiently, waiting for my answer.

"I . . . I don't know exactly. I wasn't going in a straight line. I was looking for signs of a ruin, so I zigzagged back and forth." Belatedly I realize this sounds premeditated, and therefore illegal, according to Henry. I should have said I stumbled on it by accident.

He rakes me with his eyes. "Didn't you notice the time on the way back?"

What can I say? I forgot to look at my watch? I was too excited to figure it out? "Maybe three or four hours. Like I said, I didn't find it right away. I can't remember exactly how long it took to get there, and I didn't notice how many hours I spent walking back."

He lowers the pencil and lets out a sigh. "How did you find the tomb?"

I shrug, feeling more and more uncomfortable under the cold light of his gaze. "Sam talked about lava tubes up there. He said the tomb might be located in one of them."

"Did he." Richter's voice sends a sliver of ice down my spine. "I'll have to talk to Sam about that."

"He didn't know I would go looking for them," I hurry to explain. "He didn't have anything to do with that."

"I'm relieved to hear it. But you still haven't answered my question."

I twist in the chair, wishing I could stand and pace around the tent while I talk about the trek across the mesa. Instead I struggle to remain still and describe the hike toward the volcanic cone, its orientation to the pyramid and the surrounding terrain. I tell him about the mound halfway to the cone on the horizon, and the spill of broken basalt that indicated an opening to a lava tube.

"And that's it? You followed a line that's twenty or thirty miles long and you somehow happened across a tomb that's been undiscovered for centuries? I'd call that more than luck. It borders on the supernatural."

I can feel the heat rise from my feet to my scalp. If my past has already been the subject of rumors in camp, I'm not going to dig that hole any deeper. Richter sits on the edge of the work table, staring down at me, enjoying himself. Underneath the contempt, there's something sexual in his gaze, something invasive as it wanders up and down the length of my body, probing me, inspecting me as if he were a plantation owner and I were a slave in need of correction.

When I remain silent he continues, the smile fading from his lips. "Tell me what the mound looked like on your approach."

"It didn't look like anything at first. Just another bump in a mesa full of bumps and dips."

His eyes narrow. "So what tipped you off?"

What tipped me off was a throbbing heat in my palms, an electric thrill that sizzled up my spine, but I'll never admit that to Richter. He'd never believe my skin was on fire with the nearness of bones. Nor would he appreciate hearing about the dream that showed me a parade of costumed warriors and their grief for the child they carried. To say I experienced a leap of intuition up there would be like telling him I was led to the tomb by a flying saucer. He's just like Spencer Rowland: cold, analytical, and skeptical of anything but facts and figures.

So I lie. "The mound looked different, more symmetrical, not like the other outcroppings. More like a dome."

His eyes pierce me as he taps his pencil, waiting for more. Even to my ears, the explanation sounds weak.

"I paced off the dome, and it was about fifty feet across in every direction, covered in grama grass and slabs of basalt. You'll see cholla and prickly pear on the south side of the mound. A few anthills in between the cactus. The clumps of grass are thicker on the north slope."

"Did you see an opening?"

"Yes, but it's barely big enough for a rabbit. There were a few rocks the size of bowling balls covering one side of it. When you pull the stones away, you'll see a larger shaft."

"Did you disturb the dirt around the hole?"

I hesitate. "Yes. I scooped a little dirt aside so I could enter the hole."

He gives me a long, level stare. The silence is so dense I can hear the pounding surf of my pulse in my eardrum.

"I put the dirt back," I add lamely, realizing how ridiculous that must sound. "And I replaced the stones. You won't see a hole. It's completely covered."

Richter glances at his wrist, and the crystal of his watch throws a perfect circle of light against the canvas wall of the tent. I can see the thought flash through his mind: he's wasted enough time talking to me. I'm useless to him, and therefore I cease to exist. He tosses the legal pad and pencil on the table, turns his back on me and lifts a gray backpack from behind the desk chair.

The nightmare of my professional future rises before me. Unless I can change his mind in the next thirty seconds, I'm doomed. No more work in the field I love, not after this, not after I've been fired by the all-powerful Dr. Richter. If I can't exonerate myself, the word will go out on the jungle telegraph that knits the forensic community together, and every potential employer in archaeology will see the black ball next to my name.

But if Richter and I spend a few hours together, I could show him I'm a hard working member of his team, a skilled forensic anthropologist who will help him. Not a nut-job with her own agenda.

It's a feeble hope, but I open my mouth for one last attempt. "Please. If you take me with you, I guarantee you'll save at least three or four hours. I'm not trying to threaten you, but there's a good chance you won't find the tomb, not in one day. There are no major landmarks near the ruin. Let me help you."

He examines me for a moment before he picks up the blank legal pad on the table and slides it into his pack. "I'm not a gullible man, Kate. I don't believe in ESP, and I certainly don't believe you have the power to help me, given the hazy nature of your recollections. So far you've done nothing here but compromise the legal standing of this expedition. It will take me weeks to undo the damage."

What about the damage you're doing to me? I bite the inside of my cheek to stop myself from saying more, but I can't resist. "Dr. Richter, I want to help you make this expedition a success. I'm a hard worker, a good worker, and I'll do whatever it takes to remain here."

Richter lifts my notebook into his pack, along with the map marking the location of the tomb. "Apparently you have no idea how much trouble you've caused us, and that's a pity. This is the second expedition you've sabotaged because you insist on following your own whims, and I doubt anyone in the field will want you after this. You're finished here, Kate. But you're young. You can find some other work. Send Michael in, would you?"

My whole body flushes with panic at the finality of his words, and sweat prickles my back, my arms, my neck, my forehead. Adrenaline launches me from the chair, and I rush to the doorway and out, my face roasting with shame. I run toward the dense cover of the willow, desperate to hide before someone sees me and I fall apart completely.

Momentum catapults me directly into Michael, who staggers back with the force of our collision and grabs me by the shoulders to steady both of us.

"Whoa," he says. "Where's the fire?"

I try to smile, but the effort must look more like a grimace because Michael takes one look at me and his eyebrows knit in concern. "That bad, huh? Don't give up yet. This isn't the end."

The compassion in his face threatens to undo the last shred of dignity I can muster.

"He's waiting for you." My voice sounds rusty with unshed tears.

"Kate? You going to be okay?"

I shake my head, pull away and run.

I sit on the basalt slab behind my tent and hold my head in my hands. A terrible emptiness fills me, a cold hollowness that blooms until it swallows every particle of hope. *You're finished here. But you're young. You'll find some other work.* Richter's words echo over and over again in my brain, growing louder with every repetition, making me feel as worthless as a burnt match.

The last time I felt this bad was in Casas Grandes, after Spencer Rowland gutted my pride by shouting insults at me in front of the crew. Amateur. Looter. Thoughtless. Unprofessional. Stupid. I groan and cover my eyes with both hands, trying to shut out the memory of his self-righteous face towering over mine, spraying me in his fury with bad breath and spit.

After that public humiliation, one of the crew members drove me to the bus station in Paquimé. It was a silent ride as we bounced over ruts for hours in a battered Jeep, and I sat in the passenger seat with tears and snot streaming down my face. I didn't know the driver. He was a new member of the crew; he'd just arrived that day and made no attempt to comfort me.

Suddenly the memory of the driver's face fits another face, a face I've seen every day here in the Gila. Jesus. It was Sam. Sam drove me to Paquimé. That was why he looked so familiar when he picked me up at the airport. Sam saw me cry. He heard the snuffling sounds of self-pity that I couldn't control. The realization hits me like a sucker punch, adding another layer of misery.

I hear a cough from the direction of Sam's tent, then a deeper cough as he clears the phlegm from his throat. Waves of heat roll over me as I realize he's just a few feet away, listening to me groan. Pitying me, probably. I crawl into my tent and lie on my back on the sleeping bag, then squeeze my eyes shut. I breathe in and out, fighting the constriction in my rib cage, the tautness in my throat. I will not cry. Not this time.

Another squall sweeps through the canyon late in the afternoon, turning every path into a rutted stream. As I slog through the chain of puddles toward the mess tent I can hear Fiddle's voice booming over the steady percussion of rain on leaves.

"No one messes with my kitchen." When I draw closer I see Fiddle holding a canvas bundle in her fist, the bundle I saw on my first day in camp, the slotted canvas pannier for her knives. "I want it back, or somebody's going to pay."

Sylvia stands near the stove, her arms folded tightly across her chest as she skewers Fiddle with her gaze. Jason sits at the picnic bench, facing outward, leaning back against the table with legs outstretched and crossed at the ankle, while Will sits next to him, hands in his lap. Both of them watch the argument between Sylvia and Fiddle with interest.

Under the shelter of the tarp, I pull back the hood of my raincoat as Sylvia turns to me. "Apparently one of Fiddle's kitchen utensils was taken this morning. Have you seen it?"

"That was no utensil," Fiddle says. "It was an heirloom, an antique Samurai dagger. Belonged to my dad, and he got it off a Jap he killed in the Pacific. I'm not cooking another meal until I get it back."

"And you think that's a threat?" Sylvia says dryly.

I remember the dagger, and the businesslike way Fiddle quartered the rabbit with it on my first day in camp. It makes me uneasy to realize it's missing. I give Sylvia a hard look. She and her husband are the only people in camp who seem to feel no compunction about stealing other people's things, as far as I can tell.

Fiddle pins her gaze on me, her eyes narrowed. "You take it?"

"Of course not."

"You see anybody take it?"

"No." I shrug. "Sorry, I haven't seen it."

Jessie straggles in, her head uncovered, her eyes red-rimmed and damp. She smiles sadly at me, her shoulders hunched against the chill emanating from Sylvia. Michael arrives behind her, ducking into the shelter under the tarp, shaking the rain from his thick blond hair. He sees Sylvia and Fiddle glaring at each other, then glances at me and rolls his eyes.

Jessie starts to slide into the bench of the picnic table but rises again when she sees a hooded silhouette approaching through the downpour.

We watch the figure draw closer, until the features obscured by the hood become clear. It's Sam. He joins us under the tarp and shakes himself like a wet dog before wiping his face with the back of his hand. "Jesus, two nights in a row. I've never seen it rain like this in May."

Jessie sinks back to the bench as she stares beyond Sam toward the path to the mesa. "He should be back by now."

She's right. Richter has been gone for eleven hours, more than enough time to walk six miles out and six miles back across level terrain. Veils of rain gust over the cliff face overhanging the canyon, blurring the clean angles of rock. Richter may have to spend the night on the mesa—a dangerous prospect if he's not prepared.

Silence settles over us, broken only by the pounding rain on the canvas overhead. In the stillness my palms suddenly begin to sting. Heat rises from my sacrum, flowing up my spine until my head feels like it could burst into flame. When I shut my eyes I see a dark mouth. Big. Black. Deep. There's something buried within it, something hot as a burning coal, something that radiates malevolence and stares right at me. A thing with red eyes, an evil that does not want me to see it. It's close. Much closer than we realize.

My eyes fly open, and fear skitters over my skin in a wave of goose bumps as the urge to flee seizes me. I shiver and try to blink away the feeling. What the hell was that? Whatever it was, it's here in camp. Lurking.

Instinctively I take a step back, filled with the irrational urge to run, but from what? I glance at the others and see Fiddle giving Will and Jason a hard look.

"If one of you little thieving bastards took my dagger, by God I'll make you sorry. You understand me? I will hurt you."

"Will you please shut up about your knife," Sylvia snaps. "Before you accuse anyone else, I'd suggest you look in those filthy tubs of dishwater you never seem to change."

Henry tramps up the path, head bowed against the steady downpour until he reaches the sanctuary of the canvas tarp over our heads. "The creek's flooding," he says, removing his hat. "This keeps up, we might want to move our tents to higher ground."

Jessie peers down the path, craning her neck, trying to see beyond the curtain of rain. *"Gracias a Dios,"* she whispers, and then, in a louder voice, "He's here."

In the dim half-light Richter staggers toward us, shoulders bowed by the weight of his pack.

"Did you find the tomb?" Sylvia calls out, sidestepping puddles as she trots toward him.

Henry hurries after her, and the rest of us follow. "Any luck?"

Jessie approaches Richter and examines his face, looking for answers.

We reach the shelter of the kitchen, and once he's out of the rain, Richter pushes back the hood of his coat. His face is pale, drawn with fatigue. "No luck."

Sylvia wrinkles her brow. "Why? What happened?"

"It doesn't matter." He looks ill, as if he might collapse where he stands.

Sam stares evenly at him. "How will you write the proposal without an exact position for the location of the tomb?" There's no warmth in his tone.

"You have to go back up there," Henry says. "Take me with you this time. Don't worry about the tracks. With this front blowing through, the rain will start up again tomorrow and wipe out our footprints."

Richter eases the pack from his back, exhaustion spelled out in every movement.

"Adam?" Sylvia says uncertainly. "Are you all right? Do you want something to eat?"

Jessie reaches out and takes his hand in hers. He looks at her, looks at her hand clasping his. Slowly she lowers it and lets it go. "Let me make some soup for you." She brushes past Sylvia and Fiddle to light the stove.

"I'm not hungry." His voice seems different, thinner, more hesitant, and he stares at the downpour beyond the shelter without focusing. He closes his eyes and rubs them with his thumb and forefinger. "I'll ride out for Silver City first thing in the morning. The rest of you will remain here until I return. Is that clear?"

We nod and reluctantly mumble our assent, although the air is thick with unanswered questions. There's no recognition, no spark of feeling in Richter when he finally looks at his wife, his sons, Jessie, Henry, or any of us. He sounds like a robot.

A strobe of brightness flashes outside as lightning stabs the ground, and in the flashbulb glare I see his close-cropped head and dark eyes gazing at me. In the blackness that follows, an afterimage lingers, and I see his skull, with empty eye sockets that stare at me above a death's-head grin.

The image vanishes as quickly as the fork of lightning, and then the earth shakes as thunder rolls overhead. *No,* I think. I don't want to know this. I don't want to feel this. Something happened up there on the mesa, and I don't want to see any more.

CHAPTER NINE

Someone hisses my name, and the sound slowly filters through and fuses with my dream until I hear it repeated with more urgency. "Kate! Wake up!"

I struggle out of the clutch of sleep and see a shadowed figure at the door of the tent. It's Jessie. It feels like the middle of the night.

"What," I mutter.

"It's Dr. Richter. He's hurt."

I paw the floor of the tent for my watch and peer at the face. It's five-thirty in the morning. "What happened?"

"I don't know. I think he fell. He's not moving."

I squirm out of the warm cocoon of the sleeping bag, yank a sweater over my head and hitch my legs into a clean pair of jeans. It's cold. A milky, pre-dawn twilight seeps over the eastern mouth of the canyon. My fingers feel thick and clumsy as I lace up my boots, and Jessie shifts from one foot to another with barely concealed impatience.

When I emerge from the tent I can see her flannel shirt and jeans are muddy. There's a leaf in the uncombed tangle of her hair, and her face is like chalk.

"Hurry," Jessie says, and heads north, toward the saltbush scrub beyond the piñon trees, expecting me to follow. We forge through the brush to a bare slope that hugs the north wall of the canyon, and she trots ahead, glancing back over her shoulder now and again to make sure I'm keeping up.

127

The sky becomes luminous, the color of tin, and the ravens begin their dawn chorus in the sycamores. A cold breeze sifts through the weave of my sweater, and I shiver as I hurry after her. We walk through the bleached wild grass, past the scattered tents of the crew, following the steady rise of the land to the tumble of basalt boulders that lie under the cliff edge. After we've gone about a thousand yards from the camp, the palms of my hands begin to throb. I press my left thumb into the center of my right palm, trying not to believe the familiar message that tell-tale ache delivers. But my hands know.

Not hurt. Dead.

Jessie stops at a rock fall at the base of the cliff. "There," she says, pointing toward what looks like a pile of clothing twenty feet ahead of us, half-hidden by a large boulder. It's Dr. Richter. At this distance there's no sign of blood or injury, but I recognize that kind of stillness, that appearance of repose. His body lies strewn on the rocks like rubbish.

As I walk closer I see the hand, outstretched and bloody, and then his head, centered in a dark puddle. His scalp must have split open on impact, revealing the cracked and splintered bone, resulting in a terrible loss of blood. The crown of the skull has been smashed into his head, resulting in a depressed fracture involving both parietals. His legs are twisted unnaturally beneath him. There's a slight odor coming from his corpse, a sweet, sticky smell of blood. I look up at the cliff, see the overhang forty feet above us, and sit down abruptly on the rock next to the body, feeling dizzy.

Taking a deep breath, I steel myself to lift his wrist to test for rigor. There's almost no resistance. He's been dead less than an hour.

Jessie's face collapses, and large tears spill down her cheeks. "He's dead, isn't he?"

We stare at the corpse for a long silent moment. "Did you see him fall?"

"I found him like this."

My ears fill with a rushing sound, and my body begins to tremble. Images come to me, tumbling into my brain before I can stop them, and I squeeze my lids tight to ward them off. I don't want to know this. But when I examine the hand that lies outstretched and limp in mine, the evidence is clear.

"Someone pushed him, Jessie."

Her voice is hushed, as if Dr. Richter could still hear us. "How can you tell?"

I point to the sharp bloodstained grooves running from the webbing between his thumb and forefinger, diagonally across his palm to the bottom of his little finger. "Look at these cuts on his hand. See how they cross the inside of his palm? He was attacked. These are defense wounds, made by a double-bladed knife."

"Maybe he cut himself on the rocks when he fell."

I shake my head, clutching my knees to still the tremor in my legs. "Cuts like that? No. It's practically impossible. Someone pulled a knife on him, and he grabbed the blade. That's the only way he could have sliced the flesh in two clean parallel lines like that."

"What about a branch? Maybe he tried to grab one on the way down."

"There aren't any other bruises or cuts on the hand, and there would be if he'd hurt it by clutching a rock or a branch." I close my eyes for a moment, afraid I might faint. This feels completely different from the nameless casualties I've examined in Iraq, or the mummified bodies I've excavated in Central America. This is Dr. Richter. Not just an icon of modern archaeology, a scientific superman—this is the corpse of someone I knew, someone I respected, even though I didn't like him. No one liked him.

Jessie crouches by his body, her eyes round with shock. "He was wearing a pack when I found him," she says slowly, looking around. "It's gone now." She rises to her feet and scans the rocks.

Still numb, unable to absorb the catastrophe of Richter's death, I try to gather my thoughts. "We need to tell Sylvia."

Jessie nods listlessly, but we don't move. I've never had to notify anyone of a death in the family. Whenever I had to process a corpse for the army, there was a comforting cushion of officialdom between me and the grief of the survivors. Now there's nobody but Jessie and me.

She crumples to the ground beside me and lowers her head to her hands. Her shoulders shake with silent sobs, and I press my palm to her back and feel the breath rise and shudder in her lungs.

A flutter of apprehension shimmers through me. "Are you usually up this early, Jessie?"

Her body is suddenly still under my hand. She looks up at me, her eyes red-rimmed. "I knew he'd be on his way to Silver City before the sun was up. I had to see him before he left. But I was too late."

Abruptly Jessie begins to weep again, and buries her face in her hands. "Oh God," she moans. "I can't believe he's dead."

I want to hold her, comfort her, but there are too many hovering unknowns. Why did she have to see Dr. Richter? If he was already dead, she must have come across his body just minutes after he'd been pushed off the cliff.

A line of silver appears at the horizon, signaling dawn. Jessie tilts her head back, and after a moment of absolute silence her eyes well up and glisten in the rising light. Then she begins to laugh, her eyes shining with unshed tears. "You want to hear something funny? I loved him. I loved that son of a bitch."

I remain quiet, tense, half-dreading the confession she's about to make.

"I met him when he gave a lecture at UNM. I was crazy about him. We started having an affair during Thanksgiving break, two years ago."

She goes on talking, her voice wistful as she gazes at the body sprawled on the rocks in front of us. "We used to take off in his truck, go down to the Rio Grande and make love. We'd take some good bread, some pâté and a bottle of wine, then make a little fire on the beach and have a picnic." Her voice dwindles to a whisper, then stops.

A raven caws from the cliff above us, then launches its black body into space, casting a shadow over us as it passes. The wind rises, blowing Jessie's hair into a dark halo around her face. She sniffs, straightens her spine and brushes a stray lock from her eyes. "About a year ago he started sneaking around with somebody else."

"Who?"

"I don't know, but I'm sure it wasn't Sylvia. I think it was somebody from out of town. I overheard him talking to her on the phone one day last summer. I heard a lot more than I wanted to."

I let the quiet stretch between us, waiting for her to go on.

"The whole time we were together, he never said he loved me. I could accept that. But when he was talking to her, it was like I didn't exist. I was nothing." A flash of spite crosses her tear-streaked face, then subsides as she stares at the corpse. "I thought I could make him forget about her, if I stayed close and came on the dig. But it was different. He was different. And then he disappeared for five days." She looks up at me. "Where was he, Kate? Did he tell you? Why did he go?"

"I don't know." The wind gathers strength as the sun breaks

131

the surface of the mesa, and shafts of light appear in the canyon. Finally I rise unsteadily to my feet. "We have to tell Sylvia."

Jessie nods and wipes her face with the back of her hand, and we start walking toward the Richters' tent.

My mind feels jumbled, chaotic, and shock makes me reel from one jagged thought to another. Once Sylvia reports the death on the satellite phone, anybody patrolling the airwaves will hear about it. Hordes of journalists could show up within a couple of hours, and then the pyramid will be splashed all over the evening news, along with pictures of Richter's body and the grisly details of his murder.

When the forensics team culls the physical evidence from the body—hair, blood, fibers, fingerprints—the signature of the killer will probably be revealed, but that could take weeks. In the meantime, we'll be viewed as the main suspects. My heart sinks even further as I realize that when the sheriff gets here, he'll want to interview all of us.

Jessie reaches for my hand and gives it a soft, warm squeeze. "I'll tell Michael and Jason. You talk to Sylvia, okay?"

Before I can stop myself, I glance down at her hand, searching for fresh scrapes or bruises.

She gives me a disgusted look and yanks her hand away. "You think I did it?"

I hold her gaze without saying a word, and her eyes harden.

"What about you, Kate? He stole your notes and the map to the cave. He fired you, for Christ's sake. You have as much motive as anyone."

I speak quietly. "You saw me this morning. I was sound asleep."

"You could have been acting."

I shake my head. "No."

Her face tightens as she fights back tears, and a long, exhausted pause comes between us. "I know," she whispers.

"But I almost wish you were the one who killed him."

"Why?"

"Because then I wouldn't have to suspect every single person in camp."

Filled with remorse, I reach out and take her in my arms. Her body feels like wire, and tension radiates from her like a force field. For a moment she allows me to hold her, then pushes me away and strides off toward Michael's tent.

Sylvia's tent glows in the pre-dawn twilight, and as I approach I can hear the faint murmur of conversation inside.

"Sylvia?" I call out. "It's Kate. Can I come in? It's important."

Sylvia unzips the door a few inches, blocking my view of the interior. "What is it?"

"It's about Dr. Richter."

Clearly displeased, she unzips the door the rest of the way and ushers me inside. Henry sits in the butterfly chair where Dr. Richter sat the night before. His boots are off, his shirt unbuttoned, his gray hair unbound and loose around his shoulders. The smell of coffee fills the tent, and I notice an espresso pot on the table next to two tiny cups and saucers.

Sylvia tightens the belt on her robe. "Well?" she asks, smoothing her hair. Henry rises from his chair and moves toward us.

I don't want to be here. I'd rather be anywhere else on earth right now. Giving her this news is probably one of the hardest things I'll ever have to do, and there's no good way to say it. "Dr. Richter's dead."

Sylvia staggers slightly, and Henry reaches out and steadies her with a hand on her back. "No," she breathes.

"How?" he asks.

"Someone forced him off a cliff at knifepoint. He fell. His skull was crushed."

The color drains from his face. "Forced? How do you know he was forced?"

"There are defense wounds on his hand. When the forensic team arrives, I'm sure they'll tell you the same thing. This was no accident."

Sylvia's eyes fill with tears that spill over her lower lids. "Where is he?"

"About half a mile north of here, below the mesa at the foot of the cliff. You'll need to ask everyone to stay away from the body—we can't touch it until the authorities get here. Call the sheriff, and he'll arrange for a crew to process the corpse. It shouldn't take long for a helicopter to get here."

Sylvia sways on her feet, her eyes fixed, unseeing. "Adam left for Silver City about an hour ago. There must be some mistake. He was fine. He can't be—"

"You need to sit down," Henry says, guiding her tenderly toward a chair. He covers her hand with his own, and his voice drops to a tone I've never heard from him. "I'll make the call."

She stares at him, a panicked look on her face. "Why? Why would anyone want to hurt him?"

"We'll find out," he assures her.

"No," she says, flailing out at Henry, resisting his gentle pressure. "This is my fault. I have to see Adam."

"We need help," I say, shooting a look at Henry, who gives me an almost imperceptible nod. "Our best chance of catching the killer will come from whatever evidence they've left behind. Once you alert the sheriff, it won't take long for a forensic team to arrive."

Sylvia collapses into her chair and covers her face with her hands. Henry lowers himself to crouch beside her and takes both her hands in his. "We'll get through this," he says, locking his gaze to hers. "I'll help you."

"We need to make that call," I say. "Every minute that goes by means the evidence has a greater chance of evaporating or getting trampled by the crew, once they find out what happened."

Henry kisses her on the forehead, then rises and moves to a work table in the corner. Boxes are stacked underneath it, and he slides them out until he locates a steel box at the back. Lifting the metal box to the surface of the table, he opens it and takes out what looks like a laptop computer with a cell phone attached. He lifts the receiver to his ear and presses a button on the laptop. He jabs the button several times as a worried frown begins to crease his forehead.

"It's not working?" I ask.

"Try it again," Sylvia says, her voice rising, close to hysteria.

He puts the receiver back in its cradle, then opens a sliding door in the bottom of the laptop. "The battery pack is missing."

"We have extra batteries," she says. "Look in the case."

Henry takes the case in his hands and turns it upside down. It's empty.

Sylvia leaps to her feet, takes the case from Henry and paws at the interior of the box as if she could summon a battery pack by will alone, then tosses the case on the floor. She looks up at Henry, her eyes wild. "Adam was terrified the press would get wind of what we've discovered. He must have put the batteries in his pack."

The two of them look at me, and I shake my head. "If he was wearing a pack, it's gone now."

Her mouth opens as if she's about to speak, but no sound comes out. She sags into her chair, folded in on herself like an old woman. "Everything was in that pack—the map to the tomb, the notebook and the photos." She looks up at Henry, her eyes filled with confusion. "What do we do now?"

By the time Sylvia, Henry, Michael and Jason return from viewing the body, I've told Sam and Will the news of Richter's death.

We assemble in a small, hushed group at the mess tent, each face a study in shock. Seated at the picnic bench, Michael lifts a mug of coffee to his lips, and the tremor in his hand makes the cup vibrate. His skin is gray, and his eyes seem smaller, sunken in the landscape of his face.

Sylvia looks taut as a violin string about to snap. Small, sharp lines radiate from around her mouth, and not even Jason's hand on her back can soften the tension that crackles in the air around her. Her dark hair has been brushed and pulled back into a bun, giving more prominence to her long, determined nose.

Fiddle stirs oatmeal on the stove, muttering with disapproval as she raps the spoon against the edge of the pot. Jessie's nose is pink, her eyes swollen and bruised from weeping. Will sits slumped next to her, his face slack, puffy with sleep. His bandage is off, revealing an angry red wound on his scalp that probably should have been stitched up days ago.

Sam catches my eye and pats the bench between himself and Michael, and I walk over and sit down next to him, grateful to sink into the background.

One of us killed him, I think, studying each face. The image of Richter's split skull comes back to me, that terrible purple mash of tissue, blood and bone. All my anger at him was erased by that sight. And yet—if I were completely honest about it—a part of me feels released by his death. Who else feels relieved? I think of the parallel slices on Richter's palm, and the Samurai dagger missing from Fiddle's kitchen. Surreptitiously I check Sam's knuckles and fingers. They're covered in scrapes and bruises, battered by work in the tunnel. Everyone's hands look rough, covered in nicks and cuts that could come from breaking rocks with a pickax or from a battle with a doomed man.

Across the canyon, the rising sun edges the pyramid in gold, while its bulk remains in shadow. On each platform, the sculpted head of Quetzalcoatl glares out at the world, open-mouthed, a serpent ready to devour its prey, a powerful visual curse against anyone foolish enough to disturb the monument.

And now the one responsible for tunneling into the heart of the pyramid is dead.

Henry stands at the head of the table and clears his throat, and an expectant hush falls over the group. For a moment he simply stands there with his head bowed before he looks up at the rest of us. His eyes are bloodshot, and he speaks slowly, haltingly. "This is a hell of a thing. First I'd like to say how sorry I am. Michael, Jason—your dad was the best friend I ever had." His voice cracks, and he lowers his head and closes his eyes for a moment before continuing.

Jason rolls his eyes at this, while Michael continues staring into his mug.

Henry goes on with his speech. "Sylvia—whatever you need, just say the word. We'll get through this. The rest of you should know we're going to wrap up the body so Sylvia can take it into Silver City before nightfall. Any of you want to pay your last respects, we'll be heading over there now."

"You can't move the body." It comes out louder than I intend, falling into the quiet like a rock dropped in a pond.

Sylvia's voice cuts the air. "Adam deserves a decent burial."

"It's a crime scene," I say. "He was murdered."

Her eyes gleam with the full force of her pent-up fury. "You listen to me, Kate Donovan. No one murdered my husband. He was *loved*. He was *respected*. And I will not allow his body to bake in the hot sun, exposed to maggots and flies just because you have some sick need to be the center of attention."

"He was attacked. There are defense wounds on his hand," I say in a low, even voice, and everyone at the table shifts uncomfortably.

Henry lifts his palm, like a traffic cop calling a halt. "Dr. Richter had a backpack with him when he left, but there's no sign of it now. Anybody who's seen the pack—light gray, black trim—you can return it to Sylvia's tent any time, no questions asked."

"And if it doesn't show up, you'll rip our tents apart," Jessie mutters.

He stares hard at Jessie, and she meets his eyes with a challenging look. A tense silence blooms between them, until Jessie lowers her head and fixes her gaze on the table.

"What was in the pack?" Will asks.

"The map to the tomb," Sylvia says bitterly. "The notes, photographs, every shred of evidence we have."

Michael grips the mug in front of him and looks at his stepmother. "Kate should go back up there, to see if she can locate the tomb again. We'll need another map."

"You can't be serious," Sylvia says. "After all the trouble she's caused?"

"She's the only one who knows where it is," Jason murmurs in her ear. "Dad spent hours looking for it, and he couldn't locate it. Without Kate's help, it could take us weeks to find it again."

Sam nods. "We'll need another map and a full description of the tomb before they'll give us the permit to excavate."

Hope flares in me at the thought of going back to the cave. *It's a prize worth dying for,* Richter said last night, and even though the words have taken on a morbid weight, I'd give anything to see it again. Last night I never thought I'd be allowed to go back to it. Now the possibility of returning seems tantalizingly close.

"It's out of the question. Her contract has been terminated," Sylvia says, her eyes snapping with animosity.

"She can't be trusted," Henry says. "I don't want to hear another word about it. As far as we're concerned, she doesn't work here anymore."

"That's right. I don't work here anymore," I say quietly. Aware of everyone's eyes on me, I pretend to be calm, despite the throbbing of blood in my ears. "Dr. Richter fired me last night. Given the circumstances, I'd say the tomb is open to anyone who can get the permit to excavate. Dr. Sugiyama at Arizona State, Dr. Gerritson at UNM—I'm sure they'd be interested in hiring me."

Henry's eyes narrow as he absorbs the threat. "We can't let her go," he mutters to Sylvia. "We'll have to reinstate her."

"I don't trust her," Sylvia says.

"I'll go with her to the tomb," Henry whispers. "She can't get away with anything if I'm watching her. I'll take my own notes, chart an accurate map."

Sylvia stares at him, lips pressed tightly together, her spine stiffened with regal hauteur.

"What?" Henry asks.

"Adam is dead." There's no mistaking the savage determination in her whisper. "You'll have to take him to Silver City, Henry. Surely you don't think I'm going to drag a corpse out of here by myself."

"You'll have Michael and Jason," he says.

She takes a deep breath. "Henry. Listen very carefully. I'm only going to say this once. Adam stood by you for the past twenty years, and now it's time for you to show your respect and gratitude. This is not a request. This is an order."

Henry aims a long level look at Sylvia, his face dark with anger. "Fine."

"I'll go with Kate to the tomb," Sam says.

Henry shoots him a look of pure hatred, a narrow-eyed look of anger that flashes out in the open for a second before he can smother it.

Sylvia shrugs, dismissing me, making it clear to everyone that she has more important things to think about.

Henry nods briefly at Sam, and his words spit out like bullets. "Take my rifle. You come across anybody up there with a gray pack, you might need it. And make damn sure the entrance to that cave is sealed before you leave."

Chapter Ten

The silence at breakfast is broken only by the scrapes and clicks of spoons against enamelware. Michael leaves his oatmeal untouched, and after staring into his coffee mug for a few minutes, he stands abruptly and leaves the table.

Fiddle casts a reproachful eye toward his bowl and mug, her mouth a pinched line as she sweeps his dishes from the table and carries them to the pot of dishwater. Her hunched shoulders bristle with irritability, especially when she glances at her husband, who hasn't left Sylvia's side. Henry's gaze darts nervously toward his wife, but he remains protectively close to Sylvia, whose face has taken on a waxy pallor.

I follow Fiddle with my own dishes, and give them a cursory swipe in the tepid water before hurrying off after Michael.

Michael's steps look slow and uncertain as he walks through the scrub of Arizona oak and piñon-juniper. He shuffles past the scattered tents toward the western edge of the camp, hands stiff at his sides, his back stooped, as though he's carrying an invisible burden.

"Michael!" I call out, and he turns, then straightens as I catch up to him.

"I wanted to thank you for what you said to Sylvia back there," I say. "It meant a lot to me."

He gives me a brief smile. "You found the tomb, Kate. You deserve the chance to excavate it."

The sadness behind the smile tugs at my heart, and I reach

out and touch his arm. "I'm so sorry about your father."

His body begins to tremble, and the veneer of self-control dissolves as he lowers his head and his shoulders heave in a series of silent, convulsive sobs. I stroke his arm helplessly, aching with sympathy as the pain radiates from his body.

"It shouldn't have happened," he whispers in a voice so choked with emotion he can barely speak. "It never should have happened."

I reach out and wrap my arms around him.

"It's too much," he gasps. "It's only been six months since Isabelle died . . . and now this."

"It'll be all right," I whisper, patting him helplessly. "You don't have to get through this gracefully. You just have to get through it."

We stand there, mute, holding each other while a cloud of piñon jays skims over us and settles in the trees, calling to each other with mournful, worried cries. The air is warm now, a perfect late-May warmth after the cold night of rain, the kind of warmth that feels like a benediction.

Michael steps away and wipes his face with his sleeve, letting out an embarrassed laugh. "It's only pain, right? Twenty, thirty years, I'll be fine."

We stand there looking at each other, smiling awkwardly.

"Come on," he says. "Let me buy you a cup of coffee."

I touch his back. "You okay?"

"No." He clears his throat and shakes his head, struggling for control. "But I guess I'm going to have to get used to it."

We walk in silence under the shadows of the sycamores, and the creek fills the air with the sound of water rushing over rocks. Michael leads me to the canvas awning outside his tent, where a small propane stove sits on a long table, along with tripods, chamois rags, cameras and cases of film.

He lights the stove, fills a small pot with water and places it on the burner. "Have a seat," he says, gesturing to a pair of canvas chairs that face the pyramid. "All I have is instant. It won't take a minute."

The pyramid's harsh, monolithic edges look softer in the glow of morning, and the air is bright, washed clean, the kind of weather that comes after a hurricane. I sit in one of the chairs while Michael measures out the coffee. There's no lack of steadiness about him now, but he moves slowly, with an odd deliberateness in each gesture, a determined focus.

"How's Jason taking it?" I ask.

He shakes his head. "It's hard to tell. When you told us somebody took the map from your tent, I thought he might have been stupid enough to steal it. But I can't believe he's a murderer. And that's what we're talking about, isn't it? Murder?"

Michael hands me a cup before he takes the seat beside me, and I blow on the coffee to cool it, hesitating before I answer. If I were in his shoes, I'd want the truth, no matter how terrible. "There's no doubt in my mind that somebody pushed your dad off that cliff."

"Will it screw up the investigation if Sylvia takes the body to Silver City?"

"Considering the heat, and six hours on horseback—you bet. A lot of forensic evidence will be lost. But those defense wounds won't go away. The autopsy will confirm the fact that he was murdered."

"You think Sylvia will allow an autopsy?"

"She has to," I say uncertainly. "Doesn't she?"

Michael is silent, making the answer clear. After her outburst at breakfast, it's too easy to imagine her sweeping into the small town coroner's office, haughtily informing him of Dr. Richter's "accident," pressing him to release the body immediately for burial—or worse, cremation. There's no doubt Sylvia will use the full weight and power of her name to make sure no one suspects Richter was murdered.

Michael looks at me over the rim of his cup, a trace of worry in his eyes. "She's not exactly rational right now, is she? It seems crazy to cart him off to Silver City before the sheriff gets here. Maybe I can talk her into holding off."

"You don't think she had anything to do with his death, do you?"

A wry look flickers across his face. "They had their differences, but—no, I don't think so. My dad always had a powerful effect on women. Sylvia practically worshipped him."

My mind skips to the scene in her tent this morning. I think of Henry and his unbuttoned shirt, and the way he kissed Sylvia's forehead. I think of how she looked at him and asked him what they should do.

We sit in silence for a minute. Michael closes his eyes and stretches his long legs out before him, crossing them at the ankles. He looks exhausted.

"My wife was the same way." His voice is drowsy, and for a second I can't remember what we were talking about. "As far as Isabelle was concerned, Dad walked on water." With his eyes still closed, he goes on mumbling. "They were so much alike. Isabelle thought she could do anything if she wanted it bad enough. She and Dad had the same determination. They seemed invincible."

The image of Isabelle Richter hovers in my memory, a tall, fair woman with an abundance of charisma. In their last documentary on the tombs at Bahariya, she stood in front of the camera like a statue of Isis. Gracious, poised, speaking in well-articulated, fully thought-out paragraphs, she seemed impeccably organized, with a head full of facts that she could distill to simple, clear sentences. Not at all stiff or puffed up with her performance, but formidable all the same. Exactly like Dr. Richter.

Before she died, Isabelle and Michael seemed like a golden couple, blessed with wealth and fame, radiant with self-assurance. Some vestige of that self-assurance remains in Michael, but the aura of happiness has disappeared, as if her death ruptured the invisible membrane that held his good fortune. Now Michael's face is a road map of bereavement, carved by fissures of grief. There are shadows in his eyes. His hair is thinning, prematurely gray, and he looks much older than his forty years.

I shove my hands deep in my pockets, searching my mind for any memory of a news report that mentioned the reason for Isabelle's death. As far as I can recall, the cause was never publicized. "How did your wife die, Michael?"

"Diabetes. Type one diabetes. It's much more deadly than type two, the more common form. Isabelle never wanted to be controlled by her disease. She took risks."

"What kinds of risks? You mean work? Travel?"

"No." A brief, weighted silence falls between us. "Isabelle wanted to have a child. Her doctors told her it was crazy, that her body couldn't take the strain of carrying a child to term. But she was determined to go ahead. It was the pregnancy that killed her."

So he lost more than a wife, I realize. He lost a child, too.

Michael looks at me. "I'd appreciate it if you didn't talk about this with anyone. No one else in my family knows, and I'd like to keep it quiet."

"Of course." I study his face, so different from Sylvia's lean, ascetic features and narrow skull. Michael's cheeks are broader, his jaw slightly more rounded.

"Is your mom still alive?" I ask.

The ghost of a smile flits across his face. "Happily remarried, living in Phoenix. Her husband was a very big deal in office supplies until he retired."

"What's she like?"

"When I was growing up? She was small. Anxious to please. No one took much notice of her when Dad was in the room." He lifts one shoulder, lets it drop. "She's happier, now. She and Jack live on the ninth hole of their country club, play golf every day. Go to church on Sunday, vote Republican." The smile tweaks his lips. "You know—boring."

Michael takes a ruminative sip of coffee. "How about you, Kate? Do you have anybody waiting for you at home?"

Feeling suddenly shy, I swirl the liquid in my cup, avoiding his eyes. "No. I don't even own a cat."

With his eyebrows raised, he looks right at me. "But you've had your chances to settle down, I bet."

"In this business, I have to be ready to travel halfway around the world at a moment's notice. That's not what most men want in a wife."

"Ah. You're dedicated."

I let out a rueful laugh. "I had to be. In college I was so desperate to keep my scholarship that I spent most of my time at the library, studying. There wasn't much time to date."

He looks slightly skeptical, and I realize he has no idea how different my life has been from the privileged world he was born to.

"My dad owns a little tavern in Ithaca, New York. When I was growing up, I worked for him most nights and weekends, waiting tables." I take a sip of coffee to hide my face, embarrassed at how my life must look to Michael. "Not a lot of time for romance."

Maybe if I'd spent more time with any of my would-be suitors, we would have gone beyond those first dates that felt like work, those superficial conversations that seemed so full of effort. But the men I knew always wanted a little more time or attention or energy than I could afford to give, and whatever affection there was between us would usually fizzle out under the weight of our separate ambitions. If anything happened to me now, no one would mourn for long. No one would wander the earth, looking the way Michael looks when he talks about his wife.

Sam appears at the edge of the clearing, walking toward us, and Michael nods toward him. "Your escort has arrived."

I stand up too fast and knock my cup to the ground, splashing the chair with coffee. My face feels ridiculously hot. "Damn," I whisper, blotting the liquid with the flap of my shirt. "Let me get a rag and clean this up."

"Don't worry about it." An amused look crosses Michael's face as he glances at me then Sam, striding toward us. "Be careful up there, okay?"

Up on the mesa, the sun beats down on Sam and me as we trudge along, carrying packs with sleeping bags and enough food and water to last for two days, in case we can't find the tomb by nightfall. My back is already sweaty under the weight of the pack, and I stop for a drink of water before we've gone two miles.

Sam looks east and west, scanning the terrain with binoculars, then hands them to me. I aim the binoculars toward the volcano, which looks like a shallow, overturned bowl on the horizon, at least twenty miles north of us. The mesa stretches to infinity in every other direction, a vast plateau marked only by low, scattered trees, slabs of basalt and a thousand undulations that all look alike. Whatever footprints Richter left up here yesterday are gone, washed away by last night's rain.

"How much farther?" Sam asks.

"Four miles, give or take."

"Think you can find it again?"

"I have to." I put the binoculars in the pack and start walking toward the volcanic cone. Sam keeps pace, our legs covering the ground in long, smooth strides. As we walk I recognize a big agave, and beyond it a slab of basalt with a stunted piñon tree growing out of it. Intent on my goal, I hurry past the tree, pressing on toward the hummocks of rock swelling on the horizon. For nearly an hour we hike without talking, striding along slabs of rock, leaping over low clumps of barrel cactus and prickly pear, pushing toward the acres of exposed basalt ahead of us.

Finally Sam breaks the silence. "Must have been a shock, finding Richter like that."

I glance at him. "I'm okay, if that's what you're asking."

"No one was happy, were they?" Sam says. "We all had reasons for wanting him dead." He meets my eyes, holding my gaze a little longer than necessary.

My mouth feels dry, and I pick up the pace. "What about you, Sam? What was your reason for wanting him dead?"

"You don't seem too broken up about it," he says, eyeing me. "And you're still here. I'd say things worked out pretty well for you."

I stop walking, and he stops too. We stand facing each other, the wind whipping us, the high, white clouds racing over our heads.

"If you have something to say, you'd better spit it out," I tell him.

Sam shrugs. "He fired you, Kate."

"So?"

"When somebody like Richter fires you, the walls close in. You knew what it meant. You were upset."

"You think I killed him to keep my *job?*"

"One of us killed him for something. I'm thinking out loud, that's all."

I start walking again and hear him follow. Neither one of us says a word. His accusation hums in my ears, filling me with adrenaline. Up until now I thought Sam was my ally even when he was angry at me, but apparently I was wrong, and that loss hurts more than I care to admit.

For the next thirty minutes we hike in silence, until we come to a lip of rock that juts out five feet above a shallow depression in the mesa. Sam jumps down, lands lightly on the balls of his feet, then holds his arms up for me. I stand there, hands on hips, stubbornly refusing to take his hands and let him swing me down.

He tilts his head as he looks up at me. "Do you think we could put this aside and get on with the job?"

"How can you work with somebody you don't trust?"

"Hey, I'm sorry. I never should have said—oh, hell, get your butt down here." He gives me an engaging grin and waggles his fingers in the air. "Come on. I'll be nice."

Ignoring his hands, I jump down, landing hard beside him. He helps me up and steadies me for a moment, his palms warm and dry, his eyes calm as he examines my face. I look back into his eyes, eyes that are pale as shadows on snow. Beyond his face, I see the slope of the volcano.

"Damn," I mutter. "We've gone too far."

He releases my hands and turns to follow my gaze. "How can you tell?"

"See the silhouette of those trees, up on the mountain? They weren't that clear the day before yesterday. We need to back up."

He sighs, turns to face the rock and locks his hands together to give me a boost. Once I've crawled up, I reach down to help him, but he climbs easily on his own, pulling himself up until he's standing next to me.

We double back the way we've come, and I scan the ground, searching for any sign of something familiar. The ground is soft from the rain, and none of Richter's tracks remain from the day before. Every hump and dip looks the same as I crisscross the mesa, looking for the landmarks I catalogued so carefully.

Finally I set off to the southwest, and before we've gone a mile, I see a fleck of yellow in the distance, no more than a dot from where I'm standing, but the color shows up against the gray-green wash of grama grass and basalt.

"Over there," I say, pointing. "See that patch of yellow?"

"Barely."

"Let's take a closer look."

As we walk towards it, a familiar, symmetrical shape rises above the scrabble of cholla. I break into a run, impatient to reach it.

After jogging for five minutes over the rough ground, the rounded shape becomes more obvious. It's the ruin. No doubt about it. The branches I broke off to camouflage the entrance have given it away, now that the brush has gone limp and turned yellow in the morning sun, making the opening more obvious to anyone walking by.

Mortified by my error, I scatter the branches while Sam silently helps me, and we both pull away the rocks I'd placed over the entry until the dark opening is fully revealed.

Sam stares in disbelief at the hole. "That's not the way in, is it?"

"That's it."

"It's no bigger than a coyote hole."

"Do you want to go first?" I ask.

"I don't think I'll fit in there."

"You don't have to go in," I say. "I'll just do a quick inventory, and then I'll be right out."

He gives me a look. "You think I'm going to let you go in there by yourself? I've been looking for this thing a hell of a lot longer than you have." He kicks a large boulder that juts out from the top of the opening. To my alarm the rock shifts slightly in the rain-softened ground.

"Don't do that," I say sharply. "Stay here if you don't want to risk it. I'll go in and see if everything's still there." I unbuckle my pack and swing it to the ground, then rummage in it for a flashlight, a small spiral notebook and a pen.

Leaving my pack outside the hole, I grab the flashlight in one hand, notebook and pen in the other, then get on my hands and knees to enter the tunnel. I push my way into the dark shaft, ten feet, twenty feet, squirming on my belly, using my elbows to guide myself forward. It seems easier the second time, now that I know what's waiting for me. After a few seconds I can hear Sam muttering behind me as he follows me into the tunnel.

At the bottom I stand the flashlight on its end so its beam bounces off the ceiling and illuminates the room with a soft, even glow. Sam wriggles through the shaft, rises slowly to his feet and stares around the room in stunned disbelief, silently taking in the painted walls, the mummy and the array of treasure surrounding it. He walks to one wall and brushes away the dust to trace the writing on it. My skin tingles, watching his hand moving slowly, carefully, reverently across the surface. He turns and lets his gaze sweep over the remains of the jaguar and its cage, and the tall, perfectly preserved pots that come up to my waist. A slow smile spreads across his face as he makes his way around the room. Kneeling to examine the codex, he blows gently on it to reveal the painted wood of its cover, then touches it delicately with his fingertips, as if touch were more important than sight. Finally he straightens and rises to his feet, gazing at the tiny mummy on the altar in the center of the room.

I start recataloguing the contents of the tomb as quickly as I can. While I'm scribbling, Sam bends over the mummy and studies the funerary mask covering its face.

"It's a child," he says.

"Yes."

A rumble of rock crashing down on rock echoes through the cave, followed by a distant thud.

We stare at each other, frozen in alarm.

"What the hell was that?" I ask.

"I'll go see." He reaches for the flashlight next to me, then rushes toward the tunnel and enters it headfirst, leaving me in utter blackness. I hear him scrabble his way up the slope to the entrance, and then a stream of muffled curses comes floating through the darkness.

"What is it?" I call up to him.

"That rock fell over the entrance," he yells. "I can't move it."

"Are you sure?"

"It won't budge. It's wedged in there."

This can't be happening, I tell myself. It can't be as bad as Sam makes it sound. After an eternity of waiting I see the flickering light return as Sam edges back into the cavern. He pulls himself out of the tunnel and stands up, wiping dust from his face with his sleeve.

"Give me the flashlight, and I'll try," I say.

Sam's face is rigid. "I'm stronger than you are, and I couldn't move it."

"Give me that." I rip the flashlight from him.

After squirming twenty feet up the slope of the shaft, I aim the flashlight at the rock that fills the entry. A big block of basalt covers the hole, probably the same rock Sam kicked before we entered the opening. *Damn him,* I think, edging forward.

I put the flashlight down and push against the rock, but there's no shift, no movement whatsoever. Pushing uphill while lying flat on my belly is the worst possible position for trying to move anything, and I lie in the dirt, panting, trying to figure out a way to get some better leverage.

Laboriously, I work my way backwards down the thirty-feet-long shaft. When I emerge from the tunnel, Sam looks up, and I shake my head.

"I'm going to go up feet first, see if I can move it with my legs," I say.

"I'll go. You rest."

"No, save your strength. If I can't budge it, you'll go next." I leave the flashlight with him and go back into the tunnel, moving slowly and awkwardly uphill in the thick darkness, my head lower than my feet, my elbows raw by now from the friction of pushing myself over rock. When I reach the boulder wedged in the socket of the entrance, I use my legs like coiled springs to shove against it. Nothing. No shifting, no movement at all. It's too heavy. My legs begin to quiver with the strain, and a muscle jerks in my belly.

We spend the next few hours taking turns crawling up the shaft, trying to push the stone away, but it remains locked in place. Waiting for him to return is the worst part, and the opaque darkness presses in on me like a coffin until I see the wavering beam of the flashlight as he inches his way back down.

After Sam edges back down the length of the tunnel for the last time, he slumps to the floor and lies there, exhausted.

"We'll get out," he says, panting.

"How?"

"I gotta tell you, I haven't figured that one out yet."

"If you hadn't loosened that rock . . ." I mutter.

The beam of the flashlight begins to flicker. "We need to turn off the flashlight, or we're going to be stuck without any light at all," Sam says. Abruptly he picks up the flashlight and thumbs the switch, plunging us into blackness.

The sudden darkness is full of our breathing. Seconds drag by, oozing into minutes. The floor is dry and gritty underneath my fingers, and I'm aware of the weight of my clothing, how the waistband of my jeans pinches when I prop up my legs. My shoes feel heavy and tight on my feet. My eyes are open but there's no point to keeping them open; open or shut, there's nothing to see. My skin feels shredded from crawling up and down the tunnel, and I can't face going up there again.

Panic begins to glide up my torso, enveloping me, squeezing me. We're caught, trapped underground, helpless. Buried alive. *Think,* I beg myself. There has to be a way out. Something crawls across my arm and I slap it away with more force than necessary, and then I begin to shiver. I can't stop shivering. My body heat seeps away in the chill of the tomb. I stand and try to jog in place to keep warm, but it's hard to keep my balance in the blackness. The temptation to turn on the flashlight gnaws at me with a constant, pressing urgency. A hundred different scenes play out in my mind, none of them good. How long will it be before Henry realizes we're missing? Two days? Three? By the time anyone comes looking for us, we could be dead.

Sam's disembodied voice floats out of the blackness. "Talk to me, Kate."

"About what?" I can hear him moving, feeling his way blindly toward the sound of my voice.

"Anything," he says. He lowers himself awkwardly, bumping my head as he gropes for a clear space to sit on the dirt floor.

I sink down next to him. "You're not going to like what I've been thinking."

"I don't care," he says. "Talk to me."

"What if somebody followed us up here?" I ask.

"You think someone tipped that rock over the entrance on purpose? What would that accomplish?"

"Think about it. Whoever killed Dr. Richter won't balk at killing us. He could have followed us here. Four days without water, we're dead. Then he could come back, lever the rock off, crawl in here and grab the codex. What do you think a codex is worth on the black market? A million? Five million? Ten?"

"That's crazy. The others know we're up here. When we don't come back, they'll look for us."

"What if they can't find us?"

"Then we'll dig our way out."

"This cave was carved out of basalt, Sam. It's solid rock."

"Come on, Kate. Don't think about it. Being anxious will only make you feel cold."

I shiver, hugging my elbows. "I'm freezing."

"Come here, then," he says. The weight of his arm slides over my shoulders, and he gently shifts me until we're lying next to each other on the cool sand of the floor.

CHAPTER ELEVEN

Sam turns toward me until the full length of his chest and legs fits against mine in a welcome rush of heat. His hands warm my back, and I can smell a faint odor of peppermint on his breath. My face feels hot in the darkness, body tense, stomach tight with nerves.

"Relax," he whispers, stroking my back.

His thumbs press against my vertebrae, then wander up the spinal column and out to the wings of my scapula. There's an explosion of sensation in my skin, a traveling heat under the gentle pressure of his fingers, but it does nothing to dispel the tension in my shoulders. I try to soften slightly and take a deep breath.

Usually darkness is a relative thing, a gloom lifted by moonlight filtered through curtains, or the glow of city lights on the horizon, or the crack of light under a bathroom door. Ambient light leaks in. Even out in the wilderness on a moonless night, starlight lets you see the silhouette of your hand in front of your face. Here, the blackness is absolute, and the only sound in this underground vault comes from our breath, the rustle of our clothing, and the friction of Sam's hand against my back. In the silence and darkness every muscle in my body feels rigid, uncertain, robbed of all visual cues, and intensely aware of his presence.

Sam sniffs my hair. "You smell good. Did you take a bath this morning?"

"Last night. In the creek."

"In the hot springs?"

I tilt my head up, but his face remains invisible, cloaked in the blackness. "There are hot springs?"

"About a mile downstream from camp. Didn't Sylvia tell you about them?"

I remember the amused look on her face as she watched me bathe in the freezing water, and for a second I allow myself the luxury of hating her. "No, she didn't mention that."

"Must be a hundred degrees in those pools, maybe more." He cradles my head with his hand and draws it closer, until we're lying cheek to cheek. His breath feels warm against my ear. "After we get out of here, we'll go take a soak. Spend the whole day in there. Just you and me. Relaxing in the bubbles, looking up at the trees." His voice is a low rumble, a purr that vibrates my ear and weakens my knees. He squeezes me tightly, pulling me closer. "What do you say?"

Gooseflesh pricks my arms. Will we ever see trees again? I don't want my life to end here, but I know we're running out of time with every passing second. I press the stem of my watch to illuminate the dial. It's already nine o'clock. Nightfall.

"Shh," Sam says, though I haven't said a word. He chafes my arms. "We'll get out, Kate."

I don't believe him. This cold and airless place feels too much like the tomb it was always meant to be, and the weight of what lies ahead presses on me like an anvil.

"What do you think they're doing back at camp?" I ask.

"Sylvia and Henry probably left already. By tomorrow night, the others might start looking for us. Or a hiker could see our packs and call for help."

My head sags against Sam's shoulder as I calculate our chances for survival. His optimism doesn't sway me a bit—the crew won't search for us until the day after tomorrow at the earliest. Even then they might find excuses to wait another day or two before they start looking. How much longer can we last without water? Three days?

The last time I had a drink of water was up on the mesa, at least twelve hours ago. My water bottle is still in my pack, outside the entrance to the tunnel, just a few feet away from us. The thought of it makes my mouth feel dry as parchment. How could I have left it behind? I was thirsty. The water was right there. But I was so damned eager to crawl down that hole and make sure the tomb was intact, and then Sam crawled in after me.

With an almost physical effort, I tear my mind away from the thought of water. "Will Henry lead the new expedition?"

"No," Sam says quietly. "I will."

I stiffen in his arms, and the small hairs at the back of my neck start to rise. "Why you, Sam?"

"Richter and I go way back. I told you we scouted the Gila for a year before we found the pyramid. We both had a crazy kind of faith we'd find this. He put my name down as second-in-command when he wrote the grant proposals and signed the papers for the permits. If we ever get out of here, I'll lead the dig."

"If you were next in line, why did you let Henry take over when Richter was missing?"

He releases a long exhalation in my ear. "I didn't want to kick up a fuss when there was a chance Richter would come back. And he did come back."

"Henry won't like it. He'll fight you."

"There won't be a fight," Sam says. "It's all in writing. Richter knew Henry was great at mustering supplies and organizing the physical labor on a dig. But interpreting the results? No. Charming the donors? Forget it. It's completely beyond him."

Only half aware that I've been holding my breath, I let it out.

"I wish you'd told me this before."

I can feel him shrug. "It never came up."

But that's not true. I think of how we discussed Henry on my first night in camp, outside Sam's tent. When I asked Sam if Henry was really in charge, he said something about how Henry certainly thought so, and he wasn't the kind of guy you wanted to argue with.

An edgy paranoia begins to crawl over my skin, making me colder. Sam was the only one on the crew who never showed any visible reaction to Richter's death, keeping his thoughts locked up behind those guarded, ice-blue eyes. What if he was fed up with being number two? Being the leader of an expedition like this would change his life.

Whoever excavates this tomb will become a name, a celebrity, someone whose face will be on every talk show, magazine, newspaper and lecture circuit. Everyone will want the man who uncovered the richest burial ever found in the western hemisphere. Sam would be set for life. Honors would come pouring in, and money and fame would follow.

If Sam knew he was next in line to lead the excavation of this tomb, he had a reason to kill Richter. A reason he didn't bother to share with me when he was blithely pointing out why I might have killed him myself.

"Still cold?" he asks.

My misgivings form a wall between us, a wall I'm sure he can feel with his arms wrapped around me. I edge away from him slightly, separating myself from the heat of his body. "I'm a little tired. Maybe we should get some sleep."

"Kate? You all right?"

"I don't feel like talking, okay? Go to sleep."

My eyes flutter open to blackness. Sam heaves a deep sigh and rolls over, away from me. The chill of the cave has settled in the marrow of my bones, my bladder feels tight, and there's a crick in my neck. Confused, I sit up and try to orient myself.

Time is elastic in the dark, and when I push the stem of my watch to light the dial, the hands say three-thirty. It's probably the middle of the night. We left on Monday morning, so this would be early Tuesday morning. Or is it? Without the sun or moon or stars to mark the days, it feels like it might just as well be Wednesday afternoon.

Reaching out with one hand, I can feel the rough, cool surface of the wall next to me. I need to pee, and I want to do it now, while Sam is still asleep. Awkwardly I lift myself to my feet and move to the right, away from the pots, feeling my way along the wall until I reach the opposite corner of the cave. I kneel on the sand and dig a hole, then squat over it. An embarrassing rush of sound fills the cave, along with the sharp, warm odor of urine.

Sam goes on snoring as I scoop sand over the wet spot, and then I blindly make my way back to the sound of his breath. Already I feel lethargic from thirst, and my body feels haunted by an incessant whisper of anxiety about Sam. It's alarming to realize how much I don't know about him. In spite of his easy banter, he's watchful, always coolly assessing the people around him, giving the impression that nobody can penetrate the wall he keeps between himself and other people.

When I move my head the cave seems to spin. My skin feels clammy, and my pulse is slow, almost imperceptible. Leaning back against the wall, a sudden rush of vertigo makes me slump sideways, and I bump into the pot next to me. It teeters for a moment on its slender base, and I put out a hand to keep it from tipping over.

Stupid pots. They're huge. What a pain it must have been, carting them all the way from Mexico. They take up so much room in here, and every time I move I'm terrified I'm going to knock one over and break it. They're at least four feet tall, delicate as eggshells and loaded with offerings.

Thinking about them plucks at my brain, as if something I've forgotten hovers just at the border of consciousness. Every cell in my body quivers to attention, desperately reaching for the thought beginning to take form in the back of my mind.

Sam takes in a deep breath and lets it go. I can hear him shifting on the ground, turning to face me. "God, I'm thirsty," he murmurs.

I lick my lips. My tongue feels like a lump of suede. "Let's not talk about it."

He yawns. I can hear him stretch, hear his knees crack as he rolls over.

"I have a question for you." I keep my voice casual, straining for nonchalance.

"Shoot."

"This chamber and the tunnel are made from a lava tube, right?"

The cave fills with the sound of Sam scratching the growth of beard on his face. He clears his throat. "That's right. Same kind of tube they used to bury their dead in Teotihuacán."

My heartbeat picks up speed, and starts thumping against my ribs so hard I'm sure he can hear it. "Don't lava tubes follow the natural slope of the terrain, to drain the lava?"

"Sure."

"So if this is a tube, why would it stop? Why doesn't it go somewhere?"

There's a longish pause, as if he's thinking. "Rockslide. Erosion. Earthquake. Any one of those could have destroyed the rest of the tube."

Come on, Sam. Work with me. "But what if the tube didn't collapse? What if they just walled off part of it to make this room?"

Sam turns on the flashlight, and a flood of light pervades the room as he aims it at the ceiling to create a dull, even glow. I blink, almost blinded by the sudden change in illumination. The relief of seeing feels exquisite, like a miracle. Greedy for visual stimulation, I look around, memorizing the location of the artifacts. The cave seems smaller in the beam of the flashlight, instead of the black void it felt like a minute ago.

Sam rises to his feet and examines the walls of the crypt with his fingertips. I stare at the tunnel, then sight the line it would follow across the chamber if it had flowed unobstructed. If the tunnel ran in a straight line, the corresponding opening across the floor of the cavern would be behind the tall jars of corn and shells.

I stand up and grasp the center jar, the one filled with tiny corn cobs. It's surprisingly light for its size. Only dimly aware that I'm holding a million-dollar pot in my hands, I move it away from the wall. In the weak light I run my hand over the surface I've just exposed. It's plastered and delicately painted with glyphs that stop about two feet above the floor. I kneel to touch the line where the floor meets the wall. It's easy to scoop away the soft sand of the floor, and as I dig I notice a different texture to the wall, a grain unlike the plastered basalt. I take the Swiss army knife from my pocket and score the surface.

"Sam, look."

He picks up the flashlight and shines it on the line I've scored on the wall, then comes close to investigate.

"What do you think?" I ask.

He takes my knife and scrapes a pinch of dust from the surface, holding it in his palm, then touches it with the tip of his tongue.

He looks up at me. "Tastes like clay. Let's dig."

We move the artifacts aside. Sam uses an obsidian axe like a pick on the hard earthen wall, while I use a quartzite dagger to scrape away the rubble. The dagger feels cold and heavy in my palm, and the handle fits snugly against my fingers. The blade extends a full nine inches, still sharp as a razor after more than a thousand years, balanced beautifully by the weight of the grip. Armed with these ancient tools that would be prized in any museum collection, we attack the adobe wall as if it were an enemy.

We dig in the dark to save the batteries, and at first it's exciting. The tools are sharp, sturdy, and they work surprisingly well. It feels good to have a goal, to work toward rescuing ourselves. But then I begin to wonder if we were wrong about the angle of the tube. Maybe it went through the floor, or curved off to the left, or the right, and we're digging into the mesa itself. I don't say any of this out loud, but I notice Sam's movements are slower, as if he's thinking the same thing.

My tongue aches for water. After hours of digging our hole is at least four feet deep, but there's no sign that there's anything beyond it but more dirt. "How thick do you think they made it?" Sam asks. His words are slightly slurred, as if he were drunk.

I have no idea. It makes me uneasy that he'd even ask me. Lithic analysis is his field, not mine. "Six feet," I say, giving us something to aim for.

We pile our tailings in a drift against the altar that holds the mummy. *This has to work,* I tell myself. Somewhere behind this wall the lava tube has to be big enough to crawl through, a tube that extends like a magic corridor through the mesa and spills out at the bottom of a canyon. A canyon with a stream. A stream full of luscious, pure water.

We dig for another hour, and then another, and another. The chill remains constant, about fifty degrees. With no stars or moon or sun to mark the hours, the time my watch keeps takes on a surreal irrelevance since I'm never sure whether it's day or night. The hole in the wall grows bigger, and that's the only real evidence we have that time has passed.

We crouch side by side, wedged tightly against each other in the blackness as we hack at the wall, and I can smell Sam's skin, a lingering scent of soap under a sharp odor of sweat. The heat from his body gives me some comfort. At least we're active, we have a plan, and it's keeping us warm. But I'm worried about Sam. His movements have lost their rhythm, and he seems weaker. Every time he strikes the dirt with his axe, a small, stifled grunt comes out of him, as if he's in pain.

The delicate, razor sharp edges of the tools have chipped and grown dull, and the earth is so hard it feels as though I'm trying to dig through rock with a spoon. Something scuttles over my leg in the darkness, and fear crawls up and down my skin, slowly, taking its time.

Finally we stop digging. The hole is at least six feet deep, but there's no sign of a tunnel. Thirst crushes me like an iron hand at my throat, a threat I can't resist, can't fight, can't ignore. It pushes me up against the blank wall of knowing, finally, that this is where it will all end. I'll die here.

Knowing this releases an explosion of sorrow in me, a deep, terrible remorse, not for what I've done but for what I've left undone. Gliding through life toward the bones of the dead— why didn't I embrace life, instead? Why was I afraid to live? Everything I always thought was important has evaporated. Ambition, self-protection, the stubborn need to set my own course. Money. Christ. The time I've wasted worrying about money. It's all gone. It doesn't matter. It never mattered. In a matter of hours, our breath will slow, then stop. Our tongues will swell in our mouths and turn black. Our bodies will give the rest of their water to the dry air of the cave, and whatever I am will be snuffed out.

The black void around us feels as wide and deep as outer

space, a vacuum without mercy, and I lie on the dirt floor and think about water until my consciousness fades into a stupor.

I wake in the blackness, the panic of a bad dream tight in my throat, rising like a sob. The mummy lies in its wrappings on the altar beside me, a small figure that will never grow old.

I swallow in an effort to erase the taste of my fear, but I have no spit left.

When I sit up Sam lets out a snore and turns over. I envy him. It's easier to sleep, to let thirst carry me into a blankness where I'm numb. It feels as though weeks have passed in the dark, hours since we've spoken. The silence is large as an ocean, disorienting as the lack of sun or stars. I let it embrace me again and slip into a restless doze.

When I awaken again I pull myself up, feel for the flashlight and flick it on. Crawling to the hole, I pick up my dagger, lift my arm and stab the hard dirt. It's like stabbing concrete. Sam lies in the corner, drawn into a private world where I hope he doesn't feel anything because by now the dehydration is acutely painful. I keep a pebble in my mouth to secrete more saliva, but it's hard to tell the difference between the pebble's dry, grainy surface and my tongue.

Lift, stab, withdraw. Lift, stab, pull, lift, stab, pull. I count the strokes, then lose count. My arm aches, but I can't stop. To stop would mean sleep, and my dreams take me to a place that frightens me more than this.

It feels like I've been jabbing the hard wall ahead of me for most of my life. Exhausted, ready to quit, I lift the blade and stab the dirt again, and instead of an arm-jarring stop there's an unexpected lack of resistance.

The knife plunges through into open space.

Hope stirs inside me, and I strike again at the crumbling dirt.

The hole grows to the size of a porthole, then a window as the dry dirt crumbles and falls away. Frenzied now, I dig until the gap widens. Finally I lift the flashlight to peer into the cavern on the other side of the adobe wall.

"Sam," I say, my voice a rasp. "Look."

There's no reply. I scrabble my way back toward Sam's hunched figure and shake him with one hand, aiming the flashlight at his face. His eyes are open, but there's no recognition in them.

"Wake up," I say gently, as if he's only sleeping. "We have to go now." I shake him again and give him the flashlight, which he drops.

"You have to help me." I pick it up and put it in his hand, wrap his fingers around it and squeeze. "Come on."

He blinks. After a moment or two he rises slowly to his hands and knees, then pulls himself to his feet. His movements are mechanical, lifeless, like a toy whose batteries have run down. I push him toward the hole and urge him into it. He falls to his knees as I shove him toward the opening, and then I follow close behind until we squeeze through the rubble and out to the other side.

Sam draws himself to his feet with difficulty. We're in an enormous cavern, far more spacious than the one we just left. Slowly, listlessly, he scans the wide walls with the flashlight.

"It's big," he says, the first words he's spoken in hours.

"Go," I say, and push him forward. At the far end of the cavern, the weak beam of the flashlight reveals a lava tube that curves ahead into blackness like a large intestine. We walk toward the black hole of the tube, and I keep my hand on Sam's back as he stumbles ahead of me. The tunnel runs downhill at an easy angle, and I pray it won't end in a pile of rubble.

CHAPTER TWELVE

We walk on bones. Skulls litter the floor like oversized mushrooms, their eye sockets eerily empty as they stare up at me under the flickering beam of the flashlight. Ribs, tibias, ulnas, and fibulas crunch under our feet. Dozens of human skeletons have been laid out in rows in the cavernous corridor, with burial goods arranged around each corpse. A few bodies have been wrapped in layers of cloth and look like cocoons. Blankets, pots, the smaller bones and skulls of animals, vials, amulets, beads, and statues lie in drifts around them.

When I come to one of the mummies blocking the path I lift my right foot and lower it carefully on the other side, and something snaps like a twig underneath me. I hate this. I hate the voices whispering at me, the bones breaking underfoot, the kaleidoscope of ghosts filling my head, old, young, sisters, brothers, mothers, fathers, slaves and babies. It's too much. I try to shut off the receiver inside me, but I can't remember how to do it, can't remember if I ever learned. More than anything, I want to lie down with them. Being awake is painful. Thirst makes every breath scrape my throat like a razor, and my body feels like a dry husk, wavering in and out of consciousness.

"What the hell—?" Sam rasps, staring at the scores of mummies surrounding us.

Get a grip, I tell myself. *Act like a scientist.* I sink to my knees and lift a skull to examine it more closely in the faltering beam of the flashlight. A young female. The frontal bone has been stylishly flattened in the manner of her people, but there's not a mark on the skull to explain her death.

She presses her lips to the rim of a cup while her little boy watches her. She drinks deeply, then passes the cup to her child, who obediently takes his portion.

I replace the skull gently on the ground and lift myself up.

"What happened?" Sam whispers. "A plague? A massacre?"

Poison. They drank poison.

"Look at how they arranged the burial goods," I tell him. "This isn't the aftermath of a disaster. Whatever happened here, it must have been planned well in advance." I take a deep breath, fighting off vertigo. "I think they killed themselves."

"Why?"

Why do I think so? Because I can see them. Because I know there was death in the cup, and they drank it willingly.

I grope for an answer he'll accept. "Maybe they thought their connection to the gods was severed. Maybe they thought killing themselves would mean the rebirth of the empire." I swing the beam of the flashlight from one corpse to another. Death is everywhere, staring up at us with empty eyes.

"Look at that." I aim the light down the corridor, where the bodies seem to go on forever. "There must be hundreds of them." It's the final resting place for an entire culture. A catacomb.

"Come on." I put my arm around Sam and tug him forward as we step over skeletons. "These people didn't all come through that little shaft to the tomb. It's not big enough. There must be another entrance."

Sam sways on his feet, resisting. "If there was an opening, we'd see bats. I don't see any bats."

"We can't see anything with this flashlight." Exasperated, I push him forward a little more roughly than I need to, filled with an irrational anger at his lethargy. We duck between tree roots that dangle from the ceiling like ropes. The air smells dusty and stale, as if the space has been enclosed for centuries. Our flashlight flickers, noticeably weaker now, its beam dull and yellow.

The cavern narrows until we're forced to walk in single file, and I give Sam the flashlight and push him ahead while I stagger behind him. As we stumble forward through the murky darkness, Sam shakes his head repeatedly and blinks, as though he's trying to clear his vision.

"I'm seeing things, Kate," he whispers. "There aren't any fireflies in here, are there?"

"No." Flashes of light spark at the periphery of my vision, but I stubbornly refuse to admit I know what he means. If we don't get water soon, the hallucinations will get worse. Even now, the thought of water makes the darkness shimmer around me, teasing me with the phantom sound of water dripping from the ceiling.

In the dim light we climb over clumps of rocks that stick up from the floor like claws, and sidle through narrow gaps in the stone passageway. A strange numbness prickles my fingers and toes, and my eyes continue to play tricks, reducing vision to a blur. The sound of our footsteps seems muffled, indistinct and far away. When I touch Sam's back his body feels cold, and he stumbles like an old man as he shuffles along at a turtle pace ahead of me.

Suddenly he comes to a stop, and when he aims the flashlight down the corridor I can see why. A wall of rubble blocks our path. I lean against the wall, staring in disbelief at the pile of dirt and rock that fills the passage. A queasy vertigo makes the darkness spin around me, confusing my sense of up and down, right and left. The two of us can hardly stand up, and I can't imagine moving a ton of rock.

Sam sinks slowly to his knees and pitches forward, collapsing in front of me. The flashlight rolls off to one side, and its weak light casts a dull glow on the base of the rock fall. The shadows look malevolent in the gloom.

"Come on, Sam. You have to help me."

"The hell I do," he mumbles, rolling over on his back. "We're stuck, Kate."

"Don't say that." My voice cracks with fear.

"Maybe there was another entrance a thousand years ago. But a lot can happen in a thousand years. The pyramid was buried when we found it. There were earthquakes . . . rock-slides . . ." His voice trails off.

"I can't do this alone," I say. "Come on. Get up."

His voice is a hiss in the blackness. "You won't find the entrance. Think about it. If it's still out there, somebody would have stumbled across it, and this place would have been excavated a long time ago."

I struggle to remember if Sam had a drink up on the mesa, back when we stopped for a break and I drank half the water in my canteen. He's at least six inches taller than I am. His skin surface would allow for more evaporation and lead to more rapid dehydration. He's not sane. I can't listen to this.

"We're digging, Sam. You can't quit on me now."

He looks at me steadily. "Do you know how obnoxious you can be?"

"Sorry," I say, though I'm stung.

He shakes his head. "Doesn't it get old, being such a tough girl? You know we're dying here. You're just too damned stubborn to admit it."

My irritation blooms into a creeping contempt. "What do you want from me? Should I tell you how miserable I feel? Lie down and keep you company? Forget it. We're getting out of here."

"You're like a bulldozer," he goes on. "Never mind logic, or facing facts, or following rules. You bulldoze your way ahead and look down your nose at the rest of us weaklings who can't keep up."

"Sam, come on. You, a weakling? You set me up. You told me where to look for a tomb. You practically drew me a map. 'Lava tubes,' you told me. 'Look for lava tubes.' You've been pulling my strings all along. Well, here we are, baby. This is what you wanted."

He makes a snorting noise. "I didn't tell you to *look* for them. I said they were up here."

"Oh, pardon me! God forbid anybody should step out of line and actually *find* something on this expedition."

Lying flat on his back with his eyes closed, his voice dwindles to a whisper. "You're ambitious, aren't you? You have the lust to get ahead, to get attention, no matter what the cost. Never face the truth if it threatens what you want. Permits? You never heard of 'em. Thirsty? Hell no, not you. Dying? That's loser talk." He lifts one hand and waves it in a limp, dismissive gesture.

Angry now, I grab him by the wrist and try to pull him up, but he shakes me off and curls into a fetal position, tucking his head into his elbow. "Leave me alone. I'm tired."

"You're not going to sleep." My voice sounds harsh, tight. "If you go to sleep, you'll die."

"That's my choice, isn't it?" he mumbles.

Steeling myself, I take a deep breath and look behind us, where the tunnel yawns like a dark mouth. Everything I am, everything I believe, everything I ever felt or knew or experienced in this life could disappear into that black void. And that's an intolerable thought. That's why I'll go on, with him or without him.

Finally I step over Sam and climb the pile of dirt and rock. Time is another gift I've taken for granted—like water, or food, or fresh air—one of those elements I never imagined I'd run

171

out of until now. Whenever I thought about my future I always assumed there would be a bright river of days and months and years before me, extending to an invisible horizon so far away it seemed unfathomable. Now the future has distilled itself to this blackness, this close, oppressive nearness of an end I can't face.

Sam groans, and I look at him, surprised by the sound. How long have I been lying here with my arms wrapped around this stone? A minute? An hour? With a weak tug I try to dislodge the rock, and it tips to one side, teeters for a moment, then rolls down the slope of rubble toward Sam.

"Look out," I whisper, too late. The rock tumbles down and thuds against his leg, hard enough to wake him up.

He grunts in pain, and I hear him shifting, struggling to his hands and knees before he lifts himself to a sitting position. He picks up the flashlight and aims it up at me, and for a moment all I can see is the dull yellow light.

"Don't do that," I croak.

"I dreamed you were dead," he says, lowering the light.

Phantom sparks wheel across my retina, forcing me to shut my eyes. "Not yet."

Slowly Sam drags himself to his feet and pulls himself over to the heap of rubble, holding the wall for support. Like a sleepwalker, he climbs the pile and touches a rock near the ceiling of the tunnel, feebly pushing at it until it tumbles down to the floor. My arms feel like machines, pushing aside rubble and dirt, mindlessly scraping at the dead weight of the earth.

"I have a good feeling about this," Sam says, propping the flashlight on the dirt.

His words are slurred, almost inaudible, and they swim through my awareness until I let them go with the gravel in my hands.

"We're close, Kate. Almost there."

Close to what? Thoughts snap and fall in my brain like sparks from a campfire, connecting to nothing, meaning nothing. I can't remember why we're doing this. Some primal instinct has taken over, screaming *"Out! Out!"* and this is what I do to appease it.

I take a rock in my hands and pull at it, barely toppling it over. A gap appears behind it, revealing a tunnel no bigger than a coyote hole. Sam paws at the dirt around the opening until the gap looks wide enough for us to crawl into it. I take the flashlight, sink to my belly and squeeze through.

The basalt walls of the tunnel press in on me like a casket, and I struggle to stay awake, to remain conscious. How long have we been underground? My mouth feels like a desert, an endless ache of want. The urge to stop, to sleep, nearly overwhelms me. I can hear Sam moving behind me, but he seems far away.

As I crawl forward, the surrounding walls slowly become more visible, a dull, pitted gray, and the air seems warmer, fresher. Disoriented by the change, I wonder if the flashlight has been jostled into a tighter connection to the batteries. But this light is different, more diffuse than the beam of the flashlight, and as I move along the shaft the passage widens, and the ambient light grows even brighter.

A crack in the rubble and earth ahead of us splits into a jagged hole in the rock, revealing a piece of blue sky.

"Daylight," he croaks.

I scramble forward on my hands and knees before I come to a halt at the edge of the opening in the rock. The glare of sunlight assaults my eyes, making it hard to focus. Fresh air fills my lungs, and the shock of daylight pours over me, welcome as water.

Sam crowds forward, pushing me from behind.

"Stop," I say, and shove him back.

Blinking hard, I peer over the edge of the tunnel into a chasm of open space. The view increases my vertigo, and I steady myself as I lean out to study the rock wall above us. We've come out in the middle of a cliff, a sheer, vertical expanse of rock above and below. Looking down, the wall of rock melts into the tops of sycamores fifty feet underneath us, a carpet of green leaves dancing in the wind. Below the trees, a talus slope of basalt leads down to a dry creek bed. It's a horrifying drop.

I study the cliff face above us. "It looks like we're only fifteen or twenty feet from the top."

Sam closes his eyes and leans back, resting his head against the wall. "You think you can climb up?"

I start taking off my boots. "I have to."

He pokes his head out of the opening and looks up at the rock face above our window in the cliff, then shakes his head and sinks back with a shudder. "This is nuts."

For the first time in days I can see his face in daylight. It's filthy, gaunt with tension and dehydration. "You're not afraid of heights, are you?"

"No." He lets out a dry laugh. "Falling, though—that scares the hell out of me."

The sunlight on my face makes me feel better than I've felt in a long time. Thirsty, yes, God, yes, but light makes all the difference. Moving swiftly, purposefully, I peel off my socks and tuck them in the boots, then tie the laces to my belt loops so the boots dangle from my sides.

Sam leans out and takes a long look down at the treetops below us. "You're sure about this?"

"No, but what choice do we have?" Barefoot now, I'm already edging out of the hole, feeling the sun hammer my body with light and heat. Some last remnant of adrenaline kicks in, and I reach for a handhold in the rock face above, brace myself, then lift my knee and wedge it in a crack in the wall. I pull myself up, panting with effort. I can feel the distance to the ground in my gut but keep my eyes on the rock in front of me.

After ascending ten feet my legs start to vibrate, and I'm not even halfway there. The basalt under my left foot crumbles suddenly and I gasp, half-sobbing as my leg swings wide. My breath comes in harsh grunts, as if I'm wrestling a larger, stronger opponent. A rain of gravel rattles down as my handhold disintegrates. Panicked, I kick myself upward.

My body stretches into one impossible position after another as I inch my way up, legs quivering, hands blindly seeking the pits and knobs that will support my weight. My limbs hum with nerves. How much longer can I hang on? If I fall I'll pinwheel into space like a rag doll, helplessly bouncing off rock, sailing down and down until the earth shatters my bones. The same way Dr. Richter died. Clinging to the wall, I inch higher, trying not to think about the damage to his corpse, his skull crushed like an eggshell, the blood drying in a wine-dark puddle around his head.

Finally I swing my leg over the last lip of rock and heave myself up on the flat ground of the mesa. I lie in the sun, panting, trying to get some air back in my lungs. My shirt is torn, my elbows scraped and bleeding, and my fingers feel like hamburger, but I'm alive. I take a deep, jagged breath, brush the rock dust from my eyes, roll to the edge, and shout at Sam. "Hey!"

He looks up at the sound. "You made it!"

"Wait there," I call. "I'll be back as soon as I can with some help." My throat feels raw, but the clean air makes it easier to talk, easier to breathe.

"I'll be dead by then," he yells. "I'm coming up."

I cough. "It's too hard. I barely made it, and you're in worse shape than I am."

"The hell I am." Sam pulls off his boots and ties them to his belt loops, as if his mind is made up. He hunches himself out on the narrow shelf and faces the wall of rock. *Jesus,* I think. He can't do it. It's too high. Too steep. A few minutes ago he was ready to lie down and die, and now he wants to try rock climbing? He moves tentatively, lifts his knee to the crack in the rock that I used, then looks up. The rock wall is blank, smooth, nearly vertical between us.

I don't want to watch, but can't tear my eyes away. "Go back!"

"No," he grunts. "I'm coming up."

I shake my head as his arms tremble with effort. He's trying to muscle his way up, putting too much weight on his hands, holding himself too far away from the wall. "There's a little bump just a foot above your right knee," I call down. "Get your knee on it, and you won't have to stretch so far."

"It's too small," Sam says. "I don't think it will hold me."

"Test it."

He gingerly presses his knee against it and the knob holds, and he pulls himself up. The top of his head still seems impossibly far away.

"Watch out for the crumbly stuff. Test every hold before you put your full weight on it."

Sam keeps his eyes fixed on the wall in front of him, but I know the distance to the ground is vivid in his imagination.

"You're doing great," I say, but whenever he glances up at me he looks terrified, and his progress is painfully slow. Going slow only makes the ascent more dangerous, and it's impossible to believe he has the stamina for this. Clinging to the sheer face of the cliff means hugging it with all his strength while he divides his weight as evenly as possible between his hands, knees, and feet. I know exactly how hard that can be, and the knowledge makes me want to close my eyes as he approaches the worst part of the climb.

Finally Sam comes to the spot where there are no obvious footholds or handholds above him. He's stuck.

"This part is a little tricky," I say.

"God damn it! Don't tell me that."

"You can do it. You have to traverse to your left. There's a crevice over there. You'll have to scramble sideways to reach it." It's perfectly visible to me as I lean over the edge of the cliff and look down, but I know he won't be able to see it.

"I can't feel it," he yells, reaching.

"Move your right foot up to that ledge above your left knee." Sam swings his right foot over and paws the rock with his bare toes. His legs are too sturdy, too heavily muscled to make the stretch.

"A little higher," I say. "There. You feel that?"

"It's too high," he gasps. "I can't."

"You can do it. Do it fast. Don't try to balance there. Keep moving. Push yourself over to the left and up. You'll find the crevice. Hurry. Don't think about it too long or you'll freeze. Just do it."

Sam's splayed legs are vibrating like plucked guitar strings, and I know his fingertips must be screaming from the pressure of supporting his weight. What if he stops moving? What if he stays there until his fingers cramp and his arms fall asleep and his legs can't bear the strain? How long would he last? A minute or two. No more. The rocks below glint like teeth.

Shutting his eyes, Sam swings his leg up to the slight bulge in the rock, then heaves himself over toward the invisible crevice. He finds the long vertical crack, and I know it pinches his fingers, but he's closer to the top now.

"Above your head, on the right. There's another handhold. Grab it." I gesture wildly, as if I could do it for him.

Sam reaches, pulls, scrambles and claws his way up the rock. When he's two feet from the rim I grab him by the collar and help him up. He falls on top of me, panting, shaking with exhaustion.

"You did it," I say and hug him.

We roll on our sides, facing each other, breathing hard. Sam's lungs shudder in deep, gasping breaths. I can feel his heart thumping next to my ribs, beating in time to my own. A surge of gratitude courses through me, an elation so great that tears come to my eyes. The sun bathes us in warmth and light, and for the first time in what feels like forever, I'm not shivering. It's a beautiful day.

I squeeze him tightly, inhaling the sour smell of his skin and clothes, stricken with relief that he's up here with me. "God, you stink."

He leans back and grins at me, the old Sam resurfacing for a moment in the disheveled wreck I'm holding in my arms. "You should talk! You smell like a dead skunk."

Suddenly we're both laughing, heaving with dry, hacking rasps that sound like a coughing fit. For a moment the two of us float on that laughter in the shimmering air, part of the light and heat and wind. Even with my eyes closed, the sun glows orange through my lids. The heat feels like life itself, warming me, and the air is sweet. We're going to make it. I can feel it in my bones. But we're still miles from camp, and moving seems like the worst idea in the world.

"Let's go," I say, and push myself up.

As we put our boots back on I take a deep breath of the fresh air. It feels like a miracle for both of us to be outside, up on top of the mesa. The sky blazes with light. A raven rows its way across the sky above us, wings creaking. Horizon to horizon, May spreads its warm green promise across the high desert.

Sam slowly pulls himself to his feet and scans the mesa with a hand shielding his eyes. "Looks like we should head south."

I study the blue inverted bowl of the volcano in the distance, and try to gauge our location. We must have been walking southwest in the lava tube, so we're probably a few miles north of camp.

He extends a hand to help me up, and we begin walking slowly across the open range. After a few moments I notice he's limping, his hand on his belly, as if every step hurts.

"Can you make it?" I ask.

"I'll be fine when we find water. How far do you think we are from the camp?"

"I'd say we're about five miles north of camp." It seems impossibly far.

"We'll just have to take our time," he mumbles, as if he's talking to himself. "Maybe some rain collected on the rocks. We might find a puddle in the basalt."

There's a bottle of apple juice in my tent. The thought of it seems unbearably tantalizing, and I can't get it out of my head. The crisp taste. Golden, rich, sweet. I never wanted anything in my life as much as I want that apple juice.

Sam holds his side with one hand, and his steps are smaller. I throw my arm around his waist, and we stagger forward like two drunks at closing time.

"They can't all leave, not while we're still missing," he says. "Somebody must have stayed to look for us. They won't give up."

"How long do you think we've been gone?"

"Three, four days? I don't think we'd be alive if it was much longer than that."

"It seems like a month."

"I know."

The sun beats down on our heads and shimmers from the rocks, and the sky is pale with heat, so bright the glare makes me dizzy.

I lean into Sam suddenly, falling against him. "Whoa," I whisper. "Hang on." We both tumble down on a patch of grass.

When I can focus again I see Sam's head bowed over his splayed legs.

"It's hot," he says. "We're losing more fluid out here, in the sun." He looks at me strangely. "I feel weird."

I grunt at the understatement. It feels like I'm moving underwater as I haul myself to my hands and knees, then stand and help him up. We stumble on as the sun rises higher in the sky and pours heat down on our heads. The mesa undulates like the sea, endless in its expanse, the spring grass bending to the wind as if it were being stroked by invisible hands. The movement makes me feel oddly queasy, as if I were seasick. Cactus and boulders ripple at the horizon in bands of tangerine, green, rose, and silver, a rainbow of imagined light.

Pressed to the limit, it feels like every step is a battle against the nearly overwhelming urge to stop, to sleep, to end the suffering. Whenever Sam wavers and begins to slide down, I yank him back up and push him forward, and he does the same for me. We attack the distance to the camp as if it were an enemy. My eyes feel bloodshot, my face taut with a determination so fierce it feels like hate.

In the shimmering glare of the horizon two dark vertical specks coalesce. Horses. People on horses.

"Hey!" Sam shouts weakly, and falls to his knees.

"Over here!" I yell, and wave my arms. Our shouts sound like whispers. They're at least half a mile away. I take a deep breath, put thumb and forefinger to my mouth and try to whistle, but nothing comes out. My lips are too dry, too cracked. Sam waves his arms and I do the same, gasping as we try to shout, each breath scraping my throat like sandpaper.

The figures on horseback pause, turn, and begin to gallop toward us.

CHAPTER THIRTEEN

There are no words for the ecstasy of water on my parched throat, the liquid pleasure of it sliding into my mouth, cooling the fire inside. For the past few days every breath, every word, every dry swallow has scraped my throat raw, and my tongue has ached for this long cold river of water gliding into me.

I sprawl on the ground as Michael cradles me in his arms, supporting me as I drink from his canteen, while Jessie does the same for Sam. In my groggy haze they seem impossibly clean, and smell like coconut lotion and warm skin. Especially Jessie, whose t-shirt is knotted under her breasts, revealing a tanned, bare midriff. A silver ring glints at her navel, echoing the small silver loops in her ears. When I squint to focus on her face as she leans over Sam, I can see her long lashes have been darkened by mascara, and her mouth gleams with pink lipstick. For a day in the wilderness, she's all dressed up.

"Where the hell have you been?" Michael asks, squeezing my shoulder. He looks more normal than Jessie in his old faded t-shirt and jeans, with his face shaded by a baseball cap and sunglasses.

"We've been searching for you since yesterday," Jessie says. "We thought you were dead." She sounds worried, as if she's still not sure of our chances. Sam's head rolls to one side as she tilts the water bottle to his mouth, and his eyes remain closed.

Reluctantly, I lower the canteen. "We've been stuck underground for days, with no food or water. There was a cave-in at the entrance to the tomb. We had to dig through a wall and walk out through a lava tube."

"What day is it?" Sam asks, visibly straining to focus on Jessie. The water has begun to bring him back, but he sounds like a sleepwalker. Jessie looks at Michael, apparently unable to make out the slurred question.

"Thursday," Michael says, checking his watch. "Almost four p.m. And you left on Monday morning, right? It's a miracle you're still alive."

"I wouldn't be here at all if it weren't for Kate," Sam whispers.

My lips crack as I smile. "I tried to ditch you back at the cliff, but you were too stubborn. Sort of like a bulldozer."

A ghost of a smile crosses his face as he holds up one hand. "Truce."

"What are you guys talking about?" Jessie asks. "What went on down there?"

Michael unties the bandana from his neck, holds the rag to the mouth of the canteen and tips the container until a small circle of cloth darkens. Gently he swabs my face with the wet fabric, and I close my eyes, savoring the cool moisture on my skin. Delicately, tenderly, he passes the cloth over the skin around my eyes, cheeks, chin, nose and forehead. I turn my head in his lap, baring my neck. He takes his time, tracing the tendons, wiping the skin under my chin, down to my clavicle. I lie in his arms without moving, too weak to do anything but drink in the attention.

When I open my eyes, I see Jessie staring at us. She glances away quickly, her smile gone, the color rising in her cheeks. Her expression brings me a strange sense of déjà vu, a confused memory of watching the hurt on her face when Michael told her that his father would leave her and go back to Sylvia.

And just like that, the complexity of living with other people settles over me, the likes and dislikes, the quarrels and affairs, the love that blossoms when it shouldn't and fails to be returned when it should. The image of Jessie leaning over Dr. Richter's corpse comes back to me, along with the phrase *hell hath no fury.* Has she already transferred her crush from Dr. Richter to his son? I close my eyes again, suddenly exhausted by the thought of returning to live with people I don't trust.

"We can't afford to waste water." Sam's voice is sharp, full of warning. When I look up his lips are pressed together, eyes cold as granite.

"It's just a spoonful," Michael says, unperturbed. He removes the baseball cap from his head and pushes it down on my hair, arranging the bill until it shades my face. With his thumb and forefinger he takes the sunglasses from his face and delicately fits them over my eyes, sliding the stems behind my ears, pushing the bridge until it rests securely on my nose. Immediately, the world dims to a softer hue, and the sun's glare disappears.

Without his cap, his eyelashes cast sharp, pointed shadows on the skin under his eyes. A web of fine lines radiates over his cheeks as he squints at me and smiles. "Feeling better?"

The canteen I'm holding is nearly empty. "How much water did you bring?"

Michael glances at Jessie, who shakes her head. "Not enough, I'm afraid. And we don't have any food with us. We should get moving."

Looking agitated, Sam pushes himself up on his elbows, wincing. "Let's get started." He struggles to his feet, swaying for a moment as he recovers his balance. Jessie springs up beside him and steadies him with an arm around his waist, staggering under his weight.

"How far is it to the camp?" I ask.

"Four or five miles, at least," Jessie says.

Michael lifts me to my feet, and the world swims for a moment as a queasy lightheadedness overtakes me. "Put your head down," he says, gripping me so I don't fall. I let my head droop, put my hands on my knees and bend my shoulders until my vision clears.

"Henry wanted us to fire a shot if we found you," Jessie says. There's a hint of coolness in her tone as Michael strokes my back.

"Did he give you a gun?" I ask, slowly straightening.

Michael nods. "Shall I do the honors?"

"Hold the horses so they don't panic," I say. "I'm in no mood to do any more hiking."

Sam hobbles over to the horses cropping at the low grass, and Jessie follows him. They gather the reins and lead the mares a few yards away.

"Plug your ears," Michael warns us. He takes a revolver out of his knapsack and fires a shot in the air. The sound rips the silence, and the horses toss their heads and snort at the noise.

When the horses stop shifting, Sam tries to boost himself into the saddle of the nearest mare and fails to make it, nearly falling as he staggers back.

"Let me help you," Jessie says, touching his arm.

"I can do it," he mutters, shaking her off. His struggle to mount the horse goes on for another agonizing minute, until he lunges up on the horse with a desperate heave, laboriously straddling it.

"Well?" he asks, looking down at Jessie. "Are you coming or not?"

"Go ahead," Michael says, taking the reins of the other horse from her hand. "We'll be right behind you." He squints, smiling up at Sam.

Jessie takes a deep breath and lets it out, then boosts herself up easily into the saddle in front of Sam. He slaps the mare's rump with the reins, and they set off without a backward glance.

Michael lifts me into the saddle before he swings up behind

me. The horse shakes its head at the extra weight, and Michael makes a low clicking noise that calms it. When he claps his heels a few times against the mare's sides, we lurch forward into a trot, heading south, toward the camp. His chest fits the curve of my back, and his arms encircle me. I could cry with relief at the strength in his body, the promise of safety, and I sag against him, utterly spent.

By the time we descend the trail into camp, the sun casts long shadows on the ground, tipping the sagebrush with silver, turning the earth the color of blood. The coming darkness fills me with dread, and I promise myself I'll build a fire before the sun sets and feed it all night. I can't go back to the blackness of the tomb.

Henry walks out to meet us, and at first I don't recognize him. Since Richter's death three days ago, his hair seems to have turned from gray to white, and his eyes look haggard and sunken behind his spectacles. As we bring the horses to a halt twenty feet in front of him, he stands without moving, hands loose at his sides, staring at us as if we were ghosts. I wonder how he managed to avoid Sylvia's ultimatum, and why he's not helping her on the trek to Silver City. Could Sylvia have changed her mind?

"What's Henry doing here?" I whisper to Michael. "Didn't Sylvia want him to go with her? Or is she still here too?"

"She left without him," he says in a low tone. "Whatever happened between them, he's not talking about it."

Michael helps me dismount, and I let myself fall from the saddle, joints aching from the long ride. Sam and Jessie slide off their horse, and Jessie takes the reins in one hand while she strokes the mare's neck with the other, murmuring in its ear.

Henry's gaze locks on me as he accepts the reins from Michael. "You made it."

"We were lucky these guys found us," I say.

Jessie gives me a small smile. "After surviving three days underground without food or water, I'd say you guys are pretty hard to kill."

Her off-hand comment travels through me like an electric shock, and I glance at her uneasily, wondering if she's disappointed.

We walk slowly toward the mess tent, where Fiddle stands with a hand shielding her eyes, staring in our direction. She wipes her hands on her apron and walks forward to meet us, clearly dismayed by our appearance. "God Almighty, what happened to you people?"

"They're dehydrated," Henry says. "They need liquids—soup, juice, whatever we've got."

"But we made it back alive," Sam says with a crooked smile.

"Barely, I'd say," Fiddle says with a worried glance at his sunken eyes. She walks to the canned goods stacked on her work table, opens a packet of powdered lemonade and hastily mixes it with water in an empty jug, then pours out a cup for each of us. "Drink," she says, putting the mugs on the table.

I sink down on the bench by the picnic table, too weak to stand. "Go slow," Michael warns me. Fatigue settles over me so profoundly that lifting the cup takes concentrated effort, as if it weighs a hundred pounds. The drink is warm and powerfully sweet, like nectar, heavy with life-giving calories. Every swallow brings a rising tide of energy to my body and helps to dissipate the fog that clings to me.

"I have a big can of chicken noodle soup," Fiddle says. "I'll heat it up." She rattles through a box of utensils and extracts a steel can opener, then locates the can and a pot for the soup.

"Has Will left already?" Henry asks her.

"He rode out an hour ago. You'll have to water the horses yourself."

He takes the reins from Jessie and tugs at them. "I'll take them down to the creek." The mares toss their heads, then step forward eagerly when they realize he's leading them toward the smell of water.

With the mug of lemonade cradled in both hands, I sip the sweet liquid and look around at the khaki-colored tents, the scattered laundry hanging from dead piñon trees, the narrow, goat-like paths leading through the maze of willow by the creek. Everything looks the same, which disturbs me in a way I can't explain. The pyramid squats over the canyon, a blank, staring, immoveable presence. Uneasiness stirs in me at the sight of those gargoyles of Quetzalcoatl that guard every corner, frozen in an open-mouthed roar of warning against intruders. Against us.

By the time Henry returns from staking out the horses, Sam and I have finished one bowl of soup and started another. My belly feels tight as an over-inflated beach ball, but I spoon up the hot liquid with a silent, steady focus, taking small sips, determined to replace the liquid I've lost as soon as possible. My body feels like one of those compressed paper flowers that bloom when you put them in a glass of water, and every cell seems to stretch and open to replenish itself.

Sam straightens and his movements become more certain as the liquid begins to take effect. It's a dramatic change, and I can feel the distance growing between us as he continues to eat, avoiding my eyes, closing off the connection that kept us alive. The memory of the tomb feels surreal, like an urgent, despairing nightmare.

Jessie and Michael watch us eat, quietly refilling our cups until the jug is empty.

Henry approaches our table, smoothing his white hair back from his forehead and nodding toward his wife. "Fiddle got you set up?"

I raise my spoon, not bothering to answer.

"Everybody else left already," Henry says. "Sylvia and Jason took the body back to Silver City, the same day you set out for the tomb."

"Sylvia decided to go without you?" Sam asks.

"Will went with her instead." Henry's tone is flat, detached.

The last time I saw Henry and Sylvia together they were glaring at each other, and Sylvia tried to assert her authority over him by saying *This is not a request. It's an order.* Maybe Henry didn't like the switch from lover to boss. Whatever went on after that between Henry and Sylvia, they're done. It's over.

Henry goes on talking as if that moment never happened, and he uses the same tone of pompous authority he always had with the crew. "Make sure you return any tools and equipment that belong to the dig before you go. Wrap them in tarps and stash them out of sight in the tunnel, so we don't have to pack them in again. Shouldn't be too long before the dig reopens, and I'll expect all of you to show up for work, once the permits are in place."

Sam puts his spoon down on the table and looks up at him. "You won't be leading the dig, Henry."

Henry's body becomes absolutely still, and a hush descends over the rest of us. "The hell I'm not."

Sam holds his gaze. "Richter asked me to sign the forms for the permits, the funding—all of it. I'm listed as second-in-command."

"You're lying. He would have told me." Henry's voice is belligerent, but his eyes dart uncertainly toward Michael.

Fiddle's back stiffens, and I can sense Henry's radar swing toward her as she ladles more soup into our bowls. "He didn't trust you, Henry," she says quietly. "And he had good reason, didn't he?"

Henry whirls on her, eyes flashing. "He's lying, damn it!"

"All those nights you slipped off to be with her, did you really think no one would notice? Richter knew. Everyone knew. You brought this on yourself, Henry."

He stares at Sam. "If you were in charge, you would have said something before, when Richter was missing."

"You're a good field man, Henry," Sam says. "But I was the one who flew to Washington every other month, begging the NSF and the NAA for money. Richter and I spent hours together, calculating supplies, manpower, expenses. I was with him from the beginning."

"I was, too," Henry says. For a moment I almost feel sorry for him, as the gruff confidence suddenly drains from his face.

Moving slowly, deliberately, Fiddle unties her apron, pulls it off and tosses it on the work table. She folds her arms over her ample belly and leans back against the table, surveying her husband without affection, looking at him as if she knows everything about him and doesn't like what she sees. Her cheeks are flushed, and her frizz of gray hair sticks out in wild tufts all over her head, but her voice is steady. "I'm leaving today, Henry. With you or without you. And I won't be coming back, I can promise you that. So take whatever supplies you need. I've cooked my last meal in this camp." Slowly she straightens, then turns her back on him and stalks off.

"This isn't over," Henry says, brows furiously lowered as he glares at Sam. "I'll talk to Sylvia. She'll straighten this out." He looks around the table at the rest of us, and then his eyes become unfocused as he gazes beyond the sycamores to the tall outline of the pyramid. Abruptly he turns and hurries after his wife.

When they're both out of earshot, Michael gives Sam a long, speculative look. "So you're in charge of the dig now?"

Sam nods wearily. "I know I should have said something before, when your dad was missing. But Henry jumped in and took over, and I didn't want to rock the boat when there was a chance your father would come back."

Jessie stares at Sam, a stunned look on her face. "All those conversations we had about the pit houses—how you wished Henry would let us excavate them, instead of that damn tunnel—what the hell was that about, Sam? You could have said something. You could have taken over the dig and saved us all a lot of time and trouble."

He shrugs. "I'm sorry."

Her eyes burn at him, full of spite. "Fuck you."

Michael rubs his forehead with his thumb and forefinger. "So what now?"

Sam squares his shoulders and takes a deep breath. "I'll talk to the bureaucrats in Washington, get the permits and funds lined up so we can get started on the excavation. Do you think Sylvia will tell the Forest Service about the new site?"

"I doubt it," Michael says. "I don't think she'll say anything that might draw outsiders to the pyramid. Especially now the dig's closing down."

"She has to say something," I blurt out. "There was a murder here. We have to tell the Forest Service, the sheriff's office." I study their faces, waiting for one of them to agree, but they all eye me with wary scrutiny. "There has to be some kind of investigation," I say, struggling for calm. "They should be taking pictures of the place where Dr. Richter's body was found. They have to interview us. All of us."

Michael shrugs. "I could take a few pictures, if it makes you feel better."

Astounded by his lack of concern, I stare at him. "It's not about what I'd like. Don't you get it? One of us killed your father."

Michael and Jessie exchange uneasy looks, and I realize they don't believe me.

"He could have fallen," Jessie says, tracing a blemish on the wooden table. "It could have been an accident."

Is this what they really think? Could Sylvia have persuaded them it was an accident before she left, or is something more sinister going on? My mind feels frozen as I cast about helplessly for a way to convince them that the murderer must have been here, with us, living in the camp. Sam's spoon scrapes the bowl, a loud sound in the silence thickening around me. He won't look at me. None of them will look at me.

"Did you find your father's pack?" I ask Michael.

He lifts an eyebrow. "I hate to say it, but I'm afraid Jason may have taken it. He kept asking me about the codex, and how much it might be worth. Don't get me wrong—I can't believe he'd do anything to hurt our dad—but he's the only one I can think of who would steal the map to the tomb."

"Come on, Kate," Sam says, leaning back from the table and rising to his feet. "We need to get cleaned up. You guys want us for anything, we'll be at the hot springs."

He takes me by the elbow and pulls me to my feet, then hustles me away from the table, palm firmly pressed against my back.

"Excuse me," I say as he hurries us toward the tents. "I thought I was in the middle of a conversation."

"Uh-huh," he says, walking briskly, his fingers tight on my arm.

I yank it away from him. "You're hurting me." The pressure on my back remains, forcing me to stumble forward. "Sam, what's the matter with you? What's the big rush?"

"You just don't know when to let up, do you?" he mutters. "You go around telling people you suspect them of murder, what do you think will happen to you? For God's sake, Kate, ease up, or you'll wake up with a knife at your throat."

"You believe me, then. You think one of us did it."

"Yes, I believe you. But I want to get out of here in one piece before we start throwing around accusations."

"What makes you think we'll be any safer if we don't kick up a fuss?"

We pause outside my tent, and Sam lifts his fingers and rasps them against his unshaven chin. "There's no percentage in tipping our hand to a murderer. In case you haven't noticed, there's no pay phone. We can't call the cops. If you keep talking about it, who's going to stop him from trying again?"

His bossiness irritates me, considering what we just went through a few hours ago, and it rankles that he's treating me like some helpless woman he has to rescue from a burning building. "Maybe we can stop him, Sam."

He takes a deep breath and lets it out in a puff of air. "Let's argue about this while we're soaking in the hot springs. Get some clean clothes and a towel. I'll wait here."

"I don't need a bodyguard, for crying out loud. I'll meet you in front of your tent in ten minutes."

He speaks softly, looking directly into my eyes. "I'll wait."

"Sam, your tent's thirty feet away. If I need you, I'll yell. Now go on, get out of here." I flatten my hand against his chest and push.

"Five minutes," he says, backing away, holding up his index finger.

I wave him off, then squat down and unzip my tent. Knees creaking, I pull back the flap, duck inside and look around at the haphazard clutter of my belongings.

There's a small mirror in my bag, and I pull it out, open the scratched cover and look at my reflection. The face that stares back at me is gaunt, rimmed in grime from the tunnel. I sweep the stray hair away from my mouth and run my tongue over my lips, examining the chapped skin on my nose and cheeks and forehead. My eyes look like two burnt holes in a piece of paper.

I've never looked so haggard, and I close the mirror, stricken by the image of the stranger I've become.

A gust of homesickness sweeps through me, a sudden, intense longing to return to the life I know, to the simple luxury of a hot shower, my own bed and a refrigerator full of food. I want to drive up Thurston Avenue in my old reliable Ford truck, chugging up the incline slowly enough to admire the forsythia bursting above the stone walls and trailing blooms down to the street like a fountain of gold. I'd give anything to walk into my dad's tavern in Collegetown, see him polishing the bar with an old rag, his bald head shining in the dim orange glow of the overhead lamps, his solid, upright, honest face a wall between myself and trouble.

I want to go home.

CHAPTER FOURTEEN

Sam meets me outside the tent, carrying a change of clothes, a towel and two canteens, his face gleaming from the removal of three days' worth of beard. Without the stubble softening the line of his jaw, he looks more determined, and he holds himself erect, as though his run-in with Henry has revived him as much as two bowls of soup and a gallon of water. After living for four days in the blackness of the tomb, I'm still not used to looking at him in daylight, and it's oddly disconcerting to see his freshly shaved face. His vacant stare is gone, replaced by a direct gaze that crackles with new energy.

"All set?" he asks.

I nod, freshly aware of his height as he towers over me and the arresting color of his eyes, with their fringe of dark lashes and irises as pale as distant clouds.

Sam turns abruptly and sets off toward the creek, expecting me to follow. Apparently neither one of us wants to go anywhere without an ample supply of drinking water, and we both cradle a bottle in our arms as we walk down the path. Water. I hug the water bottle tightly to my chest, reveling in its weight, its volume, its comforting availability. The gurgle of the liquid sloshing back and forth in the container fills me with an exquisite sense of relief.

Every inch of my skin feels filthy, and I hang back, embarrassed by the odor of my unwashed body and a little intimidated by the new swagger in Sam's walk. Once we reach the bank of willow by the creek, he holds the whip-like branches out of the way for me as we make our way downstream, but for the most part he moves quickly, without hesitating, his legs covering the ground in long strides. He leads me down the path without glancing back to see if I'm keeping up, clearly intent on putting some distance between us and the camp as soon as possible.

The sun begins to slide below the rim of the canyon, and even though it won't set for at least an hour, my fear of darkness comes creeping back, stroking my limbs with chilly fingers. The thought swirls through my mind that someone we know will probably get away with murder, and there's nothing I can do to stop him. Or her. As the shadows deepen, an unseen threat seems to lurk behind every tree and boulder, increasing my awareness that we're trapped in the wilderness with whoever tried to kill Richter, and they could easily go on killing anyone who stands in their way.

The creek rushes along at our feet, swollen by snowmelt to the limit of its banks, splashing over rocks and cascading down the channel. It's hard to imagine hot springs capable of warming such icy water, and I shiver at the thought of bathing in it.

When we've put a few hundred yards between ourselves and the camp, Sam finally breaks his stride, glancing around before he speaks. "This is what we should do," he says in a hushed voice. "As soon as it's light tomorrow morning, we'll ride out of here. We'll talk to the guys at the Forest Service in Silver City and tell them we think Richter was murdered, then alert the sheriff and the coroner."

"I just hope we're not too late," I say.

He looks at me. "What do you mean, too late?"

I wave a hand toward the camp. "It's been four days since Richter was killed, and no investigators have shown up. That means Sylvia must have convinced the coroner it was an accidental death."

"What about the defense wounds you saw on Richter's body? The coroner would have spotted those."

"Defense wounds are tricky. They could be blamed on natural causes, especially when there's already so much trauma to the body." I don't mention the images that flooded my mind when I first saw Richter's body, and the certainty that haunts me. In my bones, I know he was murdered, but that doesn't matter in a court of law. It's not evidence. "Sylvia's had three days to sell her version of events to the coroner, and Jason's going to go along with whatever she says. She might claim he grabbed a cactus or a thorn bush on the way down, and nobody's going to contradict her. Without an investigator to examine the terrain, the coroner won't know she's lying."

"I can't believe Sylvia would go that far to whitewash his death," Sam says.

"You saw how she reacted when I told her he was pushed off that cliff. She was furious at me for even suggesting it."

There's something ruthless about Sylvia, I think, something hard. As I step over a rotten log lying across the path, the memory of her chilly disapproval washes over me, the way she always looked as if she were calculating something hidden behind her flat, narrowed eyes. No small-town coroner would want to stand up to the widow of an international celebrity like Dr. Richter. Sylvia's a respected scientist in her own right, and she probably has the home phone numbers of a dozen senators and congressmen in her files. I have no doubt she'd know how to pull the necessary strings to get whatever she wanted.

"Do you think the coroner has released Richter's body?" Sam asks.

"Probably. And if it's cremated, our only evidence will disappear."

A stray memory nudges the edge of my consciousness, something to do with the tension that hovered between Sylvia and her husband. But I can't quite retrieve it. I cast my mind back to that night in their tent, when I first met Richter. His jaw was covered in thick stubble, his face was sunburned, and his clothes were filthy. He looked as though he'd been living out in the open, not staying in a hotel room in Silver City, as he claimed.

Perhaps Richter disappeared for five days because he was afraid.

Afraid of what? And if he were afraid, why did he come back? Was it merely a coincidence that he reappeared on the day I found the tomb, or did Sylvia send him a message? I can't believe she knew where he was, after I saw her whispering with Henry, asking why he wasn't out looking for him. She was genuinely worried.

"Do you think he was killed for the map to the tomb?" I ask Sam. "Or do you think it was personal?"

"Richter wasn't exactly popular." We walk in silence for a minute, while Sam ponders the question before he goes on. "I used to watch him walk into a room, and everyone's attention would automatically turn to him. They all wanted something from him. He projected that aura, that he was a guy who could make things happen. Women were attracted to him because of it, and men were too. Everybody believed in his power, but it didn't earn him any real friends."

I can see why. When I cowered in Richter's presence for those few eternal moments in his tent, I could feel his pleasure at my discomfort. I can't imagine the softer side of him that Jessie described, but it must have been there, judging by the number of his conquests.

"Whoever killed him probably took his pack," I say, musing out loud. "Which means somebody we know has the map. The map might still be here in the camp, if Jason didn't take it. What if we create some sort of diversion, then search the tents?"

Sam ducks under a low-hanging branch, then lifts it out of the way for me. "You get caught sneaking into tents, rummaging through other people's belongings—what do you think they'll do to you?"

"What options do we have, under the circumstances? Do you want to know the truth, Sam? Or do you want to spend the next year looking at the people you work with and wondering which one of them is capable of murder?"

He looks at me over his shoulder. "I don't want you to end up in a morgue, Kate."

We let the silence envelop us for a while, escaping into our own minds. In the shadows of the evening light a garter snake slithers across our path, its tongue flicking from side to side to taste the air, and Sam holds his arm out to bar my way, letting it pass before he resumes walking.

"I can't see Sylvia killing Richter," he says suddenly. "And I don't think Jessie would kill him, either. They were both in love with him."

"Jessie seems to have recovered from his death pretty quickly," I say. "Have you seen the way her eyes sparkle when she looks at Michael? She can hardly take a deep breath around him." I think of Jessie and her sideways glances at Michael, seeking his face with her gaze, over and over, like a caress.

"Jealous?" Sam's voice is light, but it carries an edge.

"No," I say, startled. "Of course not."

"He's falling for you, Kate."

A stubborn resistance wells up in me at his needling tone. "I like Michael," I say, just to rattle him. "I think he's really nice."

Sam lets out an odd little laugh. "I'm sure he'd love it if you stopped by his tent later to tell him so."

I come to a halt, forcing him to wait while I take a long drink. "Maybe you guys should get it over with and have a pissing contest."

He lifts his canteen, unscrews the cap and tilts it to his mouth, then lowers it and wipes his mouth with the back of his wrist. "Maybe you shouldn't let your attraction get in the way of keeping an open mind."

I let out a snort of disbelief. "An open mind about what?"

Sam leans toward me, his face serious, his eyes soft. "You don't know much about him, do you? And neither one of us knows what kind of relationship he had with his father."

I roll my eyes to let him know what I think of this, and he turns and continues walking down the trail.

What I avoid telling Sam is that the feeling Michael evokes in me most often is pity. His wife's death clings to him like a ghost, and I'm always aware of that shroud of melancholy. Even when he was wiping the dust from my face up on the mesa, I could feel the sadness in him, as if he were remembering his wife. If he's interested in me, it's an idle, passing interest, and that's how I feel about him, too—friendly, but hardly smitten.

It would be so much easier if it were Michael who inspired that tell-tale flutter in my belly, that deep shift in my womb. But it isn't. Sam is the one who gets under my skin. Sam is the one I feel connected to, and it almost feels as if our long ordeal in the tomb together has bonded me to him at some molecular level. Sam is the one who makes me feel flushed and alert, and I know by the way my heart starts racing when I'm around him that my body has already made its choice.

A few minutes later the willow thins out, and we enter a clearing next to a rocky part of the river, where a deep pool has formed near the bank. Sycamores make a canopy above the water, and the surface of the pool is still as a mirror, reflecting the bright evening sky.

Sam drops his towel over a basalt boulder. "That's it," he says, nodding toward the pool. He props one foot up on the rock and starts to untie his bootlace.

I walk over to the bank, bend down and touch the water with my fingers. It's hot. Deliciously, perfectly hot. How long has it been since I've felt warm water on my skin? Nine or ten days? It seems like a year, and my skin starts to itch in anticipation.

Sam unbuttons his shirt and shrugs it off, then starts to unzip his jeans. He's not wearing any underwear, and after a fleeting glimpse I look away, suddenly frozen by the thought of undressing in front of him. Back at the tent I never gave it a second thought, but now I curse myself for not bringing a swimsuit.

A faint smile crosses his face as he steps out of his jeans. "Don't you want to take a bath, Kate?"

Out of the corner of my eye I can see the dark mat of pubic hair at the confluence of his legs, and a blur of flesh at the center. I stare at the ground, stabbed by uncertainty. The truth is, I don't want him to see the woman I saw in the mirror. I don't want him to see the stubble on my legs, or the sweat-caked grime between my breasts, or the bruises that cover my body. Something about his casual attitude makes me uneasy, and I wonder if he's soaked in these hot springs with Jessie or Sylvia.

The trouble is, I don't know Sam. I don't know what he's thinking behind those glacier-blue eyes, or how he really feels about me. I don't know anything about his past, and with a murderer at large, it's not easy to relax and give him the benefit of the doubt. Just because we were locked in the tomb together doesn't mean Sam couldn't have pushed Richter off that cliff.

"I think I'll wait," I say, lowering my eyes. "I can come back later, now that I know where the hot springs are."

"You're kidding, right?" Unabashed by his lack of clothing, he moves toward me until he's standing close enough for me to smell the toothpaste on his breath.

A bead of sweat trickles from my armpit down to my waist as I watch his bare chest rise and fall, and I feel more self-conscious with every passing moment. He has a beautiful body, with wide shoulders tapering to a slender waist, a line of muscle extending down his long, lean legs.

Tentatively he lifts the hem of my t-shirt, asking for a sign, and I clutch the shirt, stopping him.

He steps back, palms up as if he's under arrest. "Fine. You don't want a hot bath, I'll tell you all about it when I'm done."

I cast a longing look at the dark pool of water, torn by temptation.

His face becomes serious, and he moves closer. Reaching out, he touches my arm, sliding his palm slowly upward, taking his time, leaving an electrified awareness in my skin. My heart beats so loudly I'm sure he can hear it, and I can feel myself blushing to the roots of my hair. With one finger he tilts my chin up, then leans down to kiss me. His lips are warm, his breath is sweet, and when he pulls me close a flash of heat spreads through my limbs, a yearning that feels as deep as gravity, drawing me toward him.

Hesitantly, as though asking permission, he reaches behind me and lifts my shirt, slowly coaxing it up above my breasts, pulling it higher until I have to raise my arms or make him stop. *Why not?* I think. I lift my arms, letting him ease the t-shirt past my chin and over my head. He tosses the shirt on the ground, then bends down to untie my shoes. Kneeling in front of me, he unzips my jeans and tugs them down, and I step out of them. A light wind brushes my body, and my skin prickles into goosebumps.

Sam rises to his feet and wades into the water, his long pale legs disappearing, followed by his sunburned neck and arms. He lets out a whoop of pleasure as he flops into the pool, then ducks his head under and comes up spouting, gleefully shaking his wet hair.

Cautiously I step down the rocky bank into the luxuriantly

warm water, then plunge in, groaning in satisfaction as the creek curls over my shoulders. The pool is only about four and a half feet deep, and I tilt my head back to let the heat surround my neck, swaying slightly as I bob in the water. Threads of bubbles percolate through the pool, tickling my skin. After dunking my head and scrubbing my scalp and face with sand from the bottom, I come back up to see Sam watching me. He's reclining on a rock bench near the bank, up to his neck in steaming water.

"Have a drink," he says, offering me his canteen.

I stretch a creaky arm, accepting it, and join him on the bench. My body aches just enough to make sitting in the deep, hot water even more delectable. I wallow in it as I drink, absorbing water through every pore, feeling each cell in my body swell with it. My shoulders begin to unknot as the muscles go slack, softened by the heat. Every part of me is richly aware of Sam's body next to mine, the brown fur on his chest, the legs corded with muscle. I don't know what will happen between us, and there's a certain pleasure in not knowing. For the moment I relax into it, surrendering to the tug of the current, letting my eyes drift to the flash of silver and green in the sycamores as the breeze flutters through the leaves. Every sensation rippling into me feels soothing, hypnotic, and it seems impossible that Sam and I could have been in such desperate straits just a few hours ago. I lean back, resting my head against the bank, letting the hot water purl over every curve and ache in my body, reveling in the warm illusion of safety.

Sam tilts his head, studying me. "We never really got to know each other, did we?"

I lift an eyebrow and start to smile, and he splashes my face with a deft flick at the water.

"I meant the usual things. I don't know where you were born. I don't know if you have brothers or sisters, or whether your parents are still alive. I don't even know how old you are."

"I'm thirty-one."

"And you grew up in—?"

"Ithaca, New York. My dad owns a bar there."

"Any brothers? Sisters?"

I smile. "Five older brothers. Peter, Matthew, James, Scott and Luke."

Sam grins. "You must have been a tomboy."

I slip off the rubber band holding the end of my braid and begin to unravel the locks of wet hair. "I had to be. My mom died when I was nine, and we didn't have any aunts or female cousins. I don't think my father bought me a dress until I was thirteen."

The smell of mud on the bank reminds me of Ithaca, and I close my eyes briefly, letting my mind return to the light mineral odor of clay and shale and water rising from the gorge near our house. The smell brings an image of that misery of sky pressing down, heavy with clouds hanging so low you could almost reach up and touch them. The high desert of the Gila wilderness is as far away as you can get from the lush, damp green of Ithaca's fields and forests. Here the air is thin, the earth barren, the sky bottomless.

A towhee trills from the top of a sycamore, a low, mournful note of warning. For no reason at all my heartbeat accelerates, and I concentrate on the bubbles in the water to distract myself from the odd tension that's suddenly inside me.

Sam finds my hand, cradles it in his palm, then lifts it, wet, to his lips.

Silent alarms go off in my head as I study him, and I wonder if he really cares about me, or whether I'm supposed to be a good-time girl who will quietly disappear when he decides to move on. I wriggle deeper into the silky, liquid heat, trying to calm my heartbeat. I've never been good at courtship or flirting, or having affairs. I wish I were smooth, like Sam, but I'm not smooth, and the silence between us has already lasted too long. A kind of queasy uncertainty washes over me as I contemplate my choices.

His eyes are fixed in a warm, intent gaze upon my face. "I like you, Kate."

"I'm sorry," I say awkwardly, and gently disengage my hand from his. "I don't know if I can do this, Sam."

He looks stunned for a second, and then his lip quirks up in his familiar crooked smile. "Guess I should have kept my mouth shut."

"It's not you."

The cliché sounds terrible, even to me, and Sam lets out a snort of disgust as he settles deeper into the water.

"I'm not any good at this," I say. If I don't want to leap off this cliff of what might happen between us, I need to back up. Flustered, I look away, casting about for something to say that might ease us past this moment. "Tell me something about yourself," I say. "Where did you grow up?"

"Alaska," he says after a nearly imperceptible pause. He closes his eyes, and I can feel the distance stretch between us as he folds his arms across his chest. "Homer, Alaska. Pretty little place on the Kenai peninsula, west of Juneau. My mom was killed by a drunk driver when I was in the fourth grade, so I didn't get much more mothering than you did. My dad's a geologist too, worked as a sub-contractor for Exxon, and made sure I took enough math and science to get into Stanford. After that I did grad work at Penn State and UNM." His voice trails off, growing more wistful. "Anything else I can tell you that might make you feel safer? I've had all my shots. Never had the clap, tested negative for HIV—"

"I'm sorry," I say, and touch his knee.

"Hey," he says, waving a hand. "You're not interested. I can understand that."

"I am," I say, before I can stop myself. God help me, I still want him, even if he's lying to me. "I'm just scared, that's all."

He eyes me warily, checking for sarcasm.

Slowly, feeling so frightened I have to fight the impulse to run, I lift my hand and trace the line of his jaw with my finger.

Sam becomes very still, then turns toward me and examines my face. He lifts the hair at the nape of my neck, then bends down and kisses me there. His lips graze the lobe of my ear, and I shiver. Desire and relief uncurl in my belly, and I meet him as his face comes close to mine, and we kiss, tasting each other. I lean into him, half-floating in the warm water, abandoning myself to sensation. His hand cups my breast and the nipple begins to stiffen as he pulls me closer, holding me tightly. A rush of heat surges through me, a mounting need to open, to be filled, to let him into me. All my caution turns to recklessness, and suddenly I want to wrap him in my arms and legs and fingers and toes and flow over him like honey.

He pulls away, his face full of anxiety and yearning. "Do you want me to use a condom?" he asks in a husky voice.

"Unless you want to have kids right away."

He studies my face to make sure I'm kidding, and then he smiles and pulls me to my feet. "We'll have to go back, then."

There's no need to talk. Limp with heat, we rise from the pool and help each other get dressed. As we start walking back toward camp, Sam clasps my hand in his, guiding me up the rocky path, and I lean against him a little more heavily than I need to, enjoying the flex of his forearm as he ushers me ahead of him. The doubts that simmer at the back of my mind have been reduced to a whisper, and I resolutely push them away, determined to let myself have this, no matter what the consequences.

When we arrive at his tent, he leads me inside, then takes a blanket off the cot and spreads it on the floor. The tent smells like him, like the musk of his skin, a mixture of soap and sweat and piñon smoke. It's a smell I want, a smell that lulls my fear and deepens the hunger in me.

His fingers explore the top button on my shirt, undoing it slowly, as if we have all the time in the world, as if we have the rest of our lives to touch each other. My hands fumble at the buttons on his shirt, and I twist them open one by one. As I shrug off my shirt, he reaches behind me, unhooks my bra and slides it over my head. We lie down together on the blanket, and I stroke the padded muscle of his chest, the mat of dark hair that trickles down to his belly. His hands are patient, reassuring, as if he could find out about me by touch alone, the way he might examine an arrowhead or a piece of obsidian, by running his hands over the stone.

"You're beautiful, Kate," he says, sliding his hand over the curve of my waist. "You're a beautiful woman." His voice is lazy, relaxed, his touch almost idle as he runs his fingers down the length of my throat, then gathers me into his arms and kisses me. His hands cover my breasts and then his lips find them, and his teeth nibble the skin, not too hard, but grazing, gentle bites that increase my yearning for him.

Delicately, with profound tenderness, he kisses me again and again, small, searching kisses, as if my skin were Braille and he could read it and send his own message back through touch alone. The light, teasing warmth unleashes a flood of heat in my belly. Easy, slow, soft kissing slides into deeper, more firm kisses, a waterfall of sensation along every nerve in my body.

I want this affection, this physical communion. Whatever reservations I have about Sam belong to a different world, a world that has nothing to do with who we are now. I want to hold his naked body next to mine, and take what comfort I can from his skin on my skin. His breathing sounds rapid and shallow.

"You feel so good." His voice is low, husky.

I reach out blindly and touch the bare skin of his chest. He pulls me close until my breasts press up against the hard plank of his belly, the rough fur of his chest. I can feel his heart beat. Need flows through me, cascading over my limbs like a river, and I let myself sink into the feeling, not caring what will happen if I hold him as if we've been lovers forever.

Sam smiles and rolls to one side, fumbling through his shaving kit until he retrieves a foil-wrapped package.

My skin feels electric, shimmering everywhere when he touches me, and my legs begin to tremble. I cry out as he penetrates me, my head thrown back, eyes closed, pushing against him until he finds the core. He feels like silk inside me, and my body pours over his as we ride each other, surging, rising, bound and straining for release. *Now,* I think, and he takes my face in both hands and goes with me, over the edge, and we fall together into the hard rushing darkness.

CHAPTER FIFTEEN

In the morning the wind slaps the canvas and tosses the leaves, making the shadows ripple across the cloth ceiling of the tent.

"I'm hungry," I whisper.

Sam lets out a low, musical laugh that makes me turn over and run my fingers through the hair on his chest.

"What would you like?" he asks, a burr of sleep in his voice.

I close my eyes. "Blueberry pancakes. Bacon and eggs. Fresh squeezed orange juice."

"I think I have some granola left."

I stretch luxuriously. "Good. Pamper me with granola."

He grasps my wrist, pulls it toward his lips and kisses my pulse. "I want to pamper you for the rest of my life."

I roll my eyes and grin at him. "Okay."

"I mean it." He tightens his grip on my hand. "This isn't just a fling to me, Kate. Do you understand? I want you in my life."

Something about the intensity in his voice makes me look at him, a little unsettled by the seriousness of his tone. I touch his face. "I'm not going anywhere, Sam."

He relaxes slightly and, a moment later, springs to his feet to get dressed. He smiles down at me as he pulls on his jeans and shirt, tensing his biceps, puffing out his chest and assuming a Mr. America pose, glancing over his shoulder and wiggling his eyebrows at me.

I feel so *good*. In spite of all the residual aches and pains from our marathon up on the mesa—and here in the tent, last night—my energy has returned, and my whole body hums with pleasure. I roll over on my side and prop my head up on one hand to watch him flex his forearms. "My, what big muscles you have." I bat my eyelashes at him and stretch seductively.

A lopsided grin spreads across his face. "You better cut that out, or we'll never get out of here." He crouches to give me a quick kiss on the forehead. "You don't have to move an inch. I'll be right back with breakfast."

"And coffee."

He gives me a salute. "Yes, ma'am."

When he leaves the tent, some of my lightheartedness leaves with him, draining away as reality comes crowding back. In a few minutes we'll start packing up our gear, then saddle up the horses and ride toward a different world, a world of cars and stoplights and skeptical bureaucrats who probably won't believe anything we try to tell them. If we can't convince them Dr. Richter was murdered, whoever killed him will almost certainly get away with it. I don't want to think about it. I can't think about it.

Slowly, reluctantly, I rise from the warm bed and look around at Sam's things. The tent could probably sleep six people, but most of it is filled by a long table covered in broken clay pottery and stone tools, spaced in orderly rows, each artifact neatly labeled. A small metal box attached to a wide cylinder occupies the far end, and when I study its controls I realize it's a magnetometer. A stack of printouts next to it show archaeo-magnetic readings that must have come from the area surrounding the pyramid. Most well-funded expeditions rely on this machine, which can register any disturbance in the natural magnetic field of the earth, such as ashes, lumber, or oxidized earth. If Sam had used the magnetometer up on the mesa, he would have discovered the catacombs months ago. But it's a labor-intensive process to survey every few feet of ground, and he probably didn't have the time to use the magnetometer on more than a quarter-mile radius of the pyramid.

I glance idly at the radiocarbon results as I button my shirt and pull on my jeans, then lean over to study the artifacts next to the magnetometer. Most of them are from the midden in the canyon: pot shards, imperfectly knapped points of chalcedony, leftover flakes of chert, and all the rest of the lithic trash from the Teotihuacán settlement that existed here fifteen hundred years ago. It looks inconsequential compared to the treasure we saw in the tomb.

When I step back, my gaze catches a flash of color peeking out of a knapsack under the table. I crouch down to examine it and see the corner of a bright red bandana visible in the open zippered compartment. For no apparent reason my heart kicks hard, and suddenly I'm aware that I'm sweating under my arms and down my back.

I reach into the pack, touch the bandana and feel the long flat blade under the cloth. With trembling fingers I pull it out, unwrap the bundle and see Fiddle's Samurai dagger. The blade is flecked with drops of dried blood, and my bones know it's not rabbit blood.

"Kate? What are you doing?" Sam fills the doorway to the tent, bearing two enamelware mugs.

I leap up, my pulse loud in my ears.

He places the mugs on the table and comes closer, nearly touching me, and I steel myself not to recoil as he takes the dagger from my hand.

"Where did you get this, Sam?" I can hear the strain in my voice.

There's a small hesitation before he speaks. "I've never seen it before. Where did you find it?"

"It was here in your pack, under the table."

He searches my face. "It's Fiddle's missing dagger, isn't it?"

I nod, staring at it in his open hand. The double-sided blade is exactly the same width as the space between the two parallel slices on Dr. Richter's palm. He must have grabbed the blade when he was pushed off the cliff. This is the murder weapon.

"What's it doing here, Sam?"

He moves his head slowly left, then right. "Somebody must have put it here. We were gone for four days. I suppose it could have been anybody."

"Why would they plant it in your pack?"

Sam turns the blade over in his palm, testing the edge with his thumb. "I guess someone wanted you to find it." He carefully places the knife down on the work table.

"But it was wrapped up in the bandana, and that was barely visible."

"So you were going through my things?" His voice is light, but he's not joking.

"No! It was the color—I was just looking around, and I saw this red cloth, and I don't know, I just knew there was something wrapped in it, and the zipper was open, so I picked it up."

He looks at me, his eyes pale, chilly, his expression neutral.

I take a deep breath, but there's nothing I can say to bridge the chasm widening between us. My voice dies as the implications of the dagger's presence here roll over me.

His eyes bore into me. My legs turn to stone. My face is stone. I stand very still, letting the shock roll over me. The certainty that I've felt ever since Dr. Richter's death—that constant whisper at the back of my mind, muttering *he was murdered, he was murdered*—coalesces into a palpable sense of evil. It breathes in my ear, so cold and close and real it makes the hair on the back of my neck stand up. The dagger seems to glow on the table, pulsing with a dark hunger next to Sam's other trophies.

"It's been used recently," I say. "There's blood on it."

Sam lets out a brief exhalation, as if he's been holding his breath. "Son of a bitch." It comes out as a whisper.

The words almost fall out of my mouth: *Did you kill him?* But I keep my lips closed, seized by the sudden fear that saying it out loud might make it true. Sam can't be a killer. He's right—someone else must have put the dagger in here.

The air tightens around us, and I feel an overwhelming urge to go outside. "Maybe Jessie or Michael saw somebody come in here while we were gone."

"Kate." His voice holds a warning. "Don't."

"Don't what?"

"Don't go running off to Michael and Jessie. If you tell them you found the dagger in my tent, they're going to assume the worst."

"But what if they know something? What if they saw someone come in here?"

"What if one of them planted it?" he says.

"We can't pretend nothing's happened—they'll find out sooner or later that it's been recovered. It will be much worse if they know we tried to hide the fact."

His body is rigid, his face still. "Let's say you tell them you found the dagger, and you think it's been deliberately planted here in my pack. If one of them did it, why tip them off? They might do something worse next time."

I back away from him, moving toward the doorway. "Come on, Sam. Come with me. If they talk to you, they'll know you're innocent. Our only hope of clearing this up is to find out if they know anything."

He holds my gaze a moment longer. "Kate, please. Don't go. I think it's a big mistake."

Pausing in the doorway, I look at him, stricken by the swift change in the feeling between us, and the tension that hums below the surface of everything we say to each other. "I'm sorry," I say in a low voice.

He attempts a smile. "Me too."

I duck outside and rush away from the tent, my mind filled with choppy, chaotic thoughts, like the intermittent buzz of the cicadas in the clearing. The horses are staked out on a patch of grama grass under some cottonwoods, and I hurry past them, then zigzag through a clump of scattered piñons, crossing the grass flattened by the missing tents. Michael's tent stands at the western edge of the camp, and I head that way.

When I lift the door flap, I see Jessie reclining on Michael's cot, obviously naked under a thin sheet, one arm halted in mid-stretch over her head.

She looks up in surprise at the intrusion. "Kate? What happened? What's the matter?" She sits up, drawing the sheet over her breasts.

"Where's Michael?"

"Making coffee over at the mess tent. Fiddle left some supplies for us, but she's gone already. Henry told us he was going to camp out by himself on the mesa for a few days." She leans toward me, her forehead creased in a worried frown. "Is something wrong?"

"I found Fiddle's knife in Sam's tent. There's blood on it."

Jessie looks stunned. "Come on, Kate, you can't suspect Sam. Did you ask him about it? What did he say?"

"He says he never saw it before, and he doesn't know how it got there." I stop talking, suddenly assailed by doubt. Surely I would have sensed it if Sam murdered Richter. How could I have spent all that time with him and not known it, not felt it? But the blood is on the dagger, and the dagger is in his tent.

Jessie nods slowly, waiting for me to go on, her eyes bright with sympathy.

With an effort I focus on the reason I came here. "When we were gone, did you see anyone go in Sam's tent?"

She purses her lips and expels a long puff of air. "No, but Michael and I spent most of our time up on the mesa looking for you. If anyone went in Sam's tent, we wouldn't have seen a thing—we were miles away. What about Jason?"

I feel a sudden, hot catch in my throat. "Why would Jason put the knife in Sam's tent? He likes Sam, doesn't he?"

"Sam wouldn't kill Dr. Richter." Jessie says this slowly, as if asking for reassurance.

A creeping numbness overtakes me, and I sit down heavily on a camp chair by the bed. My mind floats from one scenario to another, imagining motives I don't want to think about. Without Dr. Richter standing in his way, Sam will lead the expedition to the burials in the mesa. How far would he go to grab that prize?

"I mean, I know Sam and Dr. Richter had a big fight," Jessie says thoughtfully, staring at me. "The night before he was killed, I heard them arguing." She opens her mouth as if she's about to say more, then stops and shakes her head, obviously upset.

This news rolls over me like a tidal wave, obliterating all the benchmarks of what I thought I knew about Sam. He never told me he saw Richter that night. "Do you know what they were fighting about?"

She waves a hand, dismissing it. "What I heard didn't make any sense."

I lean forward. "What did they say?"

"Sam kept yelling at him about section three. I don't know what it meant."

Whatever it meant, Sam's silence about it can't be a good thing. I can feel myself going under, overwhelmed by the evidence that seems to be mounting against him. I pinch the bridge of my nose between my thumb and forefinger and shake my head.

"Come on," Jessie says. "You don't really think Sam had

anything to do with Richter's death, do you? Don't you have feelings for him? Didn't you guys spend the night together?"

"You're right," I say, forcing myself to take a deep breath. There's no point in rambling on about my feelings for Sam, or what happened between us. Obviously Jessie can't shed any more light on the situation, and I can't afford to fall apart now.

Jessie rises from the cot and reaches for the brassiere hanging from the armrest of my chair. She stands in front of me, naked and relaxed, lifting her arms to slip the straps over her shoulders and fasten the hooks in back. Her body is deeply tanned except for a small triangle of white skin around her pubic hair and a white thread over her hips, where her thong has kept out the sun. She looks sleek and fit, like a healthy young animal, with lustrous skin and a perfectly toned belly.

She laughs as she crouches down and plucks her underpants from under the bed. "I wondered where Michael threw these." She lets out a long sigh as she straightens and pulls them on, her toes pointed. "He makes me want to howl at the moon, Kate. You know what I mean? He's terrific in bed. Better than his father by a mile."

A pang of envy pinches my heart, and for a moment I wish I'd made a different choice, before it was too late. Why couldn't I have chosen Michael? Elegant, blond, deferential, calm, easy-to-be-around Michael, who just happens to be rich and successful and apparently a wonderful lover. Why did I have to choose Sam, a dark, gruff, hot-tempered geologist who may or may not be a murderer?

Jessie stoops to pick up an unopened condom packet from the floor by the bed, then casts a sideways look at me, her lips turned up in a Mona Lisa smile. "I brought this here last night, but we didn't need to use it." Her voice drops to a low, intimate purr. "That's one of the best things about being with Michael—we don't have to use condoms."

With an effort I rouse myself. "Why not?"

"One, we've been tested and we're both clean, and two—well, you know." She holds up two fingers and snips the air. "He's been fixed."

"Fixed," I repeat.

"Kate?" The voice comes from behind me, and I look over my shoulder, startled by the sight of Michael filling the doorway to the tent. He smiles as he passes a cup of coffee to Jessie and offers the other one to me. "Here. You look like you could use some java."

"Thanks," I say, suddenly feeling bereft. I know I'm a third wheel in here, and I know Michael made the coffee for himself, and not me. Jessie gives him a coquettish look as she stands next to me, dressed only in her underwear, one knee tipped forward, her heel delicately lifted as she smiles up at him. He seems unperturbed by my presence, and gives us both the same calm, sunny smile.

"What's up?" he asks, pulling up a chair.

"Kate found the murder weapon." Jessie brings the cup to her mouth and blows on the hot liquid before she takes a sip.

Michael looks at me questioningly, his eyes alert. "Where?"

"In Sam's pack," I reply.

He leans back, his eyes fixed on mine. "You don't think . . ."

"He says he never saw it before."

"Do you believe him?"

I pause, then shrug. "Of course." My mind buzzes with thoughts that hover like wasps, threatening me with different possibilities. "Did you see anyone go in his tent while we were gone?"

"No," he says slowly. "Is that what you think? Someone else went in there and put it in his pack?"

I nod. "I think so." I look at both of them, suddenly aware of the charged silence, and the fact that neither one of them can meet my eyes.

"Well, you can't stay here with him if you're not sure," Jessie says. "Fiddle's gone, and Henry moved all his gear up to the mesa. Why don't you come to Silver City with us? You'll feel safer."

"We're ready to start packing up," Michael says. "It shouldn't take us more than an hour." He glances at Jessie, who gives him a slight nod. "We'd be happy to travel with you."

A vague memory shifts inside me, an elusive shadow I can't quite grasp. There's something odd, something wrong here, something that doesn't fit, but it refuses to take shape. My mind is a fog, and my palms ache as if they've been stung.

"Let's meet back here in an hour," Jessie says. "Can you get ready by then?"

I shrug. "Sure," I say, and give her a half-hearted smile. "I'm glad you guys are here."

"Then let's get moving," Jessie says.

Sam sits on the flat rock in front of his tent, holding a bowl of granola in one hand and a spoon in the other. He looks up as I approach, and lets the spoon fall in the bowl as he rises to his feet. "Any luck?"

I shrug. "They didn't see anything."

He settles back on the rock and scrapes at the granola half-heartedly, but doesn't lift the spoon from the bowl. "Was it worth it?" he asks quietly.

"What's section three?" My heart hammers against my ribs, and a cold dampness breaks out between my shoulder blades as I cross my arms over my chest.

Sam cocks his head and gives me a look, but his mouth remains closed.

I find a flat, steady voice to speak in and use it. "Jessie heard you and Dr. Richter fighting the night before he was killed."

He holds my gaze a moment longer, then looks away, setting the bowl down on the rock. "Section three is part of my contract with Richter."

"What does it say?"

He stares at me, his face drawn into a scowl, a spark of belligerence in his eyes. "What difference does it make?"

I stare back at him. "Maybe none. I'd just like to know why you were arguing with him, that's all."

He lets out a derisive chuckle. "Let me guess. Did Michael put you up to this?"

"No. Why would he? What does he know about it?"

"Section three lays out the chain of command on the expedition."

"Why were you arguing about it?"

He hangs his head, then turns and looks off over the sun-dappled ground. "You're not going to like it."

"Sam. Tell me."

He takes his time, pressing the palms of his hands against his eyes before he drops them and looks up at me. "I was upset about the way he and Sylvia treated you after you found the tomb. So I went over to their tent to see if I could get him to give you a second chance. But Richter had something else on his mind—he wanted to change our agreement. He wanted Michael to come on board as a full partner."

My lungs freeze, and I cannot seem to draw a deep breath. "But Michael's a filmmaker, not an archaeologist. Why—?"

"I don't know," Sam says, shaking his head. "But if I'd agreed to it—which I didn't—then Michael would be leading the dig. Not me."

"Michael doesn't even want it, does he?" I ask. "I've never heard him mention it."

"I don't care if he wants it or not. I've earned it. He hasn't."

"So how did you leave it with Dr. Richter?"

"I told him I'd sue him if he backed out of our contract."

A deep exhalation escapes me, and Sam gives me a sharp look as the resentment surfaces for a moment in his eyes. "I mortgaged my house for this trip. Every last cent I have is tied up in this expedition, and I worked my ass off for two years to make it happen. It cost me everything. And then boom, he wants to bring in his son, the golden boy, and hand it over to him on a platter."

An image sparks in my mind—Sam, struggling with Richter on the lip of the cliff. He could have intercepted Dr. Richter on his way out of camp. Maybe they argued, Sam exploded, and Richter went tumbling off the cliff. But when I picture it, my mind feels cloudy, uncertain, as if it's concocting a story out of fear.

"That fucking Michael," Sam says. "He's no scholar. He's a lightweight, an amateur. His wife carried him for years, and when she died his daddy took over." He releases a heavy sigh. "But if I sued Richter for breach of contract, he'd go ahead and excavate the tombs without me. By the time the courts settled the case, it'd be too late. Besides, I don't have any money for a long court battle. And I might have lost that, too."

I stare at him for a moment in disbelief. Why is he telling me this? If he killed Richter, wouldn't he try to minimize the argument and dismiss its importance? And if he killed Richter and kept the dagger, why didn't he wipe the blood off the blade? Nobody could be this dumb, unless they were innocent. A strange giddiness comes over me, a sense of relief so intense I almost laugh out loud.

He props up one knee on the rock and picks at a speck of dirt on his boot. "So Jessie heard us arguing? Does she think I killed him?"

"I'm not sure what she thinks, to tell you the truth. I found her in Michael's bed, and he seems to be the main thing on her mind."

His face falls, and his eyes grow serious. "You don't think I killed Richter, do you?"

He touches my hand questioningly, and I squeeze his fingers, desperately searching my mind for that stray wisp of a thought that seemed so close when I was talking to Michael and Jessie. Something Jessie said didn't make sense, and then Michael walked in. What was it? I think of her fingers snipping the air, and her mouth, smiling. *He's been fixed.*

"How could she?" I mutter, half to myself. And then the light breaks over me as a piece of the puzzle fits into place.

"It wasn't his baby," I say, looking up at Sam.

CHAPTER SIXTEEN

Jessie looks up at our approach, and murmurs something to Michael in a voice too low for us to hear. Michael's baseball cap shades his face as he goes on dismantling the tent, removing the steel rods from the framework and allowing the canvas to fall. As we draw closer, Jessie stares at us with her feet planted, hands on hips and a look of worry on her face.

"I'm surprised to see you two," Michael finally says, brushing his palms against his jeans. His expression is calm, prepared to smile as he looks at Sam. "Did you get everything straightened out?"

Sam studies Michael's face for a moment before answering. "We have a few questions for you."

Michael nods, then crouches to scoop up a handful of tent stakes, and Jessie grabs a canvas bag and steps forward so he can slide the stakes inside it.

"When did you get your vasectomy, Michael?" I ask.

There's a minute hesitation, and then he finishes loading the stakes. "I don't think that's any of your business, Kate."

Jessie throws me an irritated glance. "For God's sake, Kate, I told you that in confidence."

"Your wife was pregnant when she died," I say. "It wasn't your baby, was it, Michael?"

His face turns as white as if he's been struck, and he rises to his feet and levels a long cool look at me before he takes the bag from Jessie and tightens the drawstring. "You've been watching too many soap operas."

"Isabelle had diabetes. You told me her doctors warned her that a pregnancy might kill her, and you loved her too much to take that chance. But someone else was willing to let her take the risk."

Jessie's eyes narrow as they focus on Michael's face. "Is that true? Was she pregnant?"

For a split second his eyes spark at me, and I can see the opening of a vortex that could devour all of us. He walks over to a large duffel bag on the ground and methodically packs the bag of tent stakes into it. The sun beats down on us, and a rare silence falls over the clearing as the birds suddenly stop singing.

"I think your wife asked your father to help her get pregnant." I keep my voice low, but the sound ripples through the silence like a stone dropped in a pond. "She wanted your genes, but you refused to cooperate. You knew the pregnancy could kill her. So she went to your dad."

Michael crumples to his knees, and his shoulders sag.

"Was it your father's child, Michael?" I ask. "Was that why you killed him?"

He looks over his shoulder at me. "It wasn't like that."

Sam leans forward and speaks in a low voice that carries an unmistakable threat. "Then why don't you tell us how it was?"

Michael digs into the duffel bag, and when he removes his hand from the bag he's holding a gun. The gun Henry gave to him, the same gun he fired up on the mesa to call off the search for Sam and me. He rises to his feet with surprising speed, turns and aims the revolver at me.

My chest tightens, and Sam steps in front of me, his arms outstretched to keep me shielded behind him.

"Michael? What are you doing?" There's a tremor in Jessie's voice.

"Shut up," he snaps at her.

"You didn't—you didn't kill him, did you?"

"Just shut up for a second and let me think!" He wipes his forehead with the back of his hand and waves the gun at Jessie. "Get the tent ropes out of the bag."

"No!" she says, backing away from him.

The gunshot is unbelievably loud, a thunderclap that rips the silence and makes my eardrums ring. Jessie ducks and runs toward the piñons beyond the clearing, clutching her side, disappearing within seconds. The smell of cordite is thick in the air.

"What the hell did you do that for?" Sam shouts.

I stand motionless, confused, dazed, wired with adrenaline. "You didn't have to shoot her."

"We have to go get her," Sam says.

"I don't think that's a good idea," Michael says.

"The hell it's not," Sam says, and attempts to push past him.

Michael raises the gun and brings it down on the back of Sam's head, hard, and Sam staggers and sinks to the ground. I hurry to Sam's side, kneel in the dirt and grasp his wrist to check his pulse. After I feel the steady beat underneath the skin, I stare up at Michael.

He points the gun at me as I stand on shaky legs. I hold up my hands and back away from him, my knees weak. Terror slides over me like the shadow of a cloud, and suddenly I'm aware that we're a very long way from any kind of help.

"Get the tent ropes, Kate."

Despising myself for my helplessness, I walk over to the duffel bag and take a clump of ropes out of it. He gestures impatiently with the gun, and I walk back to Sam's unconscious body and follow Michael's terse commands, looping one of the ropes over Sam's wrists, making the knot as loose as I dare. Michael squats next to me, close enough for me to hear the breath whistle in and out of his nose. The gun is a black hyphen at the periphery of my vision, pointing at the knot.

"You'll have to do better than that, Kate," he says softly.

My mind works furiously, trying to come up with a plan. But how can we escape without abandoning Jessie? Is she already bleeding to death? Can she survive a gunshot wound out here in the wilderness, with no one to help her? The back of my neck tingles under the heat of Michael's gaze. Determined to do nothing to antagonize him, I wrap the rope again around Sam's hands and make a show of tightening it before I finish tying the knot. Sam remains limp as a sack of wheat, head sagging forward, face ashen.

The barrel of the gun swings toward my face, and my heart seems to stop.

"Now tie his feet," Michael says.

With Sam slumped in a fetal position, I bring his ankles together, using another length of rope to wrap around his boots.

"Didn't your father know a pregnancy might kill her?" I ask.

Michael lets out a small laugh. "He wanted the ego boost, I suppose. He always claimed her body could handle it. Isabelle never told me who the father was, and I never knew he had anything to do with her pregnancy until I arrived here. When Dad picked me up at the airport he started grilling me about Isabelle's death. When I told him how it happened—why it happened—he turned white. I mean, *white*. That's when I began to suspect him."

I pretend to struggle with the rope, and make a show of loosening the coils and rewrapping them. "Why did he disappear for five days?"

The barrel of the gun dips slightly and points to my chest while he considers the question. "He told me he'd spent the time wandering in the desert, thinking about the mess he'd made of his life. My life. Isabelle's life. I think he was in shock. He'd killed my wife, and he thought he loved her." His lip curls, the sarcasm obvious in his tone. "He wanted to make amends."

Slowly I finish tying the knot around Sam's feet, then pretend to yank it tight before I rise to my feet. "So you took Fiddle's knife. And when he left camp, you met him on the cliff."

"I was waiting for him. We argued." Michael's gaze softens, and he stares off toward the distant rock walls that enclose the canyon. "And then he offered me a partnership in excavating the tombs." His voice wavers as he speaks these last few words.

I keep my voice low, my body still. "But that wasn't enough to make up for what he'd done."

Michael's face hardens. "No. It wasn't. So I took the dagger, and I pushed the tip of the blade against his chest. He lost his balance, and went over."

His eyes focus on mine, bright, electric eyes, his pupils no bigger than pinpricks. "If it weren't for you, I'd be in California by now. Why did you have to make such a big deal about it, Kate? You didn't even like him."

"Do you think Isabelle would have wanted this?" I ask. "Would she like seeing you here, now, like this, holding a gun on people who never did a thing to hurt you?"

A stubborn look comes over his face. "You don't leave me much of a choice."

"Michael, whatever you're planning, it isn't going to work. Any forensics team will check our bodies for bruises on our wrists or rope fibers on our clothes. They'll know we were tied up, held against our will. You won't get away with it."

"There are lots of ways to die," he mutters. "Maybe all I need is another cliff."

"But you'd have to get close to us to push us off. We'll fight. We'll get your skin, your hair, fibers from your clothes under our fingernails. They'll identify you."

"By the time they find you, there might not be anything left but bones."

The thought chills me and lends urgency to my voice as I try to reason with him. "They can reconstruct a portrait of you from anything you do to harm us. Even if there's nothing left of us but bones. And believe me, when the bodies start to pile up, a swarm of investigators will show up on your doorstep, asking questions. Why can't you negotiate with us? If you turn yourself in, you might get off with manslaughter. I'll testify for you. We could say it was self-defense."

He smiles as if I've said something funny, then rotates the barrel of the gun in the air, gesturing for me to turn around.

"Henry must have heard the gun go off," I say, scrambling to come up with anything that might change his mind. "He can't be that far away—he's camped up on the mesa, right? He's probably on his way here right now."

"You're right," Michael says. "I'll have to head him off." Almost absentmindedly he pokes my shoulder with the snout of the gun, and I turn my back to him, desperately searching my mind for a way out.

The rope slithers over my wrists, and he ties it tightly, cutting off the circulation. Maybe Jessie wasn't hit by a bullet, I think. Maybe she can come back and untie us, after he's gone. Or maybe Henry will track us down before Michael finds him.

"Once I take care of Henry, I'll have to find Jessie," he mutters, erasing that faint hope. "I don't think she could have gone far, if she's still alive." Unceremoniously he pushes me until I fall forward heavily, bruising my face on the stony dirt. He tosses the gun down and ties my feet together. The black shape of the gun lies in front of me on the ground, just out of reach. With my hands tied behind my back, I stare at it, longing for the smooth dark heft of it, heavy in my palm. I want that gun more than anything in the world.

Michael lets out a small sigh as he gets to his feet and looks down at me. "I'll be back as soon as I can."

Panic mushrooms inside me. "And then what? You'll shoot us?"

"I won't have to. Time will take care of it."

"What are you talking about?"

"If you and Sam had spent another day or two in the tomb, we wouldn't even be having this conversation. I just need another hole in the ground," he mutters. "Something I can plug up."

The thought of returning to that kind of darkness and thirst is unbearable, and I fight back the hysteria pushing up from my chest.

Michael rubs his chin thoughtfully. "Somewhere no one will think to look. It shouldn't take long for me to find a place. I'll be back before Sleeping Beauty wakes up." He nods at Sam's trussed, inert body, then picks up the gun, adjusts the bill of his cap and walks away, disappearing in the piñons to the east, heading toward the picket line of horses.

As soon as he's out of sight I wriggle toward Sam and butt his shoulder awkwardly with my head, desperate to wake him before Michael returns. No response. His face is pale, his lips parted, his breathing nearly indiscernible.

"*Sam!*" I hiss. I knock my forehead against his chin.

His eyes flicker open. "Is he gone?" he whispers. "I thought he'd never leave."

"You've been *awake* all this time? Why didn't you do something?"

"He had a gun, didn't he? I thought we'd have a better chance if he thought I was out of it. I don't think he would have left us together if he knew I was conscious. Turn around. Let's see if we can untie these knots."

I lift my bound feet and swing them overhead, turning my back to him and hunching closer to his body until I can feel his fingers picking at the knots. "Are you okay?"

"My head hurts like hell. Otherwise, I'm fine. Quit straining. You just tightened the knot."

Even now, Sam's voice soothes me with his comfortable nagging tone and all the intimacy it implies. It's easy to imagine him nagging me to put down my book and come to bed, or to take my umbrella to work because it looks like rain. I want that future. All of it. The kids we might have together. The house with the toys scattered all over the front yard, and a big dog asleep on the porch. The kitchen that will smell like fresh coffee and cake. The bedroom I'll wake up in every morning, with Sam's comforting bulk beside me. My eyes fill with tears at the thought of losing that future, and a wall of self-pity crashes over me as I wait for him to set me free. If I ever get out of here I'll never doubt him again. My shoulders are beginning to cramp from the effort of holding my wrists together behind me, and I know it must be just as hard for him to struggle with the knot while his own hands are bound behind his back.

"We need to take a couple of horses and get out of here," he says. "We need help."

"What about Jessie? She might have been hit. We can't just leave her."

"Then we'd better hurry. After he tells Henry some fairy tale about the gunshot, Michael will come back here looking for us."

After what seems like an eternity of feeling his fingers tugging at the knot binding my wrists, there seems to be some slack in the rope, and I yank at it.

"Wait!" Sam says. "I'm not finished."

But I'm already wrestling my wrists through the constrictive loops, determined to squeeze out of them before we waste any more time. The cord bites and burns my skin, but one wrist finally pops out, and a moment later my hands are free. I pull myself up, leaning forward to undo the knot at my ankles, heart skittering, every movement jerky with fear.

I scramble to my feet and begin untying the knots around Sam's wrists, taking twice as long as I should because my hands are shaking with adrenaline, and every nerve in my body is screaming at me to run, to hide, to get away from here as fast as I can. At last I manage to undo the knot, and he hunches forward to untie his ankles. A moment later he stands up and rubs his wrists, scanning the landscape for any sign of Michael.

"I say we fight," Sam says. "Find a way to ambush him. Take the gun, tie him up and cart him back to Silver City."

"We have to find Jessie, first."

He nods, his mouth set in a grim line, his face white as he takes my hand and we hurry through the deserted camp. The tents are empty, the clearings silent, abandoned, and there's no sign of Jessie anywhere.

We come to a small clearing where the horses were staked. Sam comes to a halt, and his grip on my hand tightens as he stares at the vacant meadow.

"Damn," he mutters. "He must have taken the horses."

"All of them?" I ask, although it's clear that none remain. Without horses, we'll never be able to outrun him. My heart falls at the thought of trying to escape on foot. Out on the open mesa, he'll be able to pick us off and carry our bodies to a place where our bones will never be found. Gripping each other for support, we walk beyond the clump of piñons where Jessie disappeared. Cautiously I call out for her but there's no answer. We scour the ground along the bank of willow and finally come across a set of footprints, and we follow the trail until it vanishes in an alluvial fan of sand and gravel near the stream.

Frantic now, half expecting to see her dead body floating in the river, I cast around for any sign of her passing.

"Which way would you go if you were wounded and looking for cover?" Sam asks me.

When I close my eyes a kaleidoscope of images passes across

my internal movie screen, images that frighten me and heighten the desire to run. A blur of willow branches, rocks, rushing water, mud. My side begins to burn.

"Downstream," I say.

We scramble through the tunnel of willow, and the whip-thin branches sting my face as we plunge through the thicket. After we walk a few hundred yards, I hear a low moan that makes the hair rise on my arms. The sound comes from a stand of sycamores directly ahead of us, and when I part the willow branches I can see Jessie lying on the ground, curled up in a fetal position, softly weeping.

"Jessie," Sam whispers.

She glances up at us, her face streaked with dirt and tears. Every muscle in my body tenses, half-expecting to see Michael somewhere beyond the fringe of green, aiming at us with his gun.

"Are you okay?" Sam asks.

She lifts her shirt and shows us an angry looking streak on her side. Apparently the bullet only grazed her, leaving a black and red burn. I exhale, letting go of a breath I hadn't been aware of holding. Thank God it's a burn, not a hole.

"Bastard," she whispers, looking down at it, and her voice trembles on the verge of tears. "He could have killed me."

"But he didn't," Sam says, squatting down and giving her leg a squeeze. "You're damned lucky. We were worried about you."

"He took all the horses," she says listlessly. "I heard him ride away."

If Michael's on horseback, we can't outrun him. And if we don't get moving, he'll certainly kill us when he gets back. "We have to hide," I say.

"Yeah, but where?" Jessie asks.

I stare across the canyon at the glowing face of the pyramid, and the dark hole of the tunnel. "I have an idea."

CHAPTER SEVENTEEN

I pull the flashlight out of my pack, take off my hat and enter the dark mouth of the pyramid. The stone walls become colder as we walk down the narrow excavated passage toward the chilly air of the interior. It's a relief after the furnace-hot day outside, but the dark corridor reminds me of the claustrophobic depths of the tombs under the mesa, and I shiver from more than the drop in temperature.

We're carrying enough food and water for a three day siege. Six gallons of water, packs full of energy bars, beef jerky, fruit leather and trail mix. We probably won't need all these supplies, but Sam and I drag them in here in an irrational, tacit agreement between the two of us. We can't endure any more hunger or thirst. Not in this lifetime. I know it's crazy, but it eases some of my terror to know that the food and water is here, like an unspoken promise that we'll survive.

Sam scans the shaft with the flashlight, then takes off his baseball cap and wipes his brow, which glows with a light sheen of sweat.

"Does your head ache?" I ask.

"Like a son of a bitch." He closes his eyes, wincing as I gingerly run my fingers over the hard lump swelling on the back of his head.

"Can you count backwards from ten?"

"Yes," he says irritably, brushing my hand away. "And I know who the president is, and what year I was born. Michael didn't hit me that hard."

I unscrew the cap on one of the water jugs and offer it to him, and he takes it and drinks a pint without stopping. Even in the gloom of the tunnel, his face looks white and strained.

Jessie stares listlessly at the dirt floor, her face dull, showing no reaction to our whispered conversation or the sound of Michael's name. What a ragged looking team we are. Shot, concussed, traumatized, and still recovering from dehydration and hunger. Our chances of defeating Michael seem remote, especially when he has a gun and we look like the living dead.

"Don't give up," I tell Jessie. "We need you." I smooth her glossy dark hair with my hand, but Jessie's expression remains blank. Nothing seems to register, not the touch of my hand or the sound of my voice. But then her gaze flickers and shifts to my face.

"I never thought we'd have to dig in this goddamned tunnel again." Her expression is glum, but I'm relieved to hear her speak.

"Can you think of a better plan?"

She shakes her head.

"Then let's get busy."

The sound of a gunshot in the distance rips the air, followed by two more in quick succession. Jessie drops her shovel and runs to the mouth of the tunnel, and Sam and I both follow. Cautiously I duck my head out from the entrance. The sound came from up on the mesa, but there's nothing to see—no glint of a gun or binoculars, no silhouette on the cliff top, no movement. But images cut into my thoughts, bright and clear as the view through a camera lens. I don't want to look. I don't want to see this. *The gun in Michael's hand. Henry's open, empty eyes, his arms out flung on the dirt. A dark stain blooms on his shirt, spreading like ink across the buttons.*

"Henry's dead," I whisper to Sam.

He doesn't question how I know this. "Michael fired the shots?"

I nod.

Sam pokes his head out to look. "How many bullets do you think he has left?"

My throat constricts as I shove the fear back. I take a deep breath to steady myself and try to keep my voice even. "When he found us on the mesa yesterday he fired the gun once to let Henry know we were okay." *Yesterday.* It seems like an eternity has passed since then.

Sam glances nervously toward the mesa. "And he shot Jessie this morning. We just heard three more. That's five. The revolver takes six, right?"

"Right." There's another possibility I don't mention. If Henry is dead, Michael could take all the ammunition he needs. I try to swallow, but I have no spit left in my mouth. "I think he has only one bullet left. But I'm not sure."

"Those shots sounded like he's at least a couple miles from here," Sam says. "But he'll be here before long. We're running out of time."

In the depths of the tunnel, I dig in the dark and think about my dad. The way he wiped down the bar at the end of his shift in the tavern at home. The way he was so proud of me for landing this job. Relieved, too, not because it meant professional redemption, but because he'd been worried about me. He knew I was a mess. Not sleeping, not eating, haunted by failure and crackling with nervous energy that left everyone around me unsettled and anxious. Every time Dad looked at me, I could feel his pity, and it pains me now to realize how happy I was to run away from it.

A wave of homesickness rolls over me at the thought of his

big forearms, the comforting stink of cigars that always clung to his clothes, his thin, fluffy hair and sad Irish eyes. I think of how his good-natured face lit up in a smile whenever he saw me, and I wonder if I'll ever be lucky enough to see it light up again.

My muscles scream in protest as I dig, and my eyes sting as I think of him and how much I want to walk out of here and wrap my arms around his wrinkled old neck and hold him until we both know everything will be all right. It can't end here. My chest tightens with emotion as I blink away the rock dust and push the shovel back in the pile of rubble.

The presence of men has always meant safety, warmth, companionship. My brothers would all lay down their lives for me, and my father would walk through fire if it meant keeping me from harm. But now I hear the clank of Sam's shovel on basalt, and it means there's a man out there, a beautiful, famous, accomplished man, a man I'd thought of as a friend just a few hours ago, and he's trying to kill me. It makes my stomach tighten like a twisted rag to think about him.

The glare of my headlamp bounces off the walls of the tunnel and makes the sweat on Sam's bare arms shine. By now we've learned a lot about each other's digging style. Sam can use a pick with more force than I can, but I'll shovel dirt till the cows come home. Jessie's an Amazon once she gets going, relentless as the best digger on the expedition. *We're the best fucking digging team in the history of the universe. If there were an Olympic event for digging, we'd bring home the gold.* A sob escapes my throat as Sam's pick hammers down and Jessie and I shovel the tailings into a pile away from the edge of the hole.

We dig, and dig, and dig, until the hole is big enough to make us lean back on our tools, exhausted, our faces black with dirt. Sam sends me a swift glance, and we both look at Jessie, whose eyes show a spark of hope. Wordlessly she lifts her palm, and Sam and I take turns smacking it in a high five. My palms sting as I look into the black well we've dug. Everything depends on this.

The sun sets, and the moon rises, deepening the shadows. Michael is close. I can feel him out there. Maybe he's resting, waiting for the cover of darkness, biding his time before he kills us. The Michael I knew—the bereaved spouse, the good son, the legend that the whole world knew and loved and respected—that Michael is gone. A cold fog surrounds him now, a chill I can feel in the marrow of my bones. All that's left of him is a husk, an empty shell, a ghost with a desire to kill.

The crackle of twigs wakes me from a fitful doze, and before I've even opened my eyes, I hold my breath, waiting for the next careful step. He's coming. Jessie and Sam and I have been slumped against the tunnel wall, fighting off sleep, and now we silently rise to our feet and press ourselves back further into the shallow niche, out of sight. I squeeze Sam's leg, and he pats me lightly in return. We're as ready as we'll ever be.

I switch on the flashlight for a split second, aiming the beam at the tunnel entrance to give Michael a beacon, a sign. And then I switch it off, plunging us into darkness.

I stand about fifteen feet from the steps that lead down to the entrance, deep in the shadows, while Sam and Jessie scurry back, deeper into the tunnel, where they crouch against the wall. When Michael appears in the doorway, he scans the walls with his flashlight, slowly searching for us. With my head pressed tightly against the rock wall, I can't see the gun in his hand, but I know it's there. The beam from his flashlight misses us by inches. *Come on,* I pray. *Take another step.*

"Kate?" he calls out. "Sam? Where are you?"

Don't say a word, I think, willing Sam and Jessie to stay absolutely quiet. But what if Michael doesn't walk in far enough? The tarp is covered with a fine layer of dirt and debris, held taut by rocks set at the corners. He can't possibly see the tarp—it's mud-colored from use—but he's moving too slowly, as if he knows this is a trap.

I clear my throat. "We need a doctor." My voice quivers with strain.

He swings the flashlight toward the sound of my voice. "Come on out and we'll talk about it."

I cower against the wall, praying that the slight bulge in the rock will protect my vital organs if he shoots. "Jessie's lost a lot of blood."

"I can't help you if I can't see you," he says. "Turn on your flashlight."

This is one of the hardest things I've ever had to do, to willingly fall into the darkness surrounding him. *Breathe,* I remind myself. *Try to relax.* I close my eyes, still the panicky lurch of my heartbeat and open myself to the broken mind before me.

It's cold. So cold. Layers of ice, like armor. His heartbeat is steady, slow, unafraid. In his mind there can be only one outcome here.

"Kate?" he calls.

Go deeper, I tell myself. *Underneath the ice, down, down, deeper, deeper, into the depths below the calm, dive down as deep as you can.*

Terror claws at me as I let my mind loose in a free fall, plummeting down into Michael, into his core, until I hit bottom with a thump I can feel in my heart.

Two red eyes full of malice stare back at me. Dragon's eyes. Eyes as old as Cain. Eyes full of murder.

Come and get me, I whisper.

Squeezing myself as tightly as possible against the rock wall, I flick on the flashlight.

Michael leans forward into the next step. He seems to hover there for several minutes, peering at the cone of light in the opaque black depths of the tunnel. After an eternity of waiting, his foot finally comes down.

There's a clatter of gravel as he falls through the thin layer of canvas and plunges down into the hole.

The gun leaves his hand and flies straight up in the air, then falls like a stone and hits the bottom of the hole with a dull thud.

Michael clutches the tarp with both hands and scrambles desperately for a purchase. The hole is at least six feet deep, but the tarpaulin has caught on one of the rocks meant to hold the tarp in place. Instead of snapping free, the hem of the canvas slides slowly, too slowly, toward the hole. Before the fabric can tumble in, Michael kicks and scratches at the heavy canvas in a race to fight his way out.

"Quick," I yell, and Sam grabs the edge of a sheet of plywood stashed by the wall. We hurl it at Michael's head to cover the hole and trap him inside, but he catches a corner of the plywood. Sam and I try to tear it away from him as he flings himself over the flat surface and uses it to leverage his way up.

Michael is out. Panting, glaring at us, he staggers to his feet and edges past the hole. The gun is at the bottom of the hole, out of reach, but he's angry now, and he's coming for us.

I grab a shovel and brandish it like a club as he reaches out for me with bleeding hands. I swing the shovel at his head, but he catches it and yanks it away.

"*Bastard!*" Sam seizes a pick and goes after him. Jessie screams, frozen in terror as she sees Michael dodge him, then backhand Sam with the shovel. Jessie and I watch in horror as Sam teeters on the edge of the hole before he falls, and his body lands hard in a terrible, bruising thud of flesh hitting the ground.

Without thinking, I bolt for the entrance. Michael whirls around from the edge of the hole and tries to bar my exit with the shovel, but I barrel past it and run into the night.

Panicked, I race up the steps of the pyramid, hoping to exhaust him and lead him away from Sam and Jessie. I can hear Michael's harsh breathing as he follows me up the steps to the temple platform, to the highest tier where the human sacrifices of Teotihuacán were given to the gods.

He's stronger, faster than I thought. But I'm fast too. I can run. I can run to the top and scale the cliff where the apex of the pyramid abuts the mesa. It's steep. He'll get winded. It's a faint hope, tenuous as a spider's thread, but it's the only strategy I can think of.

My lungs ache for breath as I climb higher. I allow myself one glance over my shoulder and see his face, lit by the brightness of the moon a few feet below me, hair streaming, eyes wild, lips stretched over his teeth in a grimace of desperation and effort.

At the top of the pyramid I race across the temple platform, fling myself at the cliff wall and try to scramble up. But there's no foothold, no handhold, nothing but sheer rock. Backed up against the cliff, I'm trapped. I turn and see Michael, his face filling my vision, his arms outstretched, eager for the final clutch.

His hands go around my throat and begin to squeeze. I can't breathe. His fingers are like a vise around my neck. *This is the end,* I think. It seems impossible, ridiculous, that it's going to end this way. We fight like animals, without skill, clawing at each other, locked in a desperate struggle. I can feel the hot blast of his breath on my cheek as his hands tighten on my throat, forcing me toward the edge of the platform. Deliberately I let my muscles go slack, let my head roll back. My eyelids flutter, then close.

It works. Michael relaxes his grip and instinctively bends his head forward to look into my face. I stab his eyes with my thumbs, gouging the soft tissue as hard as I can, and he screams.

His hand snakes out and grabs my hair, and with the other

hand he punches me in the gut. In an instant I'm writhing on the ground. He shoves my face down to the rock, and a moment later I can see his booted foot swing back, ready to kick me off the edge of the platform.

"Get away from her."

The voice comes from behind us. Michael turns, and I roll off to the side, away from him, clutching my ribs.

Jessie stands motionless, holding the gun with both hands, and I realize Sam must have thrown it to her from the bottom of the hole. Gulping air, I gather myself into a ball, force myself up on my hands and knees and rise until I'm standing again on wobbly legs.

Michael gives her an engaging smile and lifts his hands. "Okay, babe. You got me."

She keeps the gun trained on him, but it quivers in her hands like a fish as she edges a few feet closer to me. I move toward her until the three of us form a triangle about twenty feet apart from each other.

He speaks casually, as if nothing has happened, nothing is wrong. "Jessie. Honey. You don't want to do this." He takes a step toward her, his voice tender, amused.

Jessie takes a step back, shaking from head to toe.

"Come on, babe. You can't shoot me. We'll get past this. I'll do whatever you want, whatever it takes." His voice is smooth as cream, and he takes another step closer.

"Stop," she says, and steps back until she wavers on the edge of the platform. There's a twenty foot drop behind her.

"Or what?" he asks, glancing at me, his smile wide, his perfect teeth gleaming in the moonlight. He turns to her, shoulders relaxed, arms spread, palms open. "You'll shoot me?" He takes another step toward her.

"Yes." She sounds uncertain.

"I don't think so, Jessie. You're still a good girl." His voice is low, seductive. "Now me, I tried to be a good man. Faithful husband, good son. No matter how hard I tried to be good, the people I loved ran right over me. They betrayed me, Jessie." He glides another step closer. "My wife cheated on me, and my father lied to me. And nothing I ever did mattered to anybody until I killed my dad. It was a terrible shock, Jessie. The first one is always a terrible shock. But then I had to kill Henry, too."

Jessie stares at him, frozen, her eyes wide in the moonlight.

Michael's dark silhouette flows toward her, closing the distance between them. "Henry wouldn't pack up and go, and I didn't have time to argue with him. So I shot him. *Poof.* Just like that." He lets out a low, easy laugh. "Jessie, I'll tell you the truth: something snapped in me when I shot him. It's amazing how easy it was, compared to watching my dad fall off that cliff."

As he talks he drifts in her direction like smoke, and his voice drops so low it's almost a whisper. "But you're a different person, Jessie. You're soft. You're sweet. Killing someone is a mortal sin, and you can't afford that weight on your conscience. It would destroy you."

"You could give yourself up," she says in a small voice, and my heart sinks.

He waves a hand. "Honey, I can't go to jail. You know that. I have nothing left to lose. Hey, it's nothing personal. I just don't have the time to argue with you." There's a sudden, unpleasant edge to his voice, and he charges toward her.

Jessie screams and draws her arm back to throw the gun across the platform, but Michael catches her wrist as the gun leaves her hand. The revolver skitters to a halt halfway between Michael and me on the black stone platform. Jessie lunges at Michael as he spins around, but he knocks her away. She totters, dazed by the blow, then sinks to her knees.

I see the gun glitter in the moonlight on the dark surface of the temple platform between us. Every muscle in my body contracts, ready to leap. The moment freezes in my mind, fixed like a photograph, clear, defined, inevitable. I spring a split second before Michael launches himself toward the gun. Weightless, I fly through the air, my bones light, my arms outstretched. The black shape of the gun fills my vision, and the world shrinks to the single bullet it contains. My heartbeat pounds in my ears, loud, a wave of heat, life, blood, and I'm there, the cold stone scraping my belly, my fingers touching the gun, gripping it, raising the barrel until it's pressed against the center of Michael's forehead.

His teeth are bared. A strange joy illuminates his face, and I see the eagerness in his eyes as he lifts both hands to wrench the gun away from me.

I pull the trigger, and the explosion shatters the night.

CHAPTER EIGHTEEN

There are no sirens, no police, no red flashing lights or uniformed men to cope with the aftermath of violence in the camp. Coyotes cry from the rim of the mesa as the stars rise in the heavens and the moon shines cold in the sky.

After we build a fire near the stream, Jessie and Sam and I lie huddled around it, wrapped in sleeping bags to ward off the chill. Around three in the morning, Jessie wakes from a restless doze, while Sam remains still, scarcely breathing, groaning from time to time in his sleep. His ankle has swelled to an alarming size, and I keep it wrapped in rags that have been dipped in the cold creek.

"You're awake," I say.

Jessie stretches in her sleeping bag, then shivers in spite of the warmth of the fire. "I dreamed of Michael," she says quietly. "I dreamed he was dead."

We exchange a long level look.

"I know," she says. "You did what you had to do." She sits up and pokes the fire with a piece of kindling. "I should have killed him myself."

But you didn't, I think. I look at her hands and remember the feel of the trigger, the kick of the gun against my palm. My thoughts cling to the image of Michael's corpse on top of the pyramid. We covered him with the tarp and weighted it down with stones, but that would give the body no more than a few hours of protection from predators.

"What do we do now?" Jessie asks.

"Wait until it's light. Then we'll pack up and leave."

"What about Michael's body?"

"We can bury him in the hole we dug. Otherwise the coyotes will get him."

"You don't think we should take the body with us?"

I shake my head. "If we show up at the trading post with a dead body, they'll hold us there until the sheriff arrives, and when we tell him what happened he'll wrap us up in red tape for days. No. You and Sam need to get to a hospital as soon as possible. Once you've been x-rayed and stitched up and bandaged, I'll tell the police about Michael."

"They won't like it," Jessie murmurs.

"The medical examiner will want to see the crime scene. The sheriff, the M.E., the Forest Service—they'll all have to come out here anyway."

"There'll be time enough in the morning to decide what to do." Sam's eyes are closed, but his voice sounds as though he's been awake for hours. His ankle has puffed up to the size of a balloon, and his face is drawn with pain as he speaks. "Maybe we should think this over."

"No," I say. "I'm worried about you."

He gives me a weak smile, though his eyes remain closed. "I'll survive."

I shiver, then toss another piece of wood on the fire. *We're safe,* I keep telling myself. *We'll all survive.* Michael is dead. He can't find us now. But my eyes are wired open, and electric currents run up and down my legs. The weight of what I've done terrifies me. It doesn't matter that I had no choice. That's what Michael said to me, when he was tying me up: *you don't leave me much choice.* There's always a choice, and I chose to kill him. How will I ever atone for this? I'm afraid to fall asleep, afraid of seeing him in my dreams.

Shortly before dawn a raven cries hoarsely from the top of the pyramid, and I turn over in my sleeping bag as a red-winged blackbird lets out a long cascade of notes. The sounds of life awaken me, and for a moment my mind is rinsed clean, empty, released from the events of the night. And then it all comes back: the fear, the struggle, the damage.

The raven is noisier now, barking the news of fresh meat from the top of the pyramid. Reluctantly, I emerge from the sleeping bag. The sky is pale. There are no clouds to reflect the rays of the rising sun. It's cold.

Jessie grunts when I shake her, and then she opens her eyes and stares up at me. Everything I felt upon waking is there in her face, the short trip from emptiness to sorrow.

"We have to move the body," I say. "The ravens are hungry."

Jessie nods and unzips her bag as I go check Sam, who is deeply asleep. His forehead is cool, and his eyelids flutter but don't open as my fingertips trace the lines of his face.

The majestic, forbidding bulk of the pyramid looms over us as Jessie and I begin to climb the high steps, and the sun rises over the apex as we near the top. Underneath the tarp, the body awaits us, a splash of unnatural color on the stone. Michael's dead face is illuminated by the dawn.

He lies on his back, his face turned to the left, his arms splayed wide, one leg extended and the other bent at the knee and drawn to one side. In the center of his forehead is a ragged black hole, with a slender thread of dried blood that trickled down one side of his face. His eyes are open, and a fly lands on the cornea. Something wells up in my throat and escapes as a breath, a sigh, an inarticulate moan. This is my doing. His life, his future—I took it away from him, in one flash of fear.

Jessie stares at him, then turns her head away and closes her eyes. The silence seems to go on forever. I can't move, or speak.

"Let's get him down," she finally says.

I take his shoulders while Jessie takes his legs, and we struggle together to lower him down the steep steps of the pyramid. The sun climbs the sapphire sky. It's quiet now, unnaturally quiet. No breeze stirs the branches of the sycamores, and the leaves hang limp as rags as we drag him down to the tunnel to bury his body.

It's an image I'll take to my grave, that grim sight of Michael's body flexed to fit the hole, just like the human sacrifice who had been buried next to the pyramid over a thousand years earlier. Did I have any choice? I ask myself. No. The responsibility of killing him had fallen to me, so I shot him. I'll never forget the expression on his face in his last moment of life. Furious. Savage. Intent upon murder. There was no other option. I had to kill, or be killed.

But the act itself—so final, so immense, so unbearable—weighs on me like a stone.

Jessie and I pack for the trip out while Sam grumbles over every knot, every buckle, every load that looks unbalanced to his expert eye. He staggers to his feet to help as I balance the pack on my horse, and I push him away with the flat of my hand pressed firmly against his chest.

"Your ankle's broken, Sam," I say. "You've been running a fever, and if you waste your strength now, you'll collapse later. Believe me, I'm being selfish. You'll be a lot more difficult to carry if you lose consciousness."

He leans back in the shade of a boulder. "You worry too much," he mutters, though he winces as he settles himself on the dirt. "I've been hurt worse than this."

My voice softens. "I don't want to lose you."

"You have no idea how strong I am," he says as he sinks back.

Jessie flashes a smile at me, but I ignore it as I lift the duffel into the sling and cinch the load tightly. I'm numb. I move like an automaton, loading the feed and grain for the horses, the canteens and water bottles, our sleeping bags and tents. If I focus on one step at a time, I'll be okay. I'll be fine.

At least Michael left his horse and Henry's staked by the stream. All I have to do is figure a way to load the two horses with the gear we'll need so we can travel without making Sam's injury worse. The horses are stoic as I adjust their saddles, and I wish I were like them, patient, detached, allowing the world to flow by in a stream of events, surrendering to it without having an opinion about any of it.

After securing the cargo in the slings that hang from the pack saddles, I turn to examine Sam. His skin is pale, his reflexes slow. The fever is down. There's no sign the infection is worse, but he needs a doctor, and quickly.

Suddenly there's nothing left to do but get on the horses and ride away, but I stand by my horse uncertainly, reluctant to leave without saying something to mark the passage of Michael's life.

"I'd like to offer a prayer for Michael before we go," Jessie says. "Is that okay?"

"Please. I need a prayer." The words catch in my throat, and I blink hard.

Sam pulls himself to his feet and takes a few experimental steps. He limps over to me and grasps my hand, then motions for Jessie to come and help him walk to the tunnel in the pyramid, where we've buried Michael.

After we've gathered around the grave, Jessie bows her head and speaks softly. *"Dios te salve Maria, llena eres de gracia, el Señor es contigo. Bendita tu eres entre todas las mujeres, y bendito es el fruto de tu vientre Jésus. Santa Maria, madre de Dios, ruega por nos otros pecodores, ahora y en la hora de nuestro muerte."*

I listen to the flow of Spanish without understanding any of it but the last word. *Muerte.* Death. As she goes on praying I think of the Psalm they always read at funerals, the one that says "The Lord is my shepherd, I shall not want." It's hazy in my memory, but I know there's something about green pastures and still waters and God restoring our souls. I wish I could believe Michael was restored.

My heart aches, and tears well in my eyes and run down my face. How fragile we are! Every human being has to live in a body that can be stopped, struck down, killed in a split second. Every bone can be broken like a twig. Every skull is delicate as a teacup. How can we love anyone when our lives depend on this bag of bones and blood? People die. And then you can't talk to them anymore, or change their minds, or atone for what you've done. You can't phone them up, or write them a letter, or smile when your eyes meet theirs. They go in the ground, and you cover their faces with dirt.

The three of us are silent, but I don't let go of Sam's hand. His warm, rough palm soothes me, and the sound of his breathing seems unbearably precious.

EPILOGUE

The tents are down, the food stowed, and Sam packs the canvas panniers while I saddle the horses for the trip out. I can't see Jessie anywhere.

"She's up there," Sam says, lifting his chin toward the pyramid.

After shading my eyes against the glare of the morning sun, I see the silhouette perched on the top platform. "I'll go get her."

A year has passed since the night I ran up the pyramid to escape Michael. Since then the pyramid has become a part of my landscape, like the mesa or the mountains, its age and bulk a comforting, fixed mark in my surroundings. As I round the corner of the monument I run my hand over the rough surface of Quetzalcoatl, the plumed serpent who guards the steep, sloped walls. His fierce stare feels protective now, as if we've been adopted by the tribe who sculpted his face.

Within a month after Richter's death, Sam assembled the necessary funding and permits to reopen the dig under his supervision. Once the press release about the site was out, it created a stir that could only be compared to the discovery of Tutankhamun's tomb. This section of wilderness was closed to the public for eleven months while an international team of archaeologists and volunteers completed the excavation.

The skeletal remains of the child-king, his retinue, and all the burial goods of Teotihuacán have already been removed from the caves under the mesa. Predictably, the Mexican government, several Pueblo tribes and a group in Santa Fe called the Children of Atlantis sued the federal government for the rights to the bones and the treasure. It will take years to litigate, but the Smithsonian hammered out a preliminary agreement with the Museo Nacional de Antropología to fund a world-wide tour to display the artifacts. Eventually they'll probably give the Mexican government half ownership of the codex and the other priceless remnants of lost Mexican history. Right now the bones and burial goods are safely locked up under twenty-four hour surveillance in a laboratory at the University of New Mexico, where a team of scientists will spend the next several years analyzing and classifying them.

Sam, Jessie and I are the only ones left from the original crew. Sylvia disappeared to Corsica, where it's rumored she's writing her husband's biography. Someone told me Jason has become a realtor, and works in Santa Fe now. Will just finished his doctoral thesis in anthropology at the University of Arizona, and he sent me an email a few months back, saying Fiddle had quit cooking and fulfilled her lifelong dream of becoming a hunting and fishing guide in the Pecos wilderness.

"Hey," Jessie says.

Breathing hard from the climb, I wave a hand toward the campsite. "We're almost ready."

Jessie pats the stone platform beside her. "Have a seat. I was just saying goodbye."

I lower myself to sit beside her and let my legs dangle off the edge while I take in the view. The canyon below us is empty of people, except for Sam. The other archaeologists and volunteers rode out this morning, while Sam, Jessie and I lingered behind to enjoy our last morning in the wilderness. The sycamores and willow are lush from the spring rains, and the wind makes the leaves ripple and flash in the morning sun.

"You can still see the bare spot where my tent used to be," she says.

I nod, although I can't see it.

"Do you ever think about that night?"

"All the time."

Jessie's eyes have a far-off look, as if she's gazing into the past. "I go over it and over it in my mind. I don't think I'll ever get rid of this feeling that I failed you that night. I should have killed Michael. I just couldn't."

I touch her back. "I think you loved him."

"Yeah, well." Her voice is gruff, but her eyes fill with tears. "I was an idiot."

"I know," I say, giving her a quick, affectionate squeeze. "But you're my idiot."

She twists away and assesses my grin. "You look suspiciously happy."

"I'm pregnant."

"My God, Kate, are you serious?"

"I took the test this morning. The stick is blue. I haven't even told Sam yet."

Jessie stares at me for a moment, then laughs with delight. "That's incredible! Did you guys plan this?"

"Not exactly."

Impulsively she reaches over, grabs me by the neck and gives me a loud kiss on the cheek. "Kate, I'm so happy for you. What an adventure."

"Compared to what we've already been through, I figure it can't be too scary." Of course this is a lie. I'm terrified.

Jessie examines my face thoughtfully. "Do you feel different?"

"I do," I say softly.

I haven't let myself take it in yet, not really. It's only been an hour since I found out, and it's too much to absorb. I cast my mind back to the child-king, and all the other martyrs of Teotihuacán. Perhaps there is a communion between the living and the dead, between those who are waiting to be born and those who have lived and died and still watch over us. Maybe this pregnancy is a sign, and I just can't read it.

It's time to go. Sam adjusts the slings to the pack saddle, then glances at me, his eyes curious as he takes in the smile I can't hide. "Are you happy to leave?"

"I'm pregnant."

He pulls me close so my back fits the curve of his chest, then lets his head come forward to rest for a moment in the crook of my neck. I can feel his cheek tighten in a smile.

"You knew," I accuse him.

"I hoped." He rubs my belly gently with the palm of his hand, and we both stare down at his fingers as they search out the new roundness of flesh. He laughs suddenly, and splays out his hands. "Look at the dirt under these nails! How can you stand me?"

I hold his hand up with my own callused palm, then turn our hands this way and that so he can see my stubby fingers, and the rime of soil embedded under my nails.

Carefully he spreads his fingers over my belly while the stillness settles over us. We've often listened like this, to ancient shards, or pots, or tools made by people from another time. By now it's as familiar as listening to thunder in the distance.

I close my eyes. At first there's nothing but the hum of bees and the whisper of wind as it rustles the leaves of the brush oak. The sun warms the top of my head as my breath deepens, and the stillness and safety of Sam's arms enclosing me brings me to that calm inner harbor where the walls of perception shimmer. The present moment shifts slightly, and I let in the other world like a breath.

In my belly I can feel my child, hardly bigger than a match

flame, but strong, and growing. And then I see a face at once strange and familiar, the face of a small brown child with a headdress of gilded wood and quetzal feathers, his skull flattened in the manner of his people. His pain disappeared long ago, and the spirit beyond his flesh is bright and alive. He's laughing, and he's looking right at me.

ABOUT THE AUTHOR

Lois Gilbert is the author of *River of Summer* (Penguin-Putnam, 1999,) *Without Mercy* (NAL Dutton, 2000,) and *Returning to Taos* (Five Star, 2006,) as well as dozens of published articles, reviews, and essays. Her work has been translated into German, Russian, and Italian. She lectures on creative writing around the world for Norwegian Cruise Line, evaluates manuscript submissions for University of New Mexico Press, and has twenty years of editorial experience.